# GLASS

## Also by Ellen Hopkins

*Crank*

*Burned*

*Impulse*

*Identical*

*Tricks*

*Fallout*

*Perfect*

*Tilt*

Margaret K. McElderry Books

# GLASS

## Ellen Hopkins

**Margaret K. McElderry Books**
NEW YORK LONDON TORONTO SYDNEY NEW DELHI

MARGARET K. MCELDERRY BOOKS

An imprint of Simon & Schuster Children's Publishing Division

1230 Avenue of the Americas, New York, New York 10020

MARGARET K. MCELDERRY BOOKS is a trademark of Simon & Schuster, Inc.

For information about special discounts for bulk purchases, please contact Simon & Schuster Special Sales at 1-866-506-1949 or business@simonandschuster.com.

The Simon & Schuster Speakers Bureau can bring authors to your live event. For more information or to book an event, contact the Simon & Schuster Speakers Bureau at 1-866-248-3049 or visit our website at www.simonspeakers.com.

Also available in a Margaret K. McElderry Books hardcover edition

Book design by Mike Rosamilia

The text for this book is set in Trade Gothic Condensed No. 18.

Manufactured in the United States of America

First Margaret K. McElderry Books paperback edition April 2009

This Margaret K. McElderry Books paperback edition August 2013

10  9  8  7  6  5  4  3

The Library of Congress has cataloged the hardcover edition as follows:

Hopkins, Ellen.

Glass / Ellen Hopkins.

p. cm.

Summary: Eighteen-year-old Kristina is determined to manage her crystal meth addiction in order to take care of her newborn son, but when the pull of the drug becomes too strong, her greatest fears are quickly realized.

ISBN 978-1-4169-4090-6 (hardcover)

[1. Methamphetamine—Fiction. 2. Drug abuse—Fiction. 3. Teenagers—Fiction. 4. Novels in verse. 5. Babies—Fiction. 6. Family problems—Fiction.] I. Title.

PZ7.5.H67 Gla 2007

[Fic]—dc22

2007299868

ISBN 978-1-4424-7182-5 (paperback)

ISBN 978-1-4391-0652-5 (eBook)

*Glass* is dedicated to Orion, Jade, Heaven, and Clyde, whose lives, through no fault of their own, have been forever marked by the monster.

I would also like to acknowledge my husband, John, whose love has kept me upright.

# Walking with the Monster

Life
was radical
right after I met

the monster.

Later, life

became

harder,
complicated.
Ultimately,

a living

hell,
like swimming
against a riptide,

walking

the wrong
direction in the fast
lane of the freeway,

waking

from sweetest
dreams to find yourself
in the middle of a

nightmare.

# 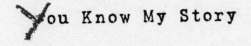You Know My Story

Don't you? All about

                    my dive

into the lair of the monster
drug some people call crank.
Crystal. Tina. Ice.
How a summer visit
to my dad sent me

                    into

the arms of a boy—a
hot-bodied hunk, my
very first love, who led
me down the path to

                    insanity.

How I came home

                    no longer

Kristina Georgia
Snow, gifted high
school junior, total
dweeb, and

                    perfect

daughter, but
instead a stranger
who called herself Bree.

How, no matter
how hard

                                    Kristina

fought her, Bree
was stronger, brighter,
better equipped to deal
with a world where
everything moved at light
speed, everyone mired
in ego. Where "everyday"

                                    became

another word
for making love with

                                    the monster.

# It Wasn't a Long Process

I went to my dad's in June, met Adam
 the very first day. It took some time
  to pry him from his girlfriend's grasp.
   But within two weeks, he introduced
    me to the monster. One time was all
     it took to want more. It's a roller-
      coaster ride. Catch the downhill
       thrill, you want to ride again,
        enough to endure the long,
         hard climb back up again.
          In days, I was hooked on
           Adam, tobacco, and meth,
            in no particular order. But
             all summer vacations must
              end. I had to come home to
               Reno. And all my new bad
                habits came with me. It was
                 a hella speed bump, oh yeah.
                  Until I hurt for it, I believed
                   I could leave the crystal behind.
                    But the crash-and-burn was more
                     than I could take. When the jet landed,
                      I was still buzzed from a good-bye binge.

My family crowded round me at the airport,
discussing summer plans and celebration dinners,
and all I wanted to do was skip off for another snort.
Mom kept trying to feed me. My stepfather, Scott, kept
trying to ask questions about my visit with Dad. My
big sister, Leigh, wanted to talk about her new girlfriend,
and my little brother, Jake, kept going on about soccer.
It didn't take long to figure out I was in serious trouble.

# Not the Kind of Trouble

You might think I'm
talking about. I was pretty
        sure I could get away with
        B.S.ing Mom and Scott.

        I'd always been such a good
        girl, they wouldn't make the
jump to "bad" too quickly.
Especially not if I stayed cool.

        I wasn't worried about
        getting busted at school
or on the street. I'd only just
begun my walk with the monster.

I still had meat on my bones,
the teeth still looked good.
        I didn't stutter yet. My mouth
        could still keep up with my brain.

No, the main thing I worried
about was how I could score
        there, at home. I'd never even
        experimented with pot, let alone

meth. Where could I go?
Who could I trust with my
money, my secrets? I couldn't
ask Leigh. She was the prettiest

lesbian you've ever seen. But
to my knowledge she had
never used anything stronger
than a hearty glass of wine.

Not Sarah, my best friend since
fourth grade, or any of my
old crowd, all of whom lived by
the code of the D.A.R.E. pledge.

I really didn't need to worry,
of course. All I had to do
was leave things up to Bree,
the goddess of persuasion.

# 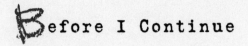efore I Continue

I just want to remind you
that turning into Bree

was a conscious decision
on my part. I never really

liked Kristina that much.
Oh, some things about her

were pretty cool—how she
was loyal to her family

and friends. How she loved
easily. How she was good

at any and all things artistic.
But she was such a brain,

with no sense of fashion
or any idea how to have fun.

So when fun presented
itself, I decided someone

new would have to take charge.
That someone was Bree.

I chose her name (not sure where
I got it), chose when to become her.

What I didn't expect was discovering
she had always been there, inside of me.

How could Kristina and Bree
live inside of one person?

How could two such different halves
make up the whole of me?

How could Bree have possibly survived,
stuck in Kristina's daily existence?

# The Funny Thing Was

Bree solved the meth dilemma on a family
    trip to Wild Waters, Scott's annual
        company picnic. Sarah came        The first was
          along to spend time with       a truly gorgeous
            Kristina. But Bree      lifeguard. Turned out
            had other things    Brendan wasn't so pretty
              in mind.    on the inside, but even Bree, who
                thrived on intuition, was clueless. Hard
             on the make, Brendan shared booze, cigarettes.

But one guy wasn't quite enough. I
    also ran into Chase Wagner that
      day. His outside wasn't as      I found out
      attractive, but inside he     soon enough that
        was fine. Of course,    both Chase and Brendan
          I didn't know    knew the score—and both
           that yet.    were interested in me. Brendan
              only wanted sex; Chase offered love.
           Either way, I had my path to the monster.

Later, I discovered that Robyn, my
old friend Trent's sister (not to
mention an "in" cheerleader),      It didn't take
tweaked to stay thin          long to immerse
and "pep up." She      myself in the lifestyle.
taught me how      Didn't take long for school
to smoke it.      to go to shit; for friendships and
dedication to family to falter. Didn't
take long to become a slave to the monster.

# My Mom and Stepfather

Tried to stop me before
it all went completely wrong.
Kristina spent almost a whole
year GUFN—grounded
until further notice.

But Bree was really good
at prying open windows
at night, lying with a straight
face, denying she had
slipped so far downhill.

Nothing slowed me down.
Not losing my virginity
to Brendan's rape. Not
spending a few days
in juvenile hall.

The only thing that kept
me sane was Chase's love,
despite all I put him through.
He even swore to love me
when I told him I was pregnant.

Pregnant. And Brendan
was the father. Bree considered
abortion. Exorcism. Kristina
understood the baby was not
the demon. His father was.

But you know this part
of the story. You followed
me on my journey through
the monster's territory.
We wound up here.

Who am I now, three
months after I left you,
standing on the deck
with me, listening to my
new baby, crying inside?

I told you then, the monster
is a way of life, one it's
difficult to leave behind,
no matter how hard you try.
I have tried, really I have.

Maybe if Chase had stayed
with me, instead of running
off to California, in search
of his dreams. Then again,
I told him to go.

Maybe if I had dreams
of my own to run off in
search of. I did once.
But now I have no plans
for a perfect tomorrow.

All I have is today.

# T for Today

I'd really like to tell you I have a nice little place with a white picket fence, flowers in the garden, and Winnie-the-Pooh, Eeyore, and Tigger, too, on baby blue nursery walls. I'd like to inform you that I am on a fast track to a college degree and a career in computer animation—something I've aimed for, ever since I found out I could draw. I'd love to let you know I left the monster screaming in my dust, shut my ears, scrambled back to my family, back to my baby, my heart. I could tell you those things, but they'd be lies—nothing new for me, true. But if all I wrote was lies, you wouldn't really know my story. I want you to know. Not a day passes when I don't think about getting high. Strung. Getting out of this deep well of monotony I'm slowly drowning in.

# I Was a Junior

When I had Hunter,
a semester away from
early graduation and a hell

of a lot farther than that
away from independence.

To find freedom that even
the magic number eighteen
can't buy, I need

a job. To get that, I need
a diploma, or at least a GED.

I have no choice but to live
at home, under the prying
eyes of my mom and Scott.

*I'll help watch the baby
until you finish school,*

is Mom's deal. *If you go on to
college, the two of you
can stay as long as you like.*

It's a pretty good arrangement,
mostly because I know jack
about babies. Mom's expertise

comes in handy, especially
in the middle of the night.

More than once, she has shaken
me awake. *Hunter's crying.
I'll change him. You feed him.*

Who knew babies could
be so obnoxious, wanting

to eat at all hours, that is?
Most of the time, my nipples
feel like puppy chew toys.

*Breast-feeding isn't easy. But you*
*want to give him a good start.*

A good, healthy start. I know
that, of course, and figure
I owe him at least that much.

Still, I wake up every morning
exhausted, wondering

how I can make it through
the day, let alone how I'll
manage to study for my GED.

I try to avoid mirrors. I gained
forty pounds with my pregnancy,

and Hunter only weighed in at
seven pounds, eleven ounces.
Minus placenta, water, etcetera,

that leaves about twenty pounds
of belly flab, jelly thighs,

and chipmunk cheeks I need
to lose before feeling positive
about how I look again.

And until I do that, I know
I'll never find someone new to love.

# 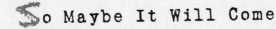So Maybe It Will Come

As no surprise to you that lately
I have been hearing the plea

of the monster, distant
at first but creeping closer.

Louder. *Come back to me,*
*Kristina. Hurry back, Bree.*

I closed my ears for a long
while, pleaded with it to please

shut up, please go away,
please leave me alone.

But I'm starting to come
around. Maybe a short

(and I mean no long-term
commitments!) stroll

with the monster might
slim me down, rev me up

and offer the impetus to slip
into my future, better equipped

to deal with the mindless
tedium that is my life.

# I Know

I should resist.
Turn
away.
Walk
away.
Run
far
away,
so far
away,
the monster will
never
find me, never
sniff
me out,
never
dare
touch
me,
never
pretend to
hear
my meager complaints,

never
        get even the slightest
taste
        of the fear in my heart,
never
        force me to
see

what I'm afraid to see.

# But Suddenly

Without
a doubt
I understand
the monster
and I are more
than friends.
We're blood
brothers.

Or maybe
blood sisters.
(Is there
such a thing?
And does
that mean
I should
include Bree?)

That is
a forever
kind of thing.

Forever.

All I need
to do is
find a way
for the two
of us

[no, most
definitely that's
three of us,
including
me, Bree]

to hook
up again.

# You Have to Remember

It has been months since
I've been out looking to

          score.

Chase is gone, Brendan
person non grata, my
Mexican Mafia

          connect

a thing of the past.
Only one person comes
to mind, and Robyn
just might be hard to

          find,

away at college in
California. And even
if I can locate my old

          party

pal, how will I ever
make it over the mountain
to the Golden State? I used
to have plenty of

          friends,

friends who could give
me rides. No more, and my
own wheels are in for a major
overhaul. I can't borrow
Mom's car to hunt down

                                        whiff.

Can I?

# I Call Trent

Robyn's brother is an old
    friend. In fact, that's how
        I know Robyn. Trent's great,
            even if he is totally straight.

Meaning he doesn't get high.
    Because when it comes to sex,
        he's 100 hundred percent gay.
            And I'm fine with things that way.

    Mrs. Rosselli answers on
        the third ring. *Hello? Oh, it's*
            *you.* Her voice is like a hail
                storm—hard, staccato, frigid.

"Hello, Mrs. Rosselli.
    Is Trent there? No?
        Well, do you know
            when he'll get home, then?"

    Long pause. Then, *I'm not*
        *really sure. Can I help*
            *you with anything else?*
                Something's up with her.

I'm not really looking
for Trent, anyway. "Yes.
Can you tell me how
to get hold of Robyn?"

Longer pause. *Uh, you*
*know, she was moving*
*out of the dorm, into*
*an apartment. I'm not sure . . .*

Things are growing clearer.
"Is there a problem, Mrs.
Rosselli? I just want to
catch up with old friends."

The longest pause of all.
*You're not their friend,*
*Kristina. You're nothing*
*but trouble they don't need.*

# tung

But not really smarting,
I could tell her that
both of her children
need all the friends

*they* can get—trouble
or not. One is eighteen
and gay, in a city where
homosexuality is almost

as dirty a word as "Democrat."
The other will be lucky
to finish her freshman year
in college—too much time

buying affection with an
omnipresent speed stash.
But saying that won't suit
either of us at the moment.

"I'm not sure what you mean,
Mrs. Rosselli. I've made some
mistakes, yes. But I'm working
hard to straighten myself out.

Having friends in my life—
good friends, on the right
track themselves—is one
thing I desperately need.

I apologize if I've ever
done anything to offend
you, or to hurt Robyn or
Trent. I don't believe I

have, but if you think
so, please let me make
it up to you." Oh yeah,
I'm back in the game,

and damn does it feel great!

# Not Only That

But it works.

*I'm sorry, Kristina.*
*I shouldn't be so judgmental.*

"That's okay, Mrs. Rosselli.
I understand your feelings."

*Trent works for a lawyer*
*after school. He usually*
*gets home around six.*

"A lawyer? Wonderful!
I know he wanted to go
to law school. . . ."

*Robyn's at UOP in*
*Stockton. She still has*
*her old cell number, 775 . . .*

"Thank you so much.
I'll call Trent later. Please
tell him I was in touch."

*I will. And how's that*
*baby? Growing like*
*corn, I'll wager.*

Growing like corn?
Whatever. "He's beautiful,
thanks. Looks just like me."

She chuckles. *I bet he*
*does. Take care, Kristina.*

"You too, Mrs. Rosselli."
I click the phone dead,

dial another number.
"Hey, Robyn. It's Kristina.

What's up?"

# She Sounds

Strung,
                    like her brain is
disconnected
                    from her mouth.
                    Don't get me
wrong.
                    I remember that
                    feeling well—
knowing
                    exactly what you
                    want to say, but
your
                    lips can't quite
                    manage the
correct
                    combination of vowels
                    and consonants
                    to form the
words.
                    Could be a bad sign.
                    Anyone that

incapable

        of cohesive language
        could very well be
        crashing—another way

of saying

        Robyn is definitely
        still using, but might
        be out at the moment,

a sentence

        worse than death for
        a regular tweaker.
        How bad *is* my timing?

# Let's Find Out

K-Kristina?

"C'mon, Robyn. It
hasn't been that long."

Oh, yeah, right.
Kristina. Whatcha
been up to?

"Not much. Studying
for my GED. Taking
care of my baby."

Sounds . . . like not
a lot of fun.

"Which is exactly why
I'm calling you."

Oh, yeah, right.
Well, I could maybe
help you out there.

"Very cool. I have to
see if I can borrow a car.
How about tomorrow?"

That would probably
work. I'm in class
until four.

She can do classes,
sounding like that?
"Okay. I'll work on
the car and give you
a buzz tomorrow."

*Oh, yeah, right.*
*Uh, Kristina? Come*
*alone, okay?*
Tweaker talk for
*This better not be a bust.*

"Not a problem, Robyn.
All I want is to get my head."

Thinking about it,
I'm starting to want
that real bad.

# 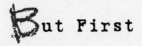ut First

I have to convince my mom to lend
me her car, and to babysit
Hunter—all on a Friday
night. Party night, for
almost every
partier in
America.
Hell, it's the
American Way, as
I think almost everyone
will agree. Get out of school
or off work, put on clean clothes,
and look for a way to escape reality—

whether that's with alcohol, weed, or
my all-time favorite: speed.
Pot and beer mostly make
me tired. I only used
to use them when
I was buzzed up
real high,

didn't
mind slowing
down a little. But I
haven't done any of that
in way too long. Being good
all the time isn't just hard. It's damn
boring. There's more to life than babies

and books, and I'm overdue to go out
and find a little fun. First things
first. I have to find a way
to Stockton. All it
will take, I hope,
is the perfect
little (okay,
big) lie.

# I'm Out of Practice

Not having had to manufacture
a lie in quite a long time.

I have to say, that isn't a bad
place to be, where you don't

have to lie. Everything is just
so much easier when you don't

have to remember what you
told who, and when, and why.

What is simply is. But not
anymore, I guess. Now I have

to not only come up with a reason
to go, but also to remember exactly

what it was, no matter how tweaked
I might be when I get home.

Tweaked! It takes a modicum
of thinking, but within an hour or so,

I invent a great (I think) excuse.

# It's a Doozer

"Mom, is there any
way I could borrow
your car? There's a
college fair I want to
check out tomorrow,
over in Sacramento.          *College*
It starts around four        *fair?*
and should go until
eight. . . ." (I think       *Don't    you want me*
that will give me            *to go     along with*
plenty of time to            *you?      You've*
hook up with Robyn—          *never     driven*
even if she isn't            *that      far by your-*
exactly on time—             *self.      It's a*
score, toot a little,                   *three-*
and start back.)                        *hour trip, you*
"I'd ask you to come along, but I       *know, not easy.*
need you to watch Hunter. I can't
really take him with me. If it makes
you feel better, I'll invite Trent to
ride along. He can visit his sister."

# I Will Invite Him Too

Of course, I know he
has to work until five thirty.
But at least if it comes up

in conversation, I can
tell Mom I asked,
but he had other plans.

I call about eight.
"Hey, Trent. It's Kristina.
Long time, no talk.

"I heard you're working
for a lawyer. Hope
he's really cute!"

Trent hesitates, not
at all sure why I'm striking
up a conversation.

*He's not bad, actually.*
*But that can't be why*
*you called. What's up?*

To the point, and why
not? We haven't spoken
since before I had Hunter.

"Actually, I'm driving over
to Stockton tomorrow
afternoon and wondered

if you'd like to ride along.
I thought you might like
to drop in on Robyn."

*Thanks for thinking*
*of me, Kristina. But*
*I have to work and*

*even if I didn't, I*
*wouldn't go. Robyn*
*is on a fast track to death.*

"What do you mean?"
Like I don't know
exactly what he means.

*If you don't know, you*
*haven't seen her lately.*
*And if you haven't*

*seen her lately, I suggest*
*you steer clear. She'll*
*take you down with her.*

*Kristina, we haven't*
*hung out together*
*for a while, but you've*

*always been a good friend*
*to me. Let me offer you*
*a good friend's advice.*

*Stay away from Robyn.*
*And if you see her coming,*
*run the other way.*

# Tonight

Sleep is impossible,
anticipation swelling
and ebbing like some
sort of crazy tide.

                              Strange,

how when I close my
eyes, try to concentrate
on that little door between
them that opens into

                              dreams,

I feel high already,
locked in a battle
between the need to dive
into REM slumber and the

                              desire

to start the damn party
already! I remember
that awful tug-of-war well.
So why jump right back in,

                              release

the monster to stalk
my days, haunt my nights;
to bite through my skull
and suck on my brain?

                                        From

a purely omniscient
point of view, it makes
no sense whatsoever. I
have freed myself from

                                        physical

addiction, no rehab but
to endure sweating, puking,
and cardiovascular jumping
jacks. The mental

                                        bonds,

however, seem as strong
as ever, and the piece
of me that recognizes
that knows I might be

making a very big mistake.

# Maybe That's Why

When Hunter makes
　　　　his daily plea for
　　　　　　　a three A.M. breast
　　　　　　　　　　milk feast, I call
　　　　　　　　　　　　to Mom, "I'll handle it."
He's now four months
　　　　old, and drinking
　　　　　　　formula supplements
　　　　　　　　　　from a bottle—a conscious
　　　　　　　　　　　　decision on my part.
I had hoped to have
　　　　him weaned—and my
　　　　　　　breasts completely
　　　　　　　　　　my own again—
　　　　　　　　　　　　within five months.
My new game plan
　　　　will expedite that
　　　　　　　schedule, I realize,
　　　　　　　　　　and I have to admit,
　　　　　　　　　　　　that makes me sad.

I change his diaper,
        marveling for about
                the millionth time at
                        his perfect little body.
                                The body I created.

All clean and dry,
        I carry him back
                to my bed, cradle
                        him in one pillowed
                                arm, unbutton my top.

And as the milk begins
        to flow, so do my tears.
                "Mommy loves you,
                        Hunter Seth. No matter
                                what, Mommy loves you."

He looks up at me
        with spectacular green
                eyes and, around my
                        very sore nipple, smiles
                                a toothless baby smile.

# Now You Might Think

That tender scene might make
me change my mind, and truthfully,
I have thought twice.

But I don't want to think again.

I MapBlast directions to Robyn's
apartment, load a small ice chest
with soda, to fight the wah-wahs

sure to strike on my way home.

*If it gets too late, promise me*
*you'll stop and spend the night,*
Mom insists. *Here's some money.*

She hands me a crisp $100 bill.

Suddenly it strikes me that I
haven't even thought about the money
end of the transaction to come.

Lucky me. A hundred will just

about cover it. Still, if prices
haven't risen with inflation,
another hundred will score

an eight ball instead of a gram.

Yeah, yeah, my thought processes
have already graduated from casual
to daily use. But I don't want

to have to drive to Stockton

too often. Hell, an eight ball
will last me just about
forever. Won't it?

# 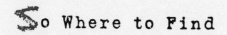So Where to Find

Another hundred dollars?
In lieu of an allowance,

Mom and Scott buy
diapers and baby formula.

My savings account is
still closed to me, and will be

until my eighteenth birthday.
That impressive turning point

is only a couple of weeks away,
but not soon enough to score

the monetary birthday rewards
I hope for from relatives, far

and near. No, only one place
comes to mind, an easy

place, all things considered—
Hunter's rainy-day piggy bank.

All those very same relatives
sent him a little cash, right

after he was born. I was going
to open a college savings

account, but haven't gotten
around to it yet. No problem.

I'll replace it as soon as I get
my birthday stash. Meanwhile,

Hunter won't miss it. And
neither, I hope, will Mom.

*Pack an overnight bag, just
in case,* she says, interrupting

my thoughts. *Always a good
idea to plan for that rainy day.*

# 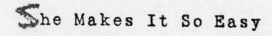 She Makes It So Easy

Handing me her keys,
helping me pack, giving
me money. I'd like to

                         blame

her for what may come,
take dead aim and whack
this big ball of

                         guilt

across the net,
into her court, wait
for her well-deserved

                         volley.

But that wouldn't
be accurate,
wouldn't be

                         right.

I know as I climb
into the SUV, crank
the engine, that what's

                         left

of Kristina will have to
battle the reemergent Bree,
that despite my plan to come

                         back

and pick up where I left
off, only more positive
and energized to go

forth,

get my GED and a great
job, find a nice little
place, make my own way,

the odds

of things ever being
quite right again are
clearly, completely,

not in my favor.

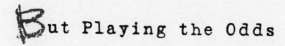

# But Playing the Odds

Is not my best thing, so
I stow every single nagging
doubt and head off to Stockton.
It's a gorgeous blue September
day, and I take my time.

South on a straight stretch
of Highway 395, turn west
on Highway 88, leaving Nevada
behind, just out of Minden.

The winding highway
carries me past Kirkwood,
my family's favorite ski resort.

Even without snow, the steep
angular mountain brings back
memories of stepping off cornices
and hanging, midair, for a scant
second before dropping down
long, deep black-diamond runs.

I can almost feel the sizzle
of adrenaline, pumping
from the back of my skull, zooming
down my spine and into my legs,
making them reach
for even more speed.
Turn. Turn. Don't fight gravity.
Suck into its jet stream.

Once in a while I'd make a mistake,
catch an edge. Or a mogul.
Most times, I corrected
before taking a tumble.

Once or twice, I wasn't so lucky,
dumping headlong down the hill,
sliding out of control
until the landscape leveled.
And that made the adrenaline
pump even faster.

Which reminds me.
I have not had an adrenaline
rush since I took my little detour,
one of nature's irresistible highs, denied

by brain chemistry gone awry,
at the claws of the monster.
I might not know the cause
of such cerebral malfunction,
if not for an article I once read.

It defined for me exactly
how crank scours
the brain's pleasure center,
scrubbing away dopamine,
adrenaline and other natural
highs. It didn't stop me,
of course, but it did slow
me down for a day or two.

Not slow enough to keep
the damage from occurring.
Now only one thing can give
me that kind of feeling—like
I have the world by its throat.

And I am on my way to it.

# Several Miles Farther West

I pass a small mountain
community, home to loggers,
retirees, and telecommuters.

My parents have friends
who live here, and for
about thirty seconds

I think about swinging
by. They have a pretty cute
son, who I once had a serious

crush on. We used to visit,
and on overnight stays Quade
and I would sneak out at night,

for nothing more than a little
conversation. Okay, we almost
kissed once. But I was such

a total tool, when he leaned
his face down close to mine,
looked into my dilated (by

the dark, not by stash, which
I still turned up my nose at)
eyes, and it came to me what

he had in mind, I actually
turned my face away, pretending
some nighttime noise

had drawn my attention.
Plain and simple, I didn't know
how to kiss and didn't want

him to know it. He was a couple
of years older, and a dark-haired
hottie who surely knew a thing

or two about kissing. Unlike me.
I didn't learn those ropes
for another year or so.

Looking back, I wish I had
had a different teacher,
one who really cared about me.

Looking back, I wish
I had parted
my lips—opened my mouth

wide and invited his tongue
inside—for Quade. Maybe
every single thing that happened

in my life after that night
would have turned out differently.
Then again, maybe not.

# Either Way

I decide not to stop by.
        My mom told me Quade plays
bass in a metal band, so he
        probably isn't as straight
as he used to be. Just like
        me. Still, I have a destination.

I jot a reminder in my
        mental notebook to look up
Quade one day very soon.
        This time, maybe I'll just
let him kiss me. I most
        definitely know how.

In fact, thinking about it
        is starting to make me
want it. I haven't let myself
        even consider going out
with a guy since Hunter
        was born. Men are trouble.

But what the hell? I'm
            looking for trouble right
now, aren't I? And one
            kind of trouble will
likely lead to another,
            at least eventually.

The more I focus on *that*
            kind of trouble, the better
it's starting to sound.
            I do still have the problem
with paunch, but crystal
            will help with that, too.

I just have to stay cool,
            keep Bree reined in.
Little lines, maybe one
            in the A.M., to wake up,
feel great, not eat
            everything in sight.

Maybe another small
       toot in the early P.M.,
just enough to limit
       dinner calories and still
be able to sleep at night.
       Or maybe go out at night.

*No, no, no!* This isn't
       about going out at night.
Isn't about partying.
       Is *not* about turning into
a lunatic again. I am
       and will remain in control.

# 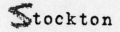tockton

Is an interesting little city—half-
artsy, half-cow town, and home

to the Asparagus Festival and other
events that take advantage of its

watery location on the delta fed by
the Sacramento and San Joaquin rivers.

Today I couldn't care less
about any of that. All I want

is to find Robyn's apartment,
not far from the University of the Pacific.

Driving by the brick-and-ivy campus,
I almost envy the students,

walking alone or sitting in groups,
looking at their books—and each other.

Guys. Girls. Tight jeans and T-shirts.
Big Gulps here. Cigarettes there.

It's all so normal. Then it comes
to me that one of those

students is Robyn, who is anything
but "normal." You can hide

a lot, or maybe just get away with
a lot, if you play your cards right.

I only hope the hand I'm about to deal
myself will hold an ace or two.

# I. Locate Robyn's Apartment

Building C-9. Third floor.
I'm early, but not too,
so I sit on the stairs to

               wait.

And wait. Four o'clock
comes and goes. Still I sit,
not too worried about
Robyn getting home

               late.

Even on her best days,
clock-watching was
never her greatest

               trait.

Did she have a greatest
trait? Oh, yeah. That's why
I'm here, huh? Patience!
Maybe she didn't come

               straight

home because she had
to make a buy on the way.
But when a watch-check says

               eight

after five, I decide I'd
better try her cell. Dumped
into voice mail,
something I

                                        hate

under any circumstances.
Just as I'm starting
to feel really pissed, this

                                        great-

looking guy starts up
the stairs. Okay, this is déja
vu-ish. I met my Adam, who
I once believed was my soul

                                        mate,

on a similar staircase. But
this guy goes way beyond
Adam—older, buffer, with

                                        slate

gray eyes that fix on me,
eliciting chills that I can't
describe. He looks at me
like a barracuda, scoping

bait.

Ravenous. Suspicious.
Curious. Delicious. (Him,
not me.) I feel like a

freight

train has steamed right
into me, and when he smiles
a hungry smile, I decide Robyn's
tardiness must be

fate.

# ⊥ Watch Him

Climb the stairs past me,
try to keep all hint of drool
inside my mouth, where it belongs.
Guess whose door he knocks on.
"Robyn isn't home yet."

He turns, eyes narrowing
into discerning slits. *She's always
late. I swear she gets lost,
driving ten blocks from school
to home. The name's Trey.*

"Hey, Trey. I'm Kri . . .
[Bree!] The voice inside
my brain practically shouts.
"Br . . ." No, I'm not her
anymore. "Kristina."

Trey smiles. *Good to meet
you, Kri-Br-Kristina. You a friend
of Robyn's?* He saunters over,
plops down next to me,
leg touching mine.

My heart picks up its pace.
Can he hear it? If he doesn't,
he's deaf! Around the pounding,
I manage, "I'm an old friend
of Robyn's, just here for a visit."

His grin says everything.
*I see. Well, Robyn's friends*
*generally only "visit" for one*
*of two reasons. Stash. Or money.*
*Wonder which one you're after.*

I'm not copping to anything.
"Do you include yourself
on that list? Or are you after
something else completely?"
I'm trolling, and he knows it.

*Guess you'll have to hang*
*around to find out. Oh, look.*
*Here she comes now. Time*
*for the party to start.*
*You up for it, little girl?*

No one has called me that
in a very long time. I like
how it makes me feel.
"Oh, yeah. I'm up for it."
And a whole lot more.

Suddenly I'm very glad
I wore butt-slimming jeans,
a baggy shirt that covers
my tummy, and for the first
time in months, a little makeup.

# Robyn Greets Trey

With a massive, soggy kiss,
one meant to impress.
(But impress him or me?)

> All I get is a lukewarm,
> *Hey, Kristina. Long time*
> *no see. You look good.*

No hug? No warm, fuzzy
friendship to rekindle? Oh, well.
Not like we were ever the best

of friends. More like snorting
buddies. She used me. I used
her, and I'm using her now.

"You look great too, Robyn."
Yeah. Great. Like bones,
in a bag of jaundiced skin.

> Robyn opens the door.
> *Sorry about the mess.*
> *I've been kind of busy.*

*Anyway, housework is*
*such a waste. It never*
*frigging ends, does it?*

The smell—dirty ashtrays,
sweat, and a slight hint
of mildew—almost knocks

me over and I enter at my
own risk. "Mess" does not
describe the battlefield

I've just walked into.
The living room is strewn
with dirty clothes, designer

shoes, and smeared paper
plates. Attached is a small
dining nook. Books (text-

and other) spatter the table,
along with beads, pastels,
and various art supplies.

*I've always got two or three
projects going on at once,*
explains Robyn. *Some for art*

*class, others just to stroke
my creative side. Unfortunately,
I don't finish many.*

Trey laughs. *Spoken like
a true tweaker. Oh, and
speaking of tweak . . .*

He reaches down into his sock
and produces a plastic bag
with some serious-looking crystal.

So Robyn wasn't scoring
for Trey. He was scoring for
her! Very interesting.

# Robyn Is Making

A sizeable buy. I sit, growing more anxious with every

passing second, watching her weigh a half ounce of meth

into eight balls. She's into the deal, heavy. I mean, there

she is, holding enough crystal to send her away for a very,

very long time. My hands shimmy as I reach for the bindle

Robyn passes me. It's different from the meth making the

rounds last year. This is hard little rocks and not much powder.

Robyn pulls out a glass pipe, but I ask, "Can we do some

lines?" I long for that punch to my sinuses. The one that

hard-core users can no longer handle because of the gaping

sinus-cavity holes. Trey gives me a strange look, and Robyn

says, *Jeez, it* has *been awhile since you've used, huh? You* can't snort glass, Kristina. You have to smoke this . . . or

shoot it. You're not into needles by any chance, are you?

Trey laughs at my over-the-top horror. Needles? No way.

And, apparently, no fine white lines to watch disappear

into my nose. "Is it all like this now?" I ask, ignorant.

Trey answers with a shake of his head. *You can still*

*find street-lab crank. This is Mexican meth, as*

*good as it comes, maybe 90 percent pure.*

*It's pricey, of course. And worth every damn penny.*

How much is that, I want to know, but before I can query,

Robyn drops a sparkling rock into her pipe. She lights

a Bic, holds it well under the glass, and a fine plume of

methamphetamine smoke lifts to greet her open mouth.

The pipe travels next to Trey, who indulges, then passes

it on to me. My hand trembles, anticipating treasure.

Long-lost treasure. One slow, easy inhale sparks little

explosions inside my brain, firing directly into the pleasure

center, igniting ecstatic bursts from eyebrows to toenails.

Trey was right. Whatever it costs, it's worth it. I want

to feel this great all the time. With one hit, the life I have

worked so hard to make normal perverts itself again.

I came here, meaning to go home reenergized. But now

I don't want to return to the artificial "home" created by

my parents, my child. All of a sudden I feel more at home

with a forgotten friend and a complete, very cute stranger.

# That Idea

Vanishes
instantly,
with the
mere mention of money.
Trey said the glass was pricey.
Now he clarifies, *So the eight
ball is three hundred.*
I suck in breath like
it hurts to find it,
confess, "I only have
two hundred with me."
Trey tsks. *Can't do a
ball for a deuce. More
like a couple of g's.*
Two grams is plenty.
But the monster is a
greedy prick. "Can't
we work something
out? I'm good for the
rest, I swear." Trey
gives an *uh-huh* look.
But he says, *Well, I do
get to Reno sometimes.*
*Why not?*
Why not?
Why not!

# Why Not?

Can I really have established
       a new connection so easily?

Nothing in life is that simple.
       So I ask, just to make sure,

"Are you sure? Because I can
       bring the money to you."

Not that I can really tell him
       when, or how. But still . . .

       But he says, *I really do get to Reno,
       more often than I'd like, in fact.*

       *I'll have to come over in the next
       week or two. We can hook up then.*

       *But you'd better be good for the rest,
       or else . . .* He pounds one fist against

       the opposite palm, but his smile
       lets me know he's only joking.

       His smile. His incredible smile.
       Stop it, Kristina! [No, don't.]

# What I Don't Really Get

Is just *why* he's being
so accommodating.
Just what, exactly, is his

game?

Can he possibly be
interested in me, baby
blubber and all? I want
to be back in the

game.

Lately, I think about it
more and more. Like
a sick little kid, I want
to go outside and

play.

But I've never been
especially good at
choosing play
partners. Is Trey

the game

I'm after, and is he
after me? If so, I need
to learn the rules of his
game so I can

play it well.

# I Meant to Pick Up a Stash

Make a quick about-face,
    head back to Reno. Like
        I couldn't have guessed it
            might not turn out that way.
                But I haven't talked to anyone
                    my age in months. Between
                        that and the toot, my mouth
                            won't stop working.
One bowl. Robyn and I talk
    about Reno, how life used
        to be. Two bowls. We talk
            about how life is now—
                too many classes for her,
                    too much home for me.
                        Still another bowl. We
                            talk about our gay siblings.
Trey perks up at that.
    Apparently he wasn't
        privy to Robyn's more
            personal information,
                and gay relatives are
                    always interesting to
                        those who don't happen
                            to have any of them.

Another toke. Trey sits
    between Robyn and me. His
        knee rests against mine.
            The warmth of it fights
                the crystal's chills, and
                    turns me on completely.
                        My face flares a deep,
                            noticeable crimson.
Robyn flashes a tweaker's
    smile, one that says, *Don't*
        *fuck with me, or I'll pay*
            *you back good. In fact,*
                *I'll pay you back first.*
                    But what comes out of
                        her mouth is, *So, tell*
                            *me all about your baby.*

# Purposely

Haven't mentioned Hunter.
I mean, it's not like the first
thing you do when you meet
an incredible guy is tell
him you've got a baby.

But Trey seems more
interested than offended.
*Baby, huh? You're not
married, are you?*

His curiosity, and Robyn's
evil glare, make me smile.
"Nope, not married . . ."
Even spun, the thought
brings me up short.

*So, where's Daddy? You
living with him or what?
Is he watching Baby tonight?*

The meth monster threatens
to pounce, but I rein it in.
Not a single vicious comment
about Daddy the rapist.
"I live with my parents.
My mom babysits Hunter
when I'm not around."

             *You still live with your*
             *parents? Mine would have*
             *kicked me out. But hey,*
             *they kicked me out, anyway.*

Bree laughs, loving
how it makes Robyn squirm.
Kristina knows it isn't very
nice, so she blames it
on the crank, which fuels
a very long ramble, Trey's
knee still sizzling against mine.

"I'd like to move out
but I need a job, and to get one
I need my GED, which I'm
still working on. And even if
if I get a job, I need someone
I trust to take care of Hunter."

Trey gives me an odd
look, one I cannot
decipher. But all he says
is, *Makes sense to me.*

Very little makes sense
to me at this moment.
All I can think about
is how great it is to feel
so alive, so in lust again.

# 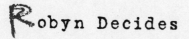obyn Decides

To break up the party.
*It's great to see you again.*
she says. *But it's getting late and
I do have some projects to finish.*

"Late? How late?" I still
have to drive all the way home.
I twist Trey's arm until
his watch reveals the time:

nineteen minutes past one.
No wonder my boobs hurt,
having not been emptied
in so many hours. They're

hard as stones and leaking
a little. Another twinge
of guilt. No more
breast milk for Hunter.

Trey hands me a scrap of paper.
*Here's my number, and give
me yours, too, okay?
In case you forget to call.*

His hand brushes mine
like a summer kiss. Heightened
by the meth spinning circles
in my brain, his simple touch—

not to mention his request—
sparks shivers, thigh to neck.
But it *is* time to go. I spent
my motel money, and anyway,

I'm much too buzzed
to sleep. Might as well drive
on home. Three hours will
go by like nothing, this buzzed.

"Thanks for everything, Robyn.
Awesome meeting you, Trey.
Hope to see you again soon."
Real, real soon.

# Start to Leave

Reconsider, knowing I'll
        want to stop for a small
                pick-me-up along
                        the long road home.

                    "Oh, hey. Can you spare
            a piece of tinfoil and
      maybe a straw? I've got
zip for paraphernalia.

*Let's make you a pipe,* Trey
        tells me. *How about a light*
                *bulb, Robyn?* She obliges,
                        and in a matter of minutes,

                    Trey turns it into a smoking
            device. *Be careful. It will get*
      *really hot. Oh, and you'll*
*probably need this, too.*

He reaches into his pocket,
   extracts a lighter. *Now just*
     *drop a rock, right in here. . . .*
      He demonstrates with one

     of Robyn's. *Hold the lighter*
    *right about here. . . .* A thin
  plume of smoke lifts, and
Trey is quick to inhale.

As Robyn and I help him
   finish it, Trey says, *So,*
    *Kristina, next time*
     *you're up for the score,*

     *call me. This shit travels*
    *the US-95 corridor up from*
  *Mexico. My connection lives*
*near Reno. Ironic, huh?*

No wonder Trey gets
        to Reno sometimes.
                Ironic barely covers
                        it. But hey, next time

                        I won't have to drive
            all the way to Stockton.
        (Let alone have to deal
with Robyn's evil eye.)

"That's good to know,
        Trey," says Kristina.
                Then Bree takes over.
                        "Next time you come

                        over the mountain, be
                sure to give *me* a call.
        I'll pay you back the
hundred. And if you talk

real nice, I just might
          add a little interest."
                    Holy crap. Team Bree
                              with the monster, you


never know what you
          might get. But Trey
                    laughs. *And just what
                              do you have in mind?*


                    This is Bree's game. So
          why does she disappear
     now? I shrug. "For me to
know and you to find out."


*Guess I'll have to make
          it soon, then. The curiosity
                    might do me in.* He wraps
                              the hot bulb in a napkin,


                    walks me to the door, bends
          to bring his lips close to my
     ear. *Careful driving home. I
want you all in one piece.*

# He Wants Me

All in one piece.
But does that mean
he wants me?

        I take the stairs slowly,
        head turning cartwheels.

It's been so long
since anyone has
wanted me.

        At the bottom of the stairs,
        I turn to look over my shoulder.

I want to believe
that he wants me.
But it's impossible.

        Trey's backlit silhouette
        is still in the doorway.

Maybe it isn't
impossible. Only
highly unlikely.

He raises a hand, waves
a good-bye. Closes the door.

I never used to
second-guess
myself. What's up?

The porch light winks out.
Is Trey staying the night?

Well, of course he is.
Why do you think
Robyn wanted you gone?

Jealousy wells up inside.
I want him to stay with me.

Wanting and getting
are two totally
different things.

I want him to take me in
his arms and kiss me.

Why must I torture
myself? He's with
Robyn. Right now.

I want him to touch
me all over my body.

Cut it out, Kristina.
You're just making
things worse.

I want him to tell me
he needs me. Loves me.

What am I thinking?
I don't want
that at all.

Yes I do want that.
I want to be in love.

Stop it! Don't you
know talking to yourself
is a sign of insanity?

# It Is a Clear

Not quite warm
September night,
the obsidian sky

brimming

with stars. An orange
harvest moon lights
the semideserted
highway, and my

confidence

in my ability to
reach home, all in
one piece, grows with
every mile left

dissolved

in my wake. I am
wide awake, buzzed
to the nth degree.
I drive slowly, lost

in thoughts

of Hunter, hopefully
sleeping soundly;
of the things that led
up to having him;

of what life

                would be like if he had
                never been conceived.
                I would never have
                thought I

could

                consider living without
                him; never would have
                thought I might

easily

                distance myself from
                him. But I want
                someone—other than
                a baby—to love, and

soon.

                I miss feeling special.
                Miss feeling beautiful.
                I only hope I haven't

become

                impossible for a guy to look
                at with lust in his eyes.

# Halfway Home I Stop

For a small pick-me-up,
not because I particularly
need it (my eyes are wide,
wide open), but because I can.
I have stash. It's talking to me.

One little hit, my heart revs
high, then settles into quick-
step mode. How I've missed
that race and pound. How
I've missed the lack of control.

It makes no sense. I know
that. But I'm sick of making
sense. Sick of being sensible.
As I consider that, it hits me
that I haven't called Mom.

Now it's much too late.
Is she pacing the floor, ready
to pounce when I walk
through the door? Has she gone
to sleep, assuming I stayed

overnight and forgot
the cell phone in my purse?
Cell phone! I yank it out,
and sure enough, there's
a voice mail message

waiting for me. *When you
get this, please call and let
us know you're safe. I don't
care what time it is.* Mom
is pissed, and rightly so.

I look at the time. Two
twenty. Screw it, I'd better
call. Mom answers on
the second ring. *Hello?
Kristina, is that you?*

Who else would it be? "Yes,
it's me. I'm fine. I stayed
late at Robyn's, decided
to come on home. No worries.
I've had gallons of coffee."

*No worries? Kristina Georgia*
*Snow! Have you no consideration*
*whatsoever for your family?*
*We've been so worried!*
*One simple phone call . . .*

She's right. Of course she is.
But I don't feel like giving much
ground. "I'm sorry, Mom.
Go on to bed. I'll be home
soon." I hang up without

even asking about Hunter. I'll
have to eat a table full of crow
in the morning, but why
worry about it the rest
of the way home?

# I'm Totally in the Wrong

And I totally know it.
And I totally don't care.
That's the monster talking
and I totally know that, too. But
I'm totally ready to listen to every
word, every excuse, every suggestion.

I feel great, for the first time in months.
I feel positive about the future, like
I actually might have a future
beyond babies and books. I
feel like I've got the world
by the balls. I just have

to remain cool, calm
down my parents, regain
my power. I ask the monster
how to manage that and he replies,
*Simple. You need money.* Money! Of
course. Can't have much of a life without

a steady supply of the green stuff. I
I do need money, and that means
a job. But what kind of job?
Only one thought comes
readily to mind.

# I Get Home

A little before four. The house
is dark. Silent. Everyone fast
asleep. Except me, of course.

Rather than chance waking up
Hunter, I think I'll run on down
to the all-night convenience

mart and pick up an application.
Almost every kid in the valley
works at the Sev for a month or two,

while waiting to go off to college,
get married, or find a better job. It
pays minimum wage, and the work

sucks, but beggars cannot be choosers.
I park off to one side, check out who's
inside. Believe it or not, there's a guy

playing a slot machine. They have slots
in Nevada 7-Elevens. And grocery
stores, airports. Anywhere people get bored.

Even up-all-night bored. Turns out I know
the guy behind the counter. Grady's a year
older than me and a total loser type.

He'll probably never work anywhere
but at the Sev, which is doubtless
just fine by him. "Hey, Grady," I say.

>He gives me a total loser smile,
>the kind that gives you the creeps.
>*Hey, Kristina. You're up early.*

"I haven't been to bed yet,
actually." Those seven words say
much more than he needs to know.

>Grady looks at my eyes, and his
>grin grows real wide. *Oh, yeah.*
>*I can see it perfectly now.*

Whatever. If he knows, it's because
he gets high too. "I came
by to pick up an application."

*Funny time of the day for that.*
*Let me see if I can dig one up.*
He goes into the back room.

It takes a few minutes, but he
finally returns, application in hand.
*You sure you want to work here?*

*Mostly what's open is graveyard.*
*You'd have to put up with people*
*like him.* He points to the slot addict.

        The guy doesn't even turn around.
        *Fuck you,* he says, feeding
        a ten into the money reader.

"It's not like I really want to
work here, but I need a job
and my choices are limited."

The monster goes on to tell him all
about Hunter. About living with my
parents, studying for my GED,

and wanting a way to escape.
"I'll be eighteen in a couple
of weeks. But I can't do anything

until I can save up enough
for a little place. Food. Diapers."
I smile. "Miscellaneous."

> Yeah, well, if you ever need help
> hooking up with that, give me
> a buzz. You know where to find me.

# All the Way to Stockton

And it was right here,
          practically under my
nose (ha-ha) all the time?

          As I start out the door,
the slot machine freak lights
          a cigarette. Now, I haven't

indulged that habit in quite
          a while either. I quit when I
was pregnant—figured I

          was eighty-sixing one bad habit,
why not lose that one too?
          But meth and nicotine buddy up

real fine. The smell of fresh-
          lit tobacco sucks me right up
tight against Slot Man.

          "Could I bum one of those?"
I'm flat out of cash at
          the moment, and still under

eighteen. Grady might
            stroke me by pretending
he doesn't know my age,

            but the cameras are rolling
and stings for selling booze
            or smokes to underage people

are common. I don't want
            to get him in trouble, not when
he might be helpful in the future.

            Besides, one cancer stick, with
no more in a drawer, won't
            get me hooked again. Right?

Slot dude smiles a knowing
            smile, shakes one from the
hard pack. *You owe me one.*

            Yech. He's scruffy. Kind
of smelly. I definitely hope
            he doesn't think I owe him.

Grady hands me some matches.
        No law against that, right?
"Thanks. I'll be in touch."

        I retreat outside, into the cool
of sunless morning. My hands
        shake a bit as I fire the Camel Light.

It tastes like heaven. Like
        if I could just keep smoking
it, I'd never need to eat again.

        If you've never smoked, you won't
understand that, but if you have,
        you know exactly what I mean.

I suck the poison slowly,
        with great, immediate pleasure.
It's almost as good as . . .

        Okay, maybe not as good as
that. But it calms me,
        convinces me to go on home,

do whatever is necessary
            to keep my mom and Scott off
my back. Apologize like I'm

            really, truly sorry. And, in
several ways, I really am. But
            there's no turning back now.

# Tiptoe Through the Door

Hoping the house is still
silent, and it is. Down
the hall, into my room,
where I quietly seek
out a new stash place,
then lie down on my bed.
The pink silk quilt is almost
too soft. Part of me—a small
part, growing smaller by
the minute—demands penance.

> That small part, the Kristina
> part, keeps whispering
> what a fool the other,
> Bree part, is. "Not only
> were you stupid to sneak
> back to the monster," she
> mumbles, "but ten to one
> you're going to get caught.
> Mom and Scott will know."

The Bree part just stares
contentedly at the ceiling,
really comfortable for the
first time in too many months.
Meth. Tobacco. A chance
at a spectacular guy, even
if he does live three hours
away, over a major mountain.
*I get to Reno sometimes.*
Will he come just for me?

"Yeah, right," Kristina
says. "Trey is going to
dump Robyn (who no
doubt gives him head
after giving him money)
and drive over the Sierras
for a frumpy chick with a
baby, who lives with her
parents, who are going to
bust her anyway."

[Shut the hell up.] Bree
talking, damn her sharp,
irritating whisper. [Don't
talk too much, keep your
(my) temper in check, leave
the ranting to Mom and Scott,
you'll (we'll) be just fine.
And whatever you do,
leave your conscience—
and confessions—behind.]

I sit in bed, arguing
with myself until the sun
peeks up over the eastern
hills, eyes almost as red
as mine must be. Just about
the time the sky shimmers
light, Hunter wakes up.
I go to him quickly, hustle
into the kitchen to fix him
a bottle, kissing him quiet.

Since Mom was up so
incredibly late last night
(worrying about me!)
[hey, conscience, remember?],
she might just sleep in.
Maybe she'll be so rested
that she'll only give me
the second degree. I'm
sure not in any mood
for the third.

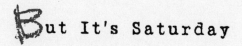
# But It's Saturday

Mom and a friend of hers
         always go to the gym early
to work out. Which means
         no way will she sleep in.
                  She pads into the kitchen,
                      notices I'm feeding Hunter.
                  *Glad to see you made it home*
                      *okay. What time did you get in?*
I suppose I could lie, but
         that's just stupid. "Around
four thirty, I guess. I'll take
         a nap when Hunter does."
                  Mom gives me a solid once-
                      over, but if she notices
                  anything, keeps it to herself.
                      *So how was the college fair?*
College fair? Oh, yeah.
         "Okay, I guess. It's a
pretty nice campus and all.
         Robyn seems to like it."
                  She looks at me harder.
                      *Robyn's at UOP, isn't she?*
                  *I thought you said the college*
                      *fair was in Sacramento.*

One thing meth is good
          for—manufacturing lies
sans hesitation. "I always mix
          up Stockton and Sacramento."
                    She stares me straight in
                              the eye. *Good thing you*
                    *didn't mix them up when*
                              *you were behind the wheel.*

"Heh-heh. Yeah, you're
          right. Oops. Smells like
Hunter's breakfast went
          right through him. . . ."
                    I start to get up, but Mom
                              puts a severe hand on my
                    arm. *One second. I need to*
                              *talk to you about something.*

I swallow hard. Does
          she hear Bree's voice
in my mouth, see the
          monster in my eyes? "What?"
                    *Leigh called. She's planning*
                              *on coming home for your*
                    *birthday. I thought it might be*
                              *a good time to baptize Hunter.*

Relief floods my face
      like a hot, red tidal wave.
"Baptize Hunter? Oh.
        Yeah. Well, I guess so."
                *Good. I'll talk to Pastor*
                  *Keith at church tomorrow*
            *morning. You should*
               *think about godparents.*

Jeez, is that it? Inquisition
      over? "Godparents. Right.
Meanwhile, diaper patrol."
      I make a hasty exit.
            Hmm. Baptize Hunter? I've
               never considered it, let alone
           who I'd want to take care
             of him, should something
bad happen to me. I don't
      have any friends who could
fill such big shoes. Mom
      and Scott? Can grandparents
           be godparents? Maybe Leigh?
              But would I have to name her
           partner, too? And how would
             Pastor Keith feel about that?

Thoughts and ideas volley
          back and forth in my head.
I put Hunter in his swing,
          watch him rock along.

I feel exhilarated. I feel rotten.
          I know I've made a terrible
mistake. I'm ecstatic that
          I found a way to make it.

# Mom Leaves for the Gym

Now I have to face Scott,
who finally comes downstairs,
"pissed" written all over his face.

*Well, look who decided to*
*grace us with her presence.*
*I can't believe how rude you are.*

I didn't have to take it from
Mom. Should I take it from
husband number two? "Sorry."

*Yeah, whatever. Just don't*
*expect to borrow one of our*
*cars again anytime soon.*

All the more reason to find
a way to keep my own vehicle
in tip-top shape. "I won't."

*Did you apologize to your*
*mother? She sat up half*
*the night, worrying about you.*

Irritation blossoms. And I'm
starting to want another
little toot. "Yes, I apologized."

*Damn straight. Kristina, you're*
*a mom yourself now. Can you*
*not relate, just a little bit?*

Like Hunter is going to
borrow a car and stay out all
night anytime soon. "Sure."

Good. All it takes is a simple
phone call, okay? That's why
we gave you the cell phone.

"I'm really, truly sorry, Scott.
Robyn and I just got to par . . . uh,
talking, and I lost track of time."

Okay, Kristina. I can understand
that. I know it's been a while
since you've spent time with a friend.

He's letting me off this easy?
Unreal. "Yes, it has. Thanks
for understanding, Scott."

Just don't forget you won't find
a better friend in the world than
the friends you have in your family.

# Scott Takes Off to Play Golf

Jake is at a friend's.
I put Hunter down
for a nap, decide to try
one myself. My

                brain

might be doing
jumping jacks, but my
body is shutting down.
It feels like a lead anchor,

                sinking

in a sea of quilt,
tugging me toward repose.
I'm drifting. Sleeping?
A parade of

                faces

floats behind my closed
eyes. An ethereal Robyn
grins, her ecru face

                distorting

into a vampirelike apparition.
Right behind her comes Trey
(predator or prey?),

                handsome

and hungry as a winter-
starved coyote. Segue
to Grady, Grade-E loser,

                                        vile

convenience store
slave and crystal meth
submissive, followed
by Leigh, my absent,

                                        beautiful

sister, with her lesbian
lover, the cheerleader.
Then Mom and Scott, who
must suspect the

                                        uglier

side of last night's adventure.
So why didn't they lash
out at me, bombard me

                                        with

questions, search my stuff,
smell my breath, something?
Do they just not want
to know for sure, stress
themselves with such

                                        wisdom?

Or have they, perhaps,
simply given up
on me?

# That Feeling

Of wanting to sleep,
                desperately needing sleep,
                                fighting the monster for sleep,
reminds me of one reason
                I have been happy to leave
                                the meth in Hunter's wake.
Though it's calling to me,
                *Just one more little toot,*
                                I simply will not give in.
I *will* keep the monster in
                check. I *am* stronger
                                than any addiction. Right?
Somewhere, a telephone
                rings. I swim up into gray
                                afternoon, the inside of
my head thick as chowder,
                tug myself from bed,
                                go to find the offending bell.

I don't get there quickly
                enough. Hunter wakes
                                at the alarm, and by the time
I reach the phone, nap-wet
                baby soaking one arm,
                                the caller is midmessage.
. . . haven't been out your way
                in a long time. I figured
                                your eighteenth birthday
was a good excuse. Besides,
                I want to see my grandson
                                while he's still a baby. We
should hit Reno on the twenty-
                eighth, so save a few hours
                                to celebrate with your old man.

# My Dad

Is coming for

a visit?

(Why now, after
all these years?)
And not just

any visit,

but on the weekend
of my birthday,
when Leigh is
also coming for

an unexpected visit.

Leigh, who still
refuses to speak
to the father who
left her in his dust.

A visit now,

the same time as
Hunter's baptism?
I can just hear
Mom: *That bastard*
*has to plan*

*a visit to Reno,*

*a place your sister*
*and I figured he'd*
*forgotten about?*
*Why does he have to*
*remember it now?*

# I Expect Her to Say

Exactly that. She doesn't.
But what she *does* say is enough
to make you cover your ears.

I never knew my mom could
have such a foul mouth! You
fill in the blanks. They scare me!

*That mother——ing sonofabitch!*
*Did he spend all year, waiting*
*for just the right ——sucking*

*moment to f— up what should*
*be a perfect day? He has no*
*——ing right! No right at all.*

*I simply cannot believe*
*that pr— would dare show*
*his face around here,*

*not after last year. And as for*
*his wanting to play "grandpa,"*
*I really don't think so!*

I'm conflicted about his plans.
I want no confrontations, no bad
blood. (Especially not if it's going

to be spilled in the baptismal
fount, or over the icing on
my birthday cake!)

But, despite everything that
went down over my summer
in Albuquerque, I want to see

Dad again. He's a freak, true,
and a piss-poor father.
But he still belongs to me.

# Mom Is Still Ranting

And suddenly she seems to intuit
my inner turmoil, which only
serves to make her angrier still.
*You can't want him to come
here, Kristina? Do you really
want him to spoil this special day?*

What can I say but the truth?
"Why does he have to spoil
anything, Mom? You've been
divorced, like, forever. Can't
you bury the hatchet—and not
literally? Can't you just let it go?"

Hunter starts to fuss—he's still
soggy—and Mom takes him
from my arms. *I'll never forgive
him for the way he treated his
family, Kristina, or for the path
he put you on last year.*

Okay, that's just not fair.
"You can stay mad at him
forever, Mom. I don't care.
But you can't blame him for
the choices I made. He didn't
make those decisions for me."

She levels me with a single
glare. [Damn, that's a real talent.]
*I suppose that's true, and I guess
I can't stop him from coming.*
She hands me the phone.
*But* you *have to tell your sister.*

# Mom Goes to Change Hunter

I dial Leigh's number,
praying she isn't home.
No luck there. We exchange
pleasantries, chat
a few minutes. Finally,
I break the news.

Leigh takes it well.
*No fucking way! Kristina,*
*I want to be there,*
*you know I do, and I really*
*want you to meet Heather.*
*It's taken both of us this long*
*to make that meeting happen.*
*But how can we possibly come*
*now? I wouldn't know what*
*to say to Dad, or how to react*
*when I saw him. Why hasn't*
*he ever once called me, Kristina?*
*How can he care so little?*

I don't want to tell her drugs—
and maybe sex—mean more
to him than anything, though
I know in my heart that's
the truth. I don't want to tell
her that's the way of the monster.
"I don't know, Leigh. But you
have to come, okay?"

I haven't seen her in months,
and want her here for my birthday,
not to mention the baptism.
Suddenly I know what to say.
Pastor Keith will simply
have to deal with it, one way
or another. Anyway, I'm not
so sure God will have a hard
time with my choice.

"I want you and Heather
to be Hunter's godparents.
Please, Leigh. Please come."

# It's Been Almost a Week

Since Leigh reluctantly agreed

to serve as Hunter's godmother.
(Godfather? Thank goodness I don't

know all the little details. They
might make me change my mind.)

But I'm happy (and sort of surprised)
to say I've managed to keep my use

pretty much under control.
I've only indulged maybe twice

a day, and yesterday I completely
ignored the monster's whining.

Mostly because my body finally
demanded the sleep of the dead.

I claimed a flu bug was taking me
down, and Mom believed every word.

With my red eyes, sweats, and chills, no
doubt I looked the part. I slept thirteen

hours, got up and ate dinner, then crashed
back out until this morning. Of course,

the first thing I did when I got up was
sneak around back for a quick toke.

I have to admit I totally misjudged a few
things, like the crystal's effect on my mothering

capabilities. I thought it would make it
easier to segue into my daytime routine

after late-night hours cajoling Hunter
to please, please go back to sleep.

Instead, the glass tends to make me
(with apologies for the coming pun)

a tad cranky. Imagine trying to placate
a fussy baby when his crying sends

major body rushes up and down your spine,
crashing into your skull and vibrating

inside your brain. Imagine trying to hold
him against breasts hard as boulders

from all the milk left to ferment inside
and finally—blessedly—dry up completely,

leaving your boobs a whole cup size
smaller than before you got pregnant.

Imagine, when the idea of food
makes you want to retch, trying

to deal with mostly-digested
baby formula, big green glops,

smeared on a butt (even if it is a pretty
cute baby butt), all yours to clean.

Imagine trying to play This Little Piggy
when what you really want is to hook up

with a guy for a great night of smoking
and "touch me right there, please."

Yeah, yeah, I know that—and exactly
that—is what got me into this predicament

to begin with. So no lectures. But hey,
if there's a cute, available guy out there,

please, someone, please point him
in my direction.

# The Garage Calls

My car is purring like a kitten
and wants to come home.
"So what's the total?"

*Fifteen hundred eighty*
*big ones. Will that be*
*cash, check, or charge?*

Like who's got fifteen
hundred in cash lying
around? "Um, check I guess."

Mom will not be pleased,
even though she promised
she'd take care of it for me.

She's not. *That's a lot*
*of money, Kristina. How*
*are you going to repay us?*

She won't be pleased
about my answer, either.
God, just please, no

lectures! "I put in an
application at the Sev.
I should hear soon."

She tsks her tongue. *Who'd
have thought you'd end
up working there?*

"It's not the worst thing,
Mom. At least it's close.
I asked for swing shift,

but sometimes they start
you on graveyard."
Grade E's loser shift.

She shakes her head
and I know that means:
*What will people think?*

# My First Inclination

With the monster
whispering in one ear, is to snap
something rude.
But Bree, believe it or not,
reigns me in.
[Won't serve our purposes.]
Her hiss is inside
my head. [We do want Mom
to agree to pay
for our car, now don't we?]

Yes, in fact we do.
So I temper my temper and
say, "It's only for
a little while, Mom. I have
to pay you back
somehow, don't I?" I don't
mention my need
to escape the confines of her
house, but I do
confess, "And a little cash

for gas, diapers, and
incidentals (!) would be nice."
Mom melts, but
just a little. *I guess you're
right. Thank you
for taking the initiative to
apply for a job.
I don't mind watching the
baby while you
work, and I know a degree*

*of independence
is important to every young
woman. It's just
that you've always had such
big dreams. I don't
want to see you lose them.  You
made an immense
mistake, but it shouldn't mean
the demise of all you
worked so hard to accomplish.*

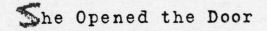

# She Opened the Door

To a real conversation and,
       fired up on twenty hours' sleep
               and a good strong whiff of quite
       excellent glass, I feel like talking.
Does she really want to listen?

"I've got lots of time to put
       my life back in order, Mom. I
           want to, really I do. But I need
       your help, and not just financially.
I want to make a good life for

Hunter, a good life for myself.
       I want to stay close to my
           family, but I also need the chance
       to leave the nest. To do that,
I need an income. I need a job."

       Her jawline turns to stone.
           *What about college, Kristina?*
               *A job is all well and fine. But*
       *to continue the lifestyle you're*
    *used to, you need a career.*

I want to scream. College?
        Career? Lifestyle? No! I
                need freedom—the freedom
        to make my own choices.
The freedom to get high.

But I know screaming
        is completely useless.
                [Counterproductive.]
        "You're absolutely right,
Mom, and I will go to

college, enter a career I
        love. But for now, going
                to work at the 7-Eleven
        seems like my best option.
Please support my decision."

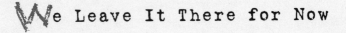

# We Leave It There for Now

She goes to get her purse [check-
book] and I run to my room for
a quick hit off my well-loved
lightbulb. I stick my head all the way
out the window, thinking about—
you guessed it—Trey, the artisan
hundred-watt soft white refinisher.

I'm still thinking about the tilt
of his shoulders, the sexy lilt in
his voice, while we drive to the
garage and Mom pays the grease
monkey. She hands me my car keys.
*Looks like Hunter is in La-La Land.*
*I'll take him home. See you in a bit.*

She's cutting me loose? Now I'm
thinking she's thinking she'd better
give me some room. She's right.
I've been cooped up for far too
long. Time to spread my wings
and let the wind carry me somewhere
new. To someone new?

The LTD chortles and the radio
plays Def Leppard, *Pour some
sugar on me* . . . I sing along, feeling
liberated despite everything. Okay,
I'm totally spun. And I plan to get
spunner, having brought along
my Trey souvenir and its glitter.

Glitter. Sugar. Ice. Glass. God!
I'm right where I want to be,
at least for now. I drive down
to the park on the river. Last time
I was here, Chase and I spent some time
getting buzzed and fooling around.
I wonder if he's all right. I miss him.

He hasn't sent me a letter in a while.
Of course, I didn't answer the last
one. It was just too painful to think
about his new life in California.
I bet *he's* got someone new.
Not that I want to know.
I'm not quite that masochistic.

There's a chill in the air when
I open the window. I watch
the cool breeze toy with the willows
along the riverbank. Take several
slow hits. Climb to a fine elevation,
listening to my favorite radio station's
new mix of classic rock and metal.

Everything changes eventually.
I know that's true, but it's hard
to wait sometimes. Sometimes
you just have to make things
happen. I'm making things happen
now. Whether they prove good or
bad simply remains to be seen.

# On the Way Home

I stop by the Sev to actually drop off
my application. (Okay, so I've only
really managed to fill it out. I've been
kind of busy the last week or so.)

Lucky me. The "big boss man"
is here, checking up on the day
crew. He looks me all up and down.
*What can I do for you, young lady?*

Okay, so he's kind of creepy. But I
know how to plaster on a smile.
"Just dropping off this application.
I live right up the hill behind here."

*Always good for our employees to live
close by. No "traffic" excuses that way.
Those really piss me off.* Here comes
the drool. But I can play that game too.

"I can imagine. But no worries
here. The only excuses I ever give
have to do with my period." OMG!
Bree has taken full-blown control.

Kevin is no match for her. He stops.
Stutters. Accepts the application
and suggests, *Let's go into the back*
*office and discuss possibilities.*

Bree and I trail him into
a big storage room, filled
with cartons and stuff. On
one table sits an old computer.

*Sit right there, Kristina Snow.*
*I see you're going to be eighteen*
*on Saturday?* He studies me like
a tough-to-crack textbook.

"That's right. So I really need
to make some money to move
out on my own. . . ." I debate telling
him about Hunter. Decide not to.

*No employment history, I see. So, no*
*cash register experience?* He doesn't
flinch at my blank stare. *Well, with*
*scanners it's easy. You can make change?*

Bree comes oozing out my pores.
"I can make just about anything,
Mr. Stewart. Change is a piece of pie."
Now I remember why I loved her.

He leans toward me, close
enough so I can see the hairs in his
nose. *Cream pie's my favorite.*
*What shift did you have in mind?*

Is he offering me—Bree—days?
One way to find out. "Well, I'd like
days, but I know you have to pay
your dues, so whatever works. . . ."

Now the drool fairly drips. *We'll*
*see what we can do about those dues,*
*but you happen to be in luck. One of*
*our day-shift people quit today.*

Unreal. The cretin *is* offering days.
And something else, too. I'll have
to consider that carefully. He's really,
truly nowhere close to my type!

He scoots his chair even closer to
mine, measures my [non] reaction.
*When can you start? I'll be happy
to come in and train you personally.*

Oh, yeah. I just bet he will.
But what will he train me *in*?
I tell him about the upcoming
celebrations. "How's Monday?"

*The shift starts at seven.* He stands,
gestures for me to precede him back
to the front of the store. I can only
guess what he's looking at from behind.

# As We Pass the Counter

The smell of fresh tobacco
almost makes me reel.
Damn, would I love a smoke!
No way can I ask for a pack
now. Kevin knows my age.
But in two more days not
only will I be old enough
to buy them, I'll have them
at my easy disposal.

Kevin pauses, extends a hand,
so sweaty it threatens to slip
from my grasp. *Welcome to
the team, Kristina. You'll be
working with Midge there.* . . . He
points to the middle-aged
redhead behind the blinking
cash register. *Say hello to
Kristina, Midge.*

She turns in my direction,
gives me a harder inspection
than Kevin himself did. And,
though she mutters an abbreviated
*hi* (can't get much shorter than
that, I know, but it came out
kind of like "h"), the almost
obscene roll of her eyes says
most eloquently, *Oh, great.*
*Here we go again.*

# Like I Care

I have my out.
I have my high.
I have more stash

                    waiting.

I have a job.
Almost have an income.
It is almost time

                    for an outstanding

eighteenth birthday.
I have earned my wings,
can't wait for my

                    test flight to freedom.

My head buzzes,
my body rushes,
electric, anxious.

                    I want a taste

of flight, a taste
of adulthood, another
small taste of ice

                    before afternoon dwindles.

The last thing on my
mind is Hunter, waiting
for his mommy.

                    I don't want to think

about Mom and Scott,
planning birthday
and baptism parties.

                    I don't want to think

about Leigh, who will
arrive soon and want
to spend time with me.

                    I don't want to think

that the monster
might have so soon
taken me hostage.

                    No, I don't want to think

such a thing
is remotely possible.
It isn't. Is it?

# o Why

Do I take a little detour,
drive up the gravel road
toward the quarry, dust
sifting over the LTD,
        find a spot under a tree,
        and, despite being pretty
        damned buzzed already,
        take another short stroll
                with the grabby monster?
                Something is different
                this time round, some
                little thing that keeps on
                        nagging at me. The
                        crystal is better, true,
                        so I know addiction
                        is even likelier than

before. That bothers
me some, yes, but like
I said, I've managed to
keep my use under control.
> Suddenly, as I inhale
> a hot, fragranced hit,
> it comes to me—the
> thing that's bugging
>> me. Before, I got high
>> as a way to socialize, to
>> fit in with the crowd, feel
>> less inhibited around guys.
>>> This time, though, I'm
>>> spending more and more
>>> of my time, getting more
>>> and more buzzed, alone.

# Tuck That Away

Into a not-so-accessible
recess of my psyche.

Everything is about to change.
I'll be out around people more.

Mingling in crowds more.
Interacting with men more.

And I'm not talking Kevin
Stewart or Grady or Slot Man.

But first I have to get through
the challenges of this weekend.

Starting with going home and
pretending I'm a perfect mom,

a decent daughter, and a loving
sister. Leigh will arrive soon,

cheerleader in tow. We'll all
have a wonderful dinner. (Will

anyone notice me, pushing
meat and veggies around on my plate

until everyone leaves the table?)
I won't sleep tonight. No way.

So tomorrow I'd better turn my
back on the monster. I'll need to

sleep before Sunday. Can't go
to church and stand up in front

of everyone bleary-eyed and
trembling, let alone take a chance

on passing out completely. Oh, yeah.
That would be one for the Good Newsletter!

# I Pull into Our Driveway

Park off to one side, where my dusty
LTD won't be in Mom's or Scott's way.
I sit a few minutes, absorbing rock
and roll rhythms, trying to slow
the race of my pulse, the hammering
of my heart. Truth be told, I'm wasted.

Finally I gather the nerve to go on
inside, and when I do, Mom hands
me a couple of large envelopes.
*Birthday loot, I'm guessing,* she says.
I open the first—fifty dollars from
Aunt Lou, who lives in Gainesville.

The second holds a hundred from
Scott's dad, my very cool Grandpa
Bill. The card reads: *Don't spend
it all in one place. Okay, you can!*
I'd hate to tell him it's already spent,
and I sure couldn't tell him what on.

Which reminds me of my promise
to myself to return the hundred to
Hunter's piggy bank. I *will* do that,
won't I? Yes, of course I will. Someday very soon. Well . . . I *do* have to cash
the checks. That could take a few days.

*And this,* says Mom, *is from Scott
and me. It would have been more, but
you never returned the hundred from
the other night. You know, the money
you didn't spend on the hotel. I'm not
sure I want to know what you* did *spend*

*it on, but anyway, happy birthday. . . .*
What does that mean? Do they
suspect the real intent behind
my visit to Robyn? They haven't
acted strangely at all, but maybe
I have. Have I? I don't think so.

Either way, she gives me a card
with daisies and puppies on the front
and two hundred dollars inside.
　　　　　I can't look her in the eye—not
with pupils the size of dimes—and
I'm afraid if I hug her she'll catch

　　　　　a solid scent of ingested crystal.
So I stand at a distance and say,
"Thanks, Mom. I promise to spend
　　　　　it wisely. Maybe I'll even put it
in my savings account. Maybe it can
even stay there, now that I've got a job."

　　　*So you got the job at 7-Eleven?*
She waits for my affirmative nod,
then adds, *I hope this doesn't mean*
　　　　　*you won't finish up your GED. You*
*need that to get anywhere, Kristina. . . .*
Tears interrupt. *You could have gone . . .*

                    I know she cares about me, wants
what's best for me. But we already
went through this once today. Anger
                    carbonates inside me, bubbles hot
and red, and if I let Bree have her way
right now, she'll say something I shouldn't.

# Luckily

The telephone rings, interrupting
a very tense situation. Mom shakes
her head and gives me a final look,

steeped with worry and something
kind of like curiosity. She knows
something, or at least intuits it.

She answers the phone, still
shaking her head a little.
*Leigh? You're here already?*

*I'll grab my purse and see you
in a half hour.* She turns to me.
*They took an early flight. I have*

*to go get them. Want to ride along?*
She wants me to, that much is
clear, but that would mean more

one-sided conversation. "I think
I'll stay here and play with Hunter.
He'll probably need another nap

soon, anyway. Car naps don't count."
The baby in question gurgles and
smiles, snug in his infant seat.

*Okay, then. We won't be long.*
She goes to the foot of the stairs.
*Jake! Come on! Leigh's waiting
for us at the airport.*

# Mom and Jake Leave

I gentle the big quilt
from its place of honor
on the living room couch,
shake it onto the floor
beneath the big picture         windows, marveling
                                for about the thousandth
                                time at the patience Mom
                                must have had to patch
                                the pieces all together.
        Then I go get Hunter,
        lay him in the center
        of the colorful fabric
        potpourri, lie down
        next to him, and marvel         for about the millionth
                                        time at how stunningly
                                        handsome he is. Pride
                                        inflates inside me, before
                                        segueing to massive guilt.

I feel spectacular. I feel
shitty. I feel on top of
the world. I feel like I'm
on my way to hell. The
ball's in my court. What          do I do? Serve? Volley?
                                   Concede? I want to be a
                                   good mom. I don't want
                                   to be a mom at all. But
                                   what choice do I have?

          Hunter coos and drools
          sweet-smelling baby spit,
          and I stroke his soft, soft
          cheeks. "Mommy loves
          you, Hunter." I really do,          and he loves me, too,
                                               with a purity that makes
                                               my eyes sting. What have
                                               I done? And more: What
                                               will I continue to do?

# Eventually

Watching dust motes play
in the afternoon light,
Hunter drifts off. I know
Mom et al will be home soon,

which gives me a small window
of opportunity to hook up with
the monster one last time.
I step out onto the patio, where,

shielded from the westerly
breeze, I can easily take a toke
and let the evidence escape
into the lengthening shadows.

Denying any earlier sense
of guilt, I ask the monster to step
up to the plate, hit an inside-the-skull
home run. It doesn't disappoint me.

Then I go to shower, douse myself
with deodorant and mouthwash.
Finally I hear the approaching party.
I zoom to meet them, at light speed.

# Leigh Has Put On a Few Pounds

And it suits her almost
as much as shedding several
suits me. (You'd be surprised
how much weight you can
lose in two weeks when you
barely eat enough to keep
a very small rodent alive.)

Anyway, it's awesome to see her
again. She hasn't visited since
before Hunter's birth. I know
she was mad at me for everything
that happened, and maybe she
had a right to be. Or maybe not.

I mean, she isn't exactly
the perfect daughter herself.
Here she comes, waltzing
down the hall on her lover's
arm—a stunning lesbian pair,
acting like they belong here.
[Belong here, together. Not
much room for us anymore!]

Bree talking, again. *Shut up!*
I tell her, and run to give Leigh
a mega mojo hug. [Good trick,
with Heather hanging on to her
like a monkey to a tree branch.]
*Shut the hell up,* I silently shout
to the bitch who lives in my brain.

Out loud I say, "God, I've
missed you. You look great.
Must be . . ." [the extra five
pounds or maybe the one
hundred twenty pounds
cemented to your right arm]
". . . did you change your hair?"

*Don't be silly. My hair has
looked exactly like this my
entire life. Although it is a
little bleached from being
out in the sun this summer.
Heather tries to tell me
it's bad for my skin, but I'm
not always so good at following
orders.  Oh! I almost forgot
to introduce you. Kristina, Heather.*

[Following orders? Can you
believe that?] I stow Bree and
give Heather a wary once-over.
"Good to finally meet you," I
venture. "Leigh has told me so
little about you. . . ." That
was mean, okay? [Not really.
Want to see "mean"?] *No!*

Heather maintains her grip
on my sister's arm. *Really?*
*Well, she's told me just*
*about everything about you.*
*Much more than I'd ever*
*choose to know, in fact.*

What does that mean? Okay,
maybe I'll just have to let
Bree out of her bottle after
all. If anyone can debate
the Cheerleader from Hell,
it's Bree. [Yeah, let me out.]
Can't. This is supposed to be
a celebration, not an insurrection.

# Truth Is

I don't know Heather
at all, but I despise her
already. It's not just that

she's freaking beautiful
or that she obviously
despises me, too.

[You're jealous.] Yeah,
yeah, that's part of it. But
what I hate most about her

is the way she seems to be
in control of my no-longer-
totally-independent sister.

*Oh, Heather, do you mind*
*if I tiptoe in to see the baby?*
*My curiosity is killing me!*

*You don't have to come*
*unless you want to. Kristina*
*will show him off later.*

Puke. Puke. Puke.
Smile that pretty girl-
on-girl smile for your

cheerleader. But don't
ask her permission to
leave the frigging room!

I mean, I guess in a same
sex relationship, someone
needs to play the guy,

and if I had to choose roles
for Leigh and Heather,
Heather would be the guy.

But hey, in any relationship,
does the guy really need
to be in charge?

# Instinct

Tells me to fall
deep into a well
of silence.

> *Keep your meth-*
> *fired mouth shut,*
> it commands.

> > [Oh, just try that
> > with the monster
> > screaming, *Let's party!*]

So I dare, "Must
you *really* ask
for permission?

> "Didn't you give
> that up when
> you left home?

> > "Is Heather your girl-
> > friend, or your
> > friggin' mommy?"

Yeah, the verbal slap
is mean. Really mean.
So why does it feel
        so damn good?
        Okay, I'm guessing
        you know exactly
                why. But the look
                on the room's collective
                face slaps me back.

*Kristina! You*
*apologize this instant,*
screeches Mom.
        *Kristina! How*
        *can you be so*
        *rude?* cries Leigh.
                Heather doesn't say a word.
                All she does is smile
                a leprechaun smile.

# Leprechauns

In case you don't know,
are cute little

        demons

with cherubic faces
and devil-born

        souls,

and when they smile,
you'd better

        run quick.

Well, Bree and I
decide no way will
the conniver make us

        run.

"Sorry," I say, but
when everyone except
Heather turns

        toward

Hunter's sudden
outburst in the living
room, I slip

        the bitch

the finger. Guess
what. She slips it back.
So now we both know
exactly where we
                    stand.
I make a mental
note to keep her
the frick out of my
bedroom, hold
                    my ground,
don't worry about
taking the high road.
Leigh's future
happiness is at stake.

# Then It Dawns on Me

If high school cheerleaders
indulge in "instant pep," college
squads probably start the party
earlier and keep it going well
after the game ends. Maybe
Heather and I have something
in common, after all.

But Leigh wouldn't go near
the stuff, would she? Secrets
between lesbians?

Hunter's still fussing
for attention. I go over
and take Leigh's hand,
making sure to turn my back
to Heather. I look into
my sister's eyes—bright
aqua, no sign of the monster
there. "Sorry. I must be
premenstrual. Come on.
I'll introduce you to Hunter."

I pull Leigh's hand, then turn
back to Heather. Close
assessment of her violet-blue
eyes yields no definitive answers,
though her pupils do look dilated.
I force a wide smile.
"Guess you can come too."

Heather takes her own
measurements, which apparently
must tally. *Why not?*

I lead the way to the living
room, where the setting sun
paints spectacular colors
on the west-facing window.
Hunter's awake, waving
his chubby fists at whatever
real or imagined air fairies
have caught his eye.

When he sees me, he smiles
his great, toothless smile.
"Hey, Sweetie," I croon.

"Meet your Auntie Leigh
and your . . ." [Uncle Heather].
The rest of my sentence sticks
around that idea. It takes all
my willpower (and you know
how much of that there is)
not to laugh out loud.

Heather shoots me a look
laced with understanding
as Leigh picks up Hunter.

She gives him a big kiss,
folds him into her arms
like she used to caress Jake
when he was a baby. *Oh, Heather.
Isn't he adorable?* she asks.

Heather gives Hunter a top
to bottom assessment, something
like how a scientist checks out
his pet lab animal. Then she pokes
my eyes with hers. *Uh-huh,* she says.
*He must resemble his father.*

# Oh Yeah, That Bites

In more ways than one. I have to admit Hunter
does look an awful lot like Brendan. I hate to
think just how much. But only two people know
the truth about Hunter's paternity—Chase and
me. When Mom asked, I told her I wasn't sure.
The "Father" line
on Hunter's birth
certificate claims:
*Unknown.* One
day, I know, he'll
ask about his dad. I'll lie to him, too.
Better I look like a sleep-around
slut than he should ever find out
he is the by-product of rape.
Anyway, Leigh
doesn't know, so
Heather doesn't
either. She did
mean to wound
me with her jab,
but not mortally.
I decide to let
it drop. At least
for a little while.

# For the Next Few Hours

Heather and I pretend
        cordiality, amidst watching
                Mom cook; Jake show off
                        his soccer trophies; and
watching Leigh play with Hunter, who
        is happy to have company.
                Which most definitely
                        stimulates not a small
amount of guilt in me.
        Since my Stockton trip,
                I must admit, I've spent
                        minimal time with him.
When my buzz starts
        to wear off, I find an
                excuse to sneak off
                        to my car, grab a toke,
maintain the very sharp
        edge I'd honed earlier.
                When I return, sucking
                        a mint, Heather smiles

the kind of smile that
        says she might be just
                the tiniest bit envious.
                        File that away for later use.
I actually *almost* think
        about offering her a whiff.
                But what if I'm wrong?
                    What if all she wants
is to double dunk me
        in a reservoir of shit?
                And anyway, on this
                    trip outside I made
a striking observation—
        there is a most definite
                dent in my stash, in
                    not quite two weeks.

# Dinner Tonight

Is interesting, to say
the least. Mom made
a huge ham, scalloped
potatoes, broccoli, rolls,
with apple pie and ice
cream for dessert.

        Jake keeps the small talk
        rolling: *Freshman English*
        *is just plain boring . . . think*
        *I'm too short to play basketball . . .*
        *Maryann Slocum is such a*
        *hot babe . . .* I've heard it all.

        But Leigh hasn't. She
        keeps prodding him for
        details, and when he
        turns red and quits giving
        them, Mom is happy to
        fill in the details she knows.

Heather and I pick at
our plates, hoping no
one will notice. But
Scott does. *Something
wrong with the ham?*
he asks, drawing much

too much attention away
from Jake and toward us.
"Nope. It's great," I say.
"I just ate too much while
we were cooking." The
explanation seems to work.

Heather chooses to flirt.
*It's delicious,* she cons,
batting her thick lashes,
*but I'm trying to lose
a few pounds.* Sure, off
an already flawless figure.

*Will someone please tell
her she's crazy?* pleads
Leigh. Then things get
really creepy, when she
turns to Heather. *You're
perfect, exactly as you are.*

Mom and Scott roll
with it. And it sails
completely over Jake's
head. Mouth stuffed
with cheesy potatoes,
he mumbles something

that sounds vaguely like
*Perfect doesn't cover it.*
He's in high school
already. How can he be
so dense? And has no one
told him about Leigh before?

[You tell him.] Luckily
Hunter starts fussing,
before I can volunteer
the information. Wrong
time, wrong place, much
to Bree's chagrin.

Leigh jumps up to pacify
the baby while Heather
goes to stick her finger
down her throat and puke
up the few calories that
have managed to make

it past her lips. Scott
gets up to read the paper.
Mom and Jake go to
do the dishes. Lucky me.
I wander outside to do
you know exactly what.

# I Won't Even Try

To sleep tonight.
I've spent all day

        climbing

to anxious heights,
me and my buddy
the glass monster,

        reaching

for a better buzz,
a taller head, one
more little whiff
(what could it hurt?),

        finally cresting

steep cliffs of speed,
rising above mundane,
towering over ordinary.

        No sense of fear,

I sit in my room,
sketching beneath
pale lamplight.

        No sense of foreboding,

I listen to Leigh
and Heather giggling
behind the too-thin
walls, doing

        whatever

girlfriends do. At
last, they fall silent.
I immerse myself
in charcoal portraiture,

        not even stressing about

the fact that it might
be a while before I have
time to sketch again,
or that I have most
definitely embarked on

        a major bender.

# But I Have

And not only that, but in
hindsight it probably wasn't a great

time for me to jump back
into the arms of the monster.

Not that there *is* a good time
to do that, and damn it all, you

know what they say about hindsight.
I mean, when I went to Stockton,

there were no plans for Hunter's
baptism, and a visit from my dad

was completely implausible,
especially at the exact same time

Leigh finally decided to schedule
one, after many distant months.

Throw in a bulimic lesbian
cheerleader with an aversion

to me, my dad's latest girlfriend,
a little brother with a major crush,

parents intent on a perfect weekend,
a pending new job, and what is left

of an eight ball of incredible speed,
and just about anything can happen.

And if Bree has her warped way,
just about anything will.

# It Is Late Friday Afternoon

When my dad pulls into our driveway,
no call to warn us of his imminent
arrival. Up till now, the day

has been relatively uneventful
except for a quick exchange
between Heather and me.

*I noticed your light was on
this morning around three,*
she says. *Up all night, huh?*

I shrug. "A lot of it.
Something about the bed-
springs creaking next door."

We left it at that and went on
about our business. Which is
a good thing. Sleep-deprived, brain

sizzling on yet another toke, my
thought processes are jumbled.
I'm not a worthy opponent.

The plan is a birthday dinner
at our favorite Italian bistro.
But dinner for six (plus room

for an infant seat) becomes suddenly
complicated when Dad's "new" '98
Montero wheezes up the driveway.

Otto barks, announcing a stranger's
arrival. Dad sits in his car a good
long while, no doubt ascertaining

his safety. Truth be told, Otto—
a hundred-pound black sable German
shepherd—would probably eat

Dad for lunch. I know he'd love
to take a big bite out of Dad's new
girlfriend, Linda Sue.

But locked safely away behind
six-foot chain-link, he won't
get the chance. Poor dog.

Once the two of them decide
Otto can't scale the fence,
Dad and Linda Sue slither

from the SUV. They stand
in the driveway, checking out
the view and ogling the house.

Five minutes of no sound
but barking, five final minutes
of peace before certain chaos.

# Jake Jumps to His Feet

Runs to the window. *Who
the heck is that?*

       Mom joins him. *Can you
       believe he didn't have
       the decency to call?*

*He? Who he?* insists Jake.
*Will someone please tell me?*

       Scott starts toward the door.
       *Did you think he would
       suddenly learn manners?*

Jake's face flares, cranberry
red over freckles. *Ahem! Who . . . ?*

       Heather peeks over Jake's
       head. *I don't know, but he sure
       looks like a shark out of water.*

*Fine! I'll just go ask him
myself!* Jake follows Scott

out the door. I glance in
Leigh's direction. Her face
is white as fresh fallen snow.

*Oh my god,* she says. *He's so
old, so . . . so . . . decrepit.*

# I Have to Admit

He looks faded,
travel-worn, threadbare.

High.

I can tell,
without getting close,
that he's sweating

speed.

Linda Sue doesn't look
the part of a serious
meth user. Only serious

pursuit

of my dad (don't ask
me why—who can say
what evil pheromones
must have been at work!)
could have dropped
her into his personal

hell

and kept her there,
smoldering at his side.
True love, between
a fairy and a troll,

bent on

proving he still has
what it takes to attract
someone ten years younger.
And both, at this moment,
look on the verge of

crashing.

# Okay, That's Bad

Even totally glazed, I know
Dad will be asking to share
what's left of my stash,

which makes me angry. Pissed.
Relieved. Some deep down straight
part of me wants to shake the monster.

Maybe I can if I quit right now.

I'll worry about it later. Right
now I'm worried about Leigh,
whose eyes are wide with emotion—
a strange mix of hate, love, and apathy.

If Mom is smart, she won't let Dad
inside. But ever the hostess, Mom
would be hard-pressed to dismiss
even a troll and his fairy

without first offering refreshments.

As they all start toward the door,
Leigh's body language changes
from curious to volatile. Every
inch of her tenses like a cheetah,

ready to pounce. Heather notices,
goes over to Leigh, strokes her hair,
kisses her lightly on the mouth.
*Don't take the offensive.*

*Don't give away your power.*

# Except for the Kiss Thing

My respect for Heather
     swells. I instruct myself
to remember that advice
     whenever I happen to sense
confrontation, or feel the
     urge to turn tail and run.

Today confrontation
     is immediate, the instant
Dad lurches through
     the front door. *Hi, honey,*
*I'm home.* The joke falters.
     And then he catches sight

        of Leigh. *Oh my God.*
          *It can't be my little Layla.*
        *You really grew into*
          *a beauty.* . . . He pauses,
        waiting for some response.
          Nothing. *Can I have a hug?*

Out come Leigh's claws.
            *I don't hug strangers.*
*Who the hell are you?*
            Her face contorts, a
subconscious effort to
            make itself less beautiful.

It fails. I steel myself
            for a lob of curses, but
Heather refuses to let
            the verbal battle begin.
She walks over to Dad,
            extends a hand, and tries

(obviously so) not to inhale
            too deeply. I can smell
Dad from across the room.
            The girl is brave. Really
brave. *Hello, Mr. Snow. I'm*
            *Leigh's partner, Heather.*

Dad checks her out too
            long. The cheerleader
facade has him completely
            confused. *Uh. Oh, yeah,
right. Partner, huh? Well,
            knock me over with a feather.*

I told you once before
            my dad was the King
of Cliché. And when
            it comes to tact, I'm
pretty sure it isn't listed
            in his internal dictionary.

# Linda Sue

Stands next to Dad, mouse
brown hair hanging in long
knobby ropes well past her
shoulders. Somewhere beneath
a thick sheet of makeup hides
a quite pretty woman.

    After a silent minute or two
    it becomes clear Dad isn't
    much for introductions either.
    Finally his new attachment
    says, *Hello. I'm Linda Sue.*
    *Sorry to barge in on you*—

        Dad interrupts, in a majorly
        rude way. *No problem, L.*
        *They knew we were coming,*
        *right gang?* He moves toward
        Leigh, who retreats slightly.
        *Well, I'm happy to see* you.

Leigh's face has gone
from ivory linen to scarlet
fleece, especially the tips
of her ears. *What took you
so long, Father? Too
busy to pick up the phone?*

*I . . . I . . . I . . .* , he stutters, his
inability to respond fueled
by the monster. [The monster,
on a crash diet of guilt.]
*I don't know what to say
except I'm sorry. Forgive me?*

This could be fun to watch,
as long as the sniping doesn't
turn into sniper fire—the battle
of the Snows. "No hello for
me, Dad?" I complain, adding,
"Nice to meet you, Linda Sue."

Everyone turns startled eyes
in my direction, as if they
can't believe I had the guts
to interfere. But a broad sense
of relief floods the room. No one
wants a battle between the Snows.

Scott takes the reins, offers,
*Let's go out on the patio.*
*Can I get you something*
*to drink? Iced tea? Lemonade?*
*We have some soda, too, I*
*think. Coke. Root beer . . .*

Dad just can't not be Dad.
*How 'bout real beer? Any*
*kind will do. We're not*
*picky, are we, Linda Sue?*
He gives her a kiss unsuitable
for mixed company.

[Not picky? Ha! Major
understatement!] I stuff Bree
back inside as Scott guides Dad
and Linda Sue outside. Mom
goes to hustle up a couple of
beers. Heather follows Leigh

upstairs. Jake and I stand here,
exchanging looks of disbelief.
Then we both break down
into a fit of uncontrollable
laughter. *Your dad is really
weird,* Jake can finally say.

Another major understatement.

# Dad and Pal

Overstay their welcome.
[Huge surprise!]

We have planned a birthday
dinner at our favorite
Italian restaurant in Reno

and as the hour of our
reservation approaches,
Mom and Scott grow a bit
antsy; Leigh and Heather

still have not reappeared;
and Hunter wakes from an overlong
nap hungry, wet, and otherwise
irritated. When I go to mitigate
that, Dad decides to tag along.

As I discard a soggy diaper
in favor of a nice dry one, Dad
says, *That boy is going to make
some woman very happy one
day! Takes after his grandpa,
in more ways than one.*

Okay, that's much more than
I want to know. "Well, I guess
he has your eyes. And not a lot
of hair. So yes, I guess he takes
after you a little bit, Dad."
We laugh as I dress Hunter
in cute overalls and a plaid shirt.

*Can I hold him?* asks Dad,
and my look is all the reply
he needs. *Hey, I'm no worse
off than you right now! Relax.
I remember how to hold a baby.
I promise I won't drop
the little guy on his head.*

He takes Hunter gently
from my arms, and though
the smell of Dad's crank
sweat makes me cringe,
Hunter doesn't seem
to notice one little bit.

Despite my trepidation,
Dad looks completely
comfortable, holding
a baby. *See?* he says.
*It ain't rocket science.*

Hunter also looks comfy
as Dad carries him back
to the living room. *Check
him out, L. Looks just like me.*

Linda Sue agrees, but everyone
else just stares at me like I've
totally lost my mind.

I'll admit I'm slipping into
the crash zone. Only one

way I know to fix that.

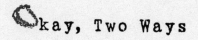

# Okay, Two Ways

And, all things considered,
I probably shouldn't try

    to sneak off for a walk
    with the monster.

        So I'll make it through
        dinner somehow (might

            even manage a nibble
            or three) and crash like a dead

                jet plane tonight. Of course,
                first we have to *get* to dinner.

*So where are you staying?*
Scott asks Dad. [Hint!]

    *Some little dive in downtown*
    *Reno,* answers Dad.

        *Figures,* Leigh whispers
        to Heather, who laughs out loud.

*It's not so bad*, offers Linda
Sue. *Small rooms, but clean.*

Mom bustles onto the scene
with her purse. *Let's go!*

*Go?* says Dad. *Do you have
plans? Don't let us interfere.*

*We weren't planning on letting
you interfere*, Leigh chimes in.

Scott moves between Leigh and
Dad. *We have dinner reservations.*

Linda Sue starts toward
the door. *Time to go, Wayne.*

*Sure*, says Dad. *Good seeing
you all. Kristina? Walk me out?*

# Dad Carries Hunter out the Door

Okay, that's really creepy. "Uh, Dad?"
I hurry after him, Linda Sue, and my
baby, but have to fight my way past

Mom. *Wayne?* she calls, wrinkling
her nose at the stench he's left
in his wake. *I'll take the baby.*

Dad turns, grinning. *You didn't think*
*I was kidnapping him, did you?*
*Sheesh. I've got enough problems!*

[No shit!] Still, both Bree and I
are relieved when he hands off Hunter
to Mom. He gestures for me to follow

him to his car. *I want to take you*
*out tomorrow night for your birthday.*
*As you can probably tell, I brought*

*a little go-fast along, but it's mostly*
*gone. I'm thinking you've got stash*
*of your own. Can you spare some?*

[Whose birthday is this, anyway?]
"I have a little I can share," I admit.
"But only about half a gram."

*If I give you some cash, can you*
*score some more?* He extracts two
wadded hundreds from a pocket.

"I'll try. But just so you know,
this was the first time I've done
any since Hunter was born."

*Okay.* He slides behind his steering
wheel. *Oh. I ran into Buddy before*
*I left. He said to send you his love.*

# Dad Drives Off

Leaves me coughing
on his exhaust fumes and shaking
at his parting remark.

I haven't stopped
to think about Buddy, aka Adam,
in a very long time.

Adam, who started me
on the highway to nowhere. And guess
where I'm standing now.

[Pretty damn close to nowhere.]

Still, remembering our
time together brings more happiness
than anything else.

They say you'll always
love your very first love. I'll always
love Adam a little.

But he's married, with
a baby just about Hunter's age. Why
would he send his love?

[Because he's a fucking player.]

Of course he's a player.
But he was my player once, at least
for a few great weeks.

Everyone piles out the
door. *We'll have to take two cars,*
says Mom. *Jake, you ride*

*with Dad. Ladies, we can*
*squeeze into mine.* But I volunteer to go
with Scott. "More room."

[Less nervous conversation.]

Jake sits up front. I take
the backseat for me, Bree, and
memories best forgotten.

Dad stirs them up too,
and something else—a big ol'
cauldron of guilt.

Two weeks and I'm most
of the way through a ball. What have I
done? Can I undo it now?

[Fat chance, now you've set me free.]

# Saturday Morning

I wake to voices in the hallway.
[Don't move. Pretend you're still asleep.]

Mom: *I'm going to wake her up.*
      Leigh: *Let her sleep. I'll take care of Hunter.*
            Heather: *She did look exhausted last night.*

Exhausted barely covers it.
[And now you'll be swamp-headed.]

Mom: *I don't know what's up with her lately.*
      Leigh: *Having a baby so young can't be easy.*
            Heather: *Her dieting must take a toll too.*

Okay, she definitely knows.
[But is she going to tell?]

Mom: *Dieting? What do you mean?*
    Heather: *She barely touched dinner last night.*
        Leigh: *And you know how she loves Italian.*

Heather barely touched dinner either.
[Yeah, but she's a better bullshitter.]

Mom: *She* has *lost a few pounds recently.*
    Leigh: *Rapid weight loss isn't good, though.*
        Heather: *I'd love to know how she's managed it.*

I'm going to kill her.
[You don't, I definitely will.]

# The Hallway Conversation

Recedes and I tug myself out of bed.
I thought I did a good con job at dinner
last night. Now I'll probably catch
an earful about rapid weight loss from Mom.

Heather is definitely on my shit list.
But apparently the loosening
of my jeans has not escaped notice.
Now if I can just run into Trey.

I'd call him about scoring for Dad,
but Stockton is too far away. So
last night, when everyone wandered
off to their bedrooms, I called Grade E.

I kept the request cryptic, of course,
and asked to meet away from the Sev.
Wouldn't do to get busted there, where
I'm supposed to start work on Monday.

Speaking of Grady, what time is it,
anyway? The clock says ten thirty.
Crap! I was supposed to meet him
at ten. I jump into clothes and dash

for my phone. Great. A message.
It's Grady, and he isn't happy.
*Where the fuck are you? It's ten
fifteen. You've got five minutes!*

I hit call return, fingers crossed.
"Hey, Grady, it's me. Sorry I'm late.
I . . . uh . . . got hung up with my mom.
I can be there in a couple of minutes."

He agrees to meet me at the state
park. *But I'll want a taste.*
I hope he means a taste of crystal,
not a taste of Kristina.

# First I've Got To

Get out the front door without
        someone stopping me. One excuse
comes easily to mind. I locate
        my keys and the money Dad gave
me and don't even stop to brush
        my teeth or hair. [Ugly picture!]
I hear everyone in the kitchen.
        Perfect. "I'll be right back," I call,
stowing the excuse for later.

I go straight for my car, jam
        the key into the ignition, and as
I back out, I notice Mom at
        the door, hands on hips. Her lips
are moving, but I wave and keep
        going. Within a quarter mile
my cell rings. Caller ID says it's
        Mom, and I consider letting
it go to voice mail. Better not.

"Hi, Mom. Yes, I know I was rude.
            Yes, I'm grateful Leigh volunteered
to get up with Hunter. Yes, I know
            we've got lots to do today. Yes, I
understand how important tomorrow
            is. Where am I going?" [Thought
she'd never ask!] "I woke up
            majorly on the rag and out of
tampons. Had to get some ASAP."

She mentions the obvious—
            that she has a box in her
bathroom. Couldn't I have
            asked instead of taking
off like a bandit in the night?
            "Heh-heh, yeah, I suppose
I could have, huh? Sorry for
            being so dense, Mom." I hold
my breath and, lucky me,

she goes for it, hook, line, and
            bobber. (I hate sinkers. My
bait always gets stuck in
            the muck when I use them.)
Anyway, I shouldn't waste
            a lot of time doing blow
with Grade E. He's parked
            at the far end of the parking
lot. And guess what.

He's not alone. From
            a distance I can see
two guys, bobbing heads.
            They're doing toot, and it
looks to me like they're
            doing it the old-fashioned
way—with a straw and mirror.

Wonder whose crank
          they're snorting. Wonder
how short the ball will
          be. [The two-hundred-dollar
price tag makes sense now.
          We're getting street crank,
not ice.] Wonder how cut

it will be. I pull into a near
          parking spot, and when I do,
the face that jumps into view
          makes me forget about every
question I had only seconds
          before. He's dark and cute
and he looks like Hunter.
          It's Brendan, and I want to puke.

# But I Can't Puke

I can't
        turn and run and
I can't
        look weak and
I can't
        even get nasty until the
deal
        is done.

        Brendan flashes a smile laced
with
        evil. I can't stand him. I despise
him.
        And now I have to look
        him in the eye?
I won't
        give him the satisfaction of turning away.
I won't
        get in his face, or out of his face.
I won't
        give up my secret.

No, I will never,
ever,
          not in a billion years,
confess
          the unimaginable result
          of his despicable act,
that
          it created beauty.

          Will never confess that
my son
          [can evil be genetic?]
is his son.

# I Had Hoped

Never to see Brendan again,
but I guess it just goes to show
that as much as Reno has grown,

it's still a compact city. And just
my luck, Brendan still lives in it.

I'll take the high road and if
the low road seems necessary,

I'll let Bree get behind the wheel.
One thing for certain, though,
I'm not getting into Grady's car.

I roll down my window; Brendan
does likewise and I speak past him.
"Hey, Grady. Thanks for waiting.

Come over here, will you please?
I'd rather handle this in private."

*Aren't you going to say hi?*
Each of Brendan's words is

a stab. *I heard you had a baby.*
Deep stabs, severing arteries.
*You look good, anyway.*

Ever chivalrous, that would be
Brendan. "Hi, Brendan. Yes,
I had a baby. And you look

exactly the same. Grady,
will you please come here?"

Grade E obliges. I shut my
window, turn my back on

Brendan. [Why didn't you do
that before?] Bree? Lecturing
me? Am I totally schizo or what?

# The Worst Thing Is

Brendan knows I'm back in the monster's snare.
And what a coincidence. [Coin cide is two
four-letter words!] Shut the hell up, Bree.

"I didn't know you and Brendan were friends,"
I say as Grade E slithers into the front seat
beside me. "I didn't know he *had* any friends."

> *I wouldn't exactly call us friends.*
> *More like business acquaintances.*
> Grady winks, hands over a bindle.

Even without opening it, I know
it's short, and I can feel it's mostly
powder. What kind is uncertain.

> The look on my face must say
> volumes. *It isn't the best*
> *crank I've ever seen, but it works.*

"You got this from"—I wag my head
backward—"him? Did he know it
was for me?" [You mean for Dad.]

The thought brings meager satisfaction,
especially after Grady says, *Um, I might
have told him. What's up, anyway?*

I shrug. "We have a history.
And it wasn't exactly romantic."
[Nope, not with him. Never was.]

Grady gets down to business. *Ahem.
So the eight ball is two hundred.
Are you going to share a little?*

I open the bindle. Short, okay.
Bree handles the clod. "Looks to me
like you already took your cut. Yes?"

His face flares but he has to admit,
*We did a couple of lines. Not much
of a finder's fee, if you ask me.*

"Not asking. Thanks for taking
care of this. Now I've got to run.
Mom's on a regular rampage."

Grady pauses a beat or two,
as if he's got something to say.
But then he exits the car silently.

Good damn thing. Not sure
I have the *cojones* (or even
that I want them!) to tell the jerk

off, but Bree most definitely does.
Let her out of her box and no
telling what might happen.

I drive away without looking back.
No good-byes for either of them.
I'll never deal with Grade E again.

As I drive home, it occurs to me
that this might just have been
for the best. Not seeing Brendan.

No, that will never be a good thing.
What I mean is, the pitiful state
of this meth. I'll go out tonight

with Dad and Linda Sue.
We'll blow through this awful
eight ball. Then I'll move

on without the monster
breathing against my neck,
begging me to do one more

little whiff. That's it, okay.
One more all-nighter, then
I'll quit cold [lukewarm] turkey.

# Dad Finally Calls

A little after four P.M. Guess
troll and fairy "rested up"
for tonight's plotted
devilry.

I spent the day with Mom
and "the girls," shopping
for Hunter's baptism
outfit.

It's adorable—a tiny white
tuxedo, with dancing Poohs
and Tiggers on the satin
cummerbund.

Afterward, we stopped by
Pastor Keith's lair. He
pounced, a white-
collared

tiger, with God's A to Z
of baptism. Who knew
it was so hard to
qualify?

On the way home I mentioned
Dad's plans for the coming
evening, omitting
you-know-what.

The scowl in the rearview
mirror said a whole
lot more than Mom
needed to.

"Jeez, Mom. I've only seen
him twice in the last
nine years. Cut me
some slack."

*That's double what I've
seen him,* says Leigh,
*and that's way
too much.*

# Still, Leigh Agreed to Watch Hunter

Dad's picking me up in an hour.
        We're supposed to have dinner,
                but I'm betting food is the last
                        thing on his mind. Mine, too,
                for that matter. After looking at
        Grade E's ten-watt crank, I want
a toke of my hundred-watt ice.

And I don't want to share it. It's
        *my* birthday. I don't have to share,
                do I? Hey, it *is* my birthday. At
                        last, today, I'm the big one-
                eight, so why don't I feel any
        different? Because I'm still
treading quicksand, that's why.

Okay, I need to get high, totally
        out-of-my-head wasted, so I
                don't keep thinking about
                        the same old shit, only
                compounded by all that's
        going on around here, not
to mention hearing about

Adam and having Brendan forced
             down my throat [not for real, only
                     figuratively], all in the space
                             of twelve hours. Talk about
                     mega déjà vu, of the not nice
             type. Happy fucking birthday
to me. Come on. Let's celebrate!

Lucky me, I'm [not even close]
             almost alone in the house. Mom
                     ran to the store, Scott ran to
                             pick up Jake from his [girl-]
                     friend's house, and Leigh took
             Hunter for a stroller walk around
the block. Heather? Who knows?

Who cares? I'm birthday partying
             with the monster, and we're
                     starting right this minute.
                             OMG. The rush is beyond
                     what I expected—hot then
             cool, and my head lights up
like casino neon. Startling.

Another whiff. Double or
          nothing, two somehow more
                    than twice as good as one.
                              I open my window to
                    let the smoke escape,
          notice Scott's car come
puttering up the street.

Can I get away with one
          more? [Go for it, quick!]
                    I turn on a fan, spray a
                              big dose of Ozium, dash
                    to the bathroom to do
          the big three—you know,
shit, shave, and shower.

Crude? Yeah. And bound to
          get cruder as the evening
                    progresses. It's Bree's
                              birthday too, and for
                    a change I'm going to
          let her cut loose. After all,
you only turn eighteen once.

# All Spiffy

I go downstairs, where
the whole crew has once
again gathered. Suddenly
everyone starts to sing,

*Happy birthday to you . . .*

Even Hunter seems to coo
along. It's enough to almost
make me feel guilty. Almost.
Leigh gives me a huge hug.

*You made it. Happy birthday.*

She hands me a big package,
all done up in chartreuse.
[Heather must have chosen
the wrapping paper. It sucks.]

*Go on. Open it,* urges Leigh.

It's a leather trench coat,
and not an inexpensive one.
"Way cool! Thanks a ton!"
I slide into it, cinch it up.

*You look great,* says Scott.

Mom comes over, puts one
hand on each shoulder,
looks me straight in the eyes.
[Dilated—will she notice?]

*I want you to know I'm proud of you.*

Okay, that has to be a lie.
But it makes me tear up
anyway. "Thanks, Mom."
[Even if I don't believe you.]

*Promise not to stay out too late.*

"I'll do my best." Okay, so
I traded a lie for a lie. No
doubt everyone knows it.
"Oh, there's Dad now."

*Don't tell him I said hi,* jokes Leigh.

At least she found her sense
of humor. I kiss Hunter on
the forehead. "Be a good boy.
Tomorrow's *your* big day."

He gurgles and smiles. He loves me.

# I Love Him, Too

But I have to admit I don't think
about him more than a couple

of times as Dad, Linda Sue, and I
dive into the half-ass crank.

Dad's got a big glass tray, which
he sets on the cracked Formica table

in their dog-eared motel room.
*Let's see what you've got there,* he says.

"It's . . ." I think about apologizing,
but decide to wait until he comments.

> He opens the bindle, says nothing
> about the powder inside. *It's what?*

"A little shy, I think. The guy I
got it from took his cut up front."

> *Ah, well, a dealer is a dealer,*
> *I guess.* Dad draws huge lines.

He hands me the straw. *The birthday*
*girl always goes first, right?*

One long, deep inhale up the right
nostril, followed by another up the left.

Oh, it's been a very long time. Probably
a good thing the purity is only maybe

60 percent. My nose complains,
anyway. [I'm complaining. I want ice.]

     *Oh, yeah,* says Dad. *That's what I'm*
     *talking about. Hey, L., how about you?*

          The fairy shakes her head. *I don't*
          *know. I don't like being high in public.*

     *You'll be fine. Everyone's high in Reno*
     *on Saturday night, right, little girl?*

"I haven't been out on Saturday night
in a long time, but I doubt it's changed

much since the last time. It's definitely
an up-all-night kind of town."

   *See?* He slides the tray under her
   face. *Anyway, tonight's a special night.*

   *A girl only turns eighteen once, you*
   *know. Let's give her a night on the town.*

I'll never forget the first night Dad
gave me a "night on the town."

Only it was really Adam that gave
it to me. Dad just tagged along.

And we didn't go anywhere except
the back room of a bowling alley.

Too many ghosts in that memory.
Oh, well. A few more lines [even

half-ass lines], I probably won't care.
In fact, I'm almost there already.

# In Reno

There are three kinds
of nights on the town:

good clean fun,

like skating or movies
or [God forbid] bowling,

boring and safe

and definitely not
what Dad's got in mind;

totally nasty,

like swap clubs or strip
clubs or titty shows,

places that check ID,

and eighteen won't get
you inside one of those;

and games of chance,

sports betting or black-
jack or slot machines,

guaranteed to suck you dry.

Eighteen isn't old enough
for casino betting either,

but all it takes is

a game plan, and dear
old Dad has already figured

a strategy.

# Dad Chooses the "Big Three"

The Silver Legacy, Eldorado,
and Circus Circus casinos
     are all connected by skyways.
                    *We can play at one for a while,*
                    *then move to another. That way*

                    *we won't draw much attention*
                    *to ourselves. Sound good?*
          Table games are riskier,
so we'll hang out in the big banks
of slots, nickels unless we get lucky.

I have to admit it's kind of exciting,
and not the unlikely idea of winning
     but of maybe getting away with playing.
                    *If you win really big, they won't*
                    *let you keep the money, but anything*

                    *that drops in the tray is yours,* Dad says.
                    *Let's take a snort, then go give it a try.*
          He pulls out his little amber bottle,
the one with the tiny silver spoon
attached to the lid by a little chain.

The crank is definitely mediocre,
but it does the job if you do enough,
keep going back—and back—for more.
                    *I'll go get some rolls of nickels.*
                    *You two scout out a quiet corner.*


                    *If a cocktail waitress comes by, I'll*
                    *take a Coors. Can't fuck that up!*
          What he means is, they bring players free
drinks—notoriously awful free drinks,
mostly mixers, to keep on the cheap.


We find a nickel slot island, well
back in one corner, away from bars,
          restaurants, and the main traffic pattern.
                    *Found you guys. Can't hide from*
                    *me,* jokes Dad, handing Linda Sue


                    and me each two rolls of nickels. *Go*
                    *ahead. Spend it all in one place.*
          We spend a good deal of time
doing exactly that. My machine
is a greedy prick, but oh, well.

I mean, I hit a few times. *Tink-
tink-tink* comes the meager payoff.
        But Dad, now, is one lucky sucker.
                *Guess it's my night,* he says, as
                the nickels keep plunking into his

                tray. *I'm thinking it's time we move
                on, with a quick pit stop, you know?*
      A pit stop, amber bottle in hand,
he means. And that's just fine by
me. This is getting boring, you know?

# Dad Really Is Lucky

Linda Sue and I follow him
from casino to casino, machines
to tables, just watching him win.
He even hits big on the Wheel
of Fortune, which has the worst
odds of anything. Oh, well, I'm
extremely buzzed and it's fun
watching *somebody* win.

No one hassles us, no one
mentions ID or that I look too
young to be standing around
watching my dad walk off with
a fair amount of casino money.
Of course, it's Saturday night—
actually Sunday morning now—
and the casinos are raking it in,

so losing a little to Dad doesn't
mean much. Besides, if *no one*
won, *no one* would ever play.
Anyway, beyond watching
Dad, I'm watching people.
It's amazing to see how eager
they are to exit Reno totally
broke. So many ATM machines,
so little time to drain them dry!

Dealers in black slacks and white
shirts. Cocktail waitresses
in tight, tiny skirts and super-
deep necklines. Janitors, in jump-
suits and spit-shined shoes.
Scowling pit bosses in perfect
tuxedoes. They're all fun to watch—
covertly, of course—as they go
about their nightly business.

People-watching in casinos
is completely consuming.
And it's only by accident
that it doesn't consume a very
important moment in Hunter's
little baby lifetime.

# See, It's Hard to Tell

If it's nighttime or day
when you're inside
a casino. The windows
are tinted almost black,
and the neon inside defies
the notion that it might be
getting light outside.

But one thing I do
finally notice is how
the restaurant lines
are growing longer.
People want breakfast.
Which means it must
be later than I thought.

"What time is it?"
I ask a passerby, and
his answer blows me
away. Six after nine.
Twenty-four minutes
until church starts.
We're going to be late!

*Just let me finish this
hand,* Dad says, watching
the blackjack dealer flip
a card and bust. *Oh, yeah!
Guess I'm cashing out.
Why am I cashing out?
I'm on a regular roll.*

"Cash out, Dad. We've
got to go. Hunter's getting
baptized in less than half
an hour. I probably ought
to be there, don't you think?"
The church isn't far as
the crow flies, but it's all
surface streets to get there.

Dad finds a cashier and
we hurry to his car, parked
in the garage at the far
casino. Round and round,
down to the exit. Straight
down Sierra Street  to
McCarran, Reno's major
loop road. Speed limit
or under all the way

(a good idea, all things
considered), we limp
into the parking lot, looking
exactly like we've stayed
up all night, at nine forty-
seven. Everyone's inside.
Everyone, that is, except

Mom.

# I Don't Think

I've *ever* seen her so pissed,
and believe me, I've seen
her pissed before. But nothing
like this. She lights into us

> before we reach the door.
> *Nice of you to show up*
> *for your own baby's baptism,*
> *Kristina Georgia. I can believe*

> *something like this from* him. . . .
> spittle foams at the corners
> of her mouth. *But not from you.*
> *Where the hell have you* been?

> > Dad jumps in with a monster-
> > fueled lie about car trouble,
> > dead cell phone batteries, and
> > more. He looks like crap

and I know I can't look much
better, but no time to worry
about that now. "Can we talk
about this later? I imagine

everyone's waiting for us."
And, of course, they totally
are. Baptisms usually happen
before the sermon, but Pastor

Keith wisely forged ahead,
assuming [praying] Hunter's
wayward mother would
appear sooner or later.

All eyes turn as we come
through the door, and I know
every single pair must ascertain
exactly what the problem is.

Better not to think about that.
Leigh has saved Mom and me
seats up front. Dad and Linda Sue
sit at the back of the sanctuary.

Somehow, we maintain
when they call the baptismal
party up to the font, repeat
a flurry of meaningless

words. Resplendent in
his white tuxedo, Hunter
smiles up at me as Pastor
Keith pours water over

his head, makes him a child
of God. I was baptized once
too, and I silently ask, "So,
Big Guy, am I still Your child?"

# Party Time

Well, actually, it's time
for the postbaptism reception.
I decide I ought to ride home with
Mom, who decides not to get into a
big discussion now, not with Leigh and
Heather in the car and a regular parade of
friends and family trailing us home. *We'll
talk about this later,* she promises, and I
think I'm glad I've turned eighteen so I
can hit the streets if I must. [Uh-huh,
right. With a baby, three hundred
dollars, and no place to crash.]
Okay, that's not the best
idea either. Oh, well.
Why worry about
it now? Just make
it through the
afternoon. Get
some sleep tonight.
Get up early tomorrow
morning, start a
not-so-exciting
job at the not-so-
exciting 7-
Eleven. Whoopee!

# 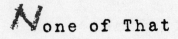None of That

                    Is so easy to do,
                    semibuzzed and
                    knowing I need to

crash,

                    knowing I most
                    definitely *will*

crash

                    as soon as everyone
                    eats and drinks their
                    fill, goes on home.

Except,

                    of course, I'll have
                    to deal with Mom's
                    wrath, Scott's

inquisition,

                    Leigh's hurt [real
                    or imagined], Heather's
                    delight at my

torment,

                    a possible [make
                    that highly probable]

confrontation

                              between all of the above
                              and my father, the troll,
                              and his
miserable

                              fairy, Linda Sue. I do
                              feel sorry for her, and
                              I'm starting to feel pretty
sorry

                              for myself, too. Okay,
                              it's looking to turn
                              out to be a
sleepless

                              toss-and-turn,
                              dissolve-slowly-
                              into-morning night
after all.

# Three Weeks and Four Days

Since Hunter became an official
candidate for the kingdom of heaven.

Three weeks and one day since
Dad and Linda Sue left Mom's insults

in their exhaust. Three weeks and two
days since Leigh and Heather flew

back to their swanky campus, leaving
me with no unequivocal answers

about cheerleaders and their diet aids
or what, exactly, lesbians do for fun.

Three weeks and three days since I
started work at the 7-Eleven.

Three weeks and three days of learning
to stock shelves, scan items, clear gas

pumps, make coffee and hot dogs. Three
weeks and three days of Kevin's leers

[not to mention "accidental" gropes]
and semirude comments about

the growing appeal of my shrinking
behind. *It even looks good covered*

*by a smock!* A nasty green smock,
over looser and looser jeans.

Not that I've been into the monster—
not much, anyway. I only have a tiny bit

left, and I haven't looked to score
more. I only take a quick toke or two

when Hunter doesn't sleep through
the night and I have to be at work

by seven. Quarter till, actually, but I rarely
punch in before 7:03 or 7:04.

The job isn't bad, actually. Not great.
Not life-changing. But not as boring

as I thought it would be. At least
it's around people. Some I even know.

Old classmates. Old teachers. [Really
old, most of them.] Old party pals.

And hey. Tomorrow is my first paycheck.
How will I celebrate? Hmm.

I have definitely vacillated about
scoring again. I want to. Don't want to.

Need to. Can't. Bree is screaming
for the monster. Kristina keeps trying

to say no. But somewhere deep inside
she thinks Bree will win.

[You know you want me to.]
The only real question is when.

# The Question Is Answered

With a phone call. Unexpected.
Anticipated. I happen to be on
a smoke break (yes, I've taken up
the habit again—big surprise)
when my cell begins to chime.

*Kristina? It's Trey. I'm*
*in Reno. Can we hook up?*

OMG! He wants to hook up
with me? My heart starts to pound,
and my hands go clammy. And
then it strikes me he probably
wants the hundred I owe him.

*I'd like to collect that debt.*
*And talk about that "interest."*

OMG! Maybe he wants more
than money. Am I prepared to give
it to him? [Hell, yeah!] "I don't
get off work until four. I could
meet up with you after that."

*Sounds like a plan. Oh, are*
*you by any chance looking?*

Looking for what? [To score,
idiot.] "Um . . ." I'm not looking,
am I? [Of course you are.]
"Well . . . uh . . . yes, actually, I guess
I am." Question answered.

*Great. I'll give you a taste*
*of what I've got. You'll love it.*

No doubt about that! And I'll
probably like the ice, too. I tell
him where he can find me, hang
up the phone, and go back inside
to stock shelves and think about Trey.

# I Can Hardly

Think about anything else
        for the rest of the day.
I haven't thought seriously
        about a guy since Chase
went away. And Trey?

I don't really believe
        I might have a chance
with him. [Well, *I* do!]
        No, I don't think Bree
really thinks so either.

He's gorgeous. Smart.
        Built. Has a spectacular
connection, unlike Grade
        E and his rapist connect.
I guess Trey's connection

could be a rapist. At least
            I won't have to know
about it from firsthand
            experience. [Speaking
of hands, wonder how his

will feel, touching me.]
            Hold on now. I still don't
know that's what he has
            in mind. [Come on. Of course
it's what he's got in mind.]

Just stop. Won't do to get
            all hot and bothered on
a definite maybe. Anyway,
            I've got to concentrate,
get through this shift.

# I Do

But somehow my drawer comes
up a little short. No problem. I'll
make good on it. Oh my god,
the anticipation is making me
        totally insane!
        Every   nerve
        in   my   body
        buzzes, high-
        voltage want.
        I want to get
        high.  I  want
        to  be  kissed.
        (How  long  it
        has   been!)  I
        want   to   give
        myself   away.
        I  want  to  be
        stunned     by
passion  so  intense  it  knocks
me right off my feet, down to
my knees, where I know I'll
surrender to this luscious i n s a n i t y.

# I Grab a Few Dollars

From the cash stash in my purse,
round out my drawer, stow
my inelegant green smock on a hook
in the back room, run to the bathroom

to take a quick peek in the mirror.
My hair is pulled back in a tight
ponytail. I let it loose, and it falls
past my shoulders, shiny and smooth.

Mascara! I search my purse, to no
avail. Guess what I've got left
from this morning will have to do.
I don't look bad, don't look great.

Oh, well. Trey will be here anytime. Luckily, I keep my birthday
bread in my wallet. I count out
a hundred, tuck it into my jeans.

I wish I was wearing the tight
ones. These leave plenty to
the imagination, a defense
against Kevin's obnoxious stares.

Okay, breath mints. A spritz of nice
perfume. (Jake's unexpected
birthday gift—who told him
how to shop for fragrance?)

I walk out the door just as Trey
pulls up in a stunning new
black-on-black Mustang.
Guess he's doing okay.

He exits his car, comes over,
and gulps me into his arms like
we're forever friends. *Great to see
you. Let's go for a drive.*

"Nice ride. Guess I wouldn't
mind checking it out."
[Way to play it cool. But
I can't wait to heat things up.]

# He Cruises Slowly

Up Virginia Grade,
a well-kept gravel road
into the boonies. I study

his face,

chiseled and handsome,
even in profile, the not-
quite-black shade of

his eyes.

He asks how I've been,
what all I've been up to,
and my focus shifts to

his lips,

pouting and perfect. As I
outline the last three weeks,
I notice the breadth of

his shoulders.

He's built, so he must do
something besides deal,
something physical.

His biceps

don't deny that notion.
They tense as he shifts,
making me tense too.

His thighs

lean but strong, make
me even more tense.
[Go on. Touch them.]

                              He's the whole package,

okay, and I want to unwrap
it, explore what's inside,
under the denim.

# He Finds a Secluded Parking Place

*This looks okay, don't you think?*
I agree, "Looks good to me."

*Hope you're ready to rocket.*
I give a brisk nod. "Way overdue."

*Excellent.* He loads his pipe, hands
it to me. I can't help but smile

at the meth—a clear shard of glass.
I inhale gently, gratefully, pass

it back for him to do the same,
close my eyes to ride the giant rush.

Trey is generous. Within a few minutes,
I have climbed to a very tall buzz.

*So what do you think? Was I lying?*
"It's the best meth I've ever done."

He touches my knee. *You want more?*
"Absolutely." [And more glass, too.]

*The price drops a lot for a quantity.*
Heat pulses at my temples. "Like . . . ?"

*We could get a half for eight hundred.*
If we split that, double last time, for . . .

*It's just sitting there, waiting for us.*
I owe him a hundred, plus four . . .

To help my decision, he passes the pipe.
"I get paid tomorrow. Can you wait?"

*I'll be here. But I don't want to wait for . . .*
We're kissing. Long. Deep. Amazing.

My head spins and my heart pounds
and Bree is demanding more, more,

and suddenly, there is no Adam, no
Chase, and there never, ever was.

# Stop

|  | Before things go overboard. |
| --- | --- |
| *Stop?* | |
| | Stop before we go all the way. |
| *Stop?* | |
| | Stop before I want to. |
| *Can't stop.* | |
| | "Don't," I plead. "I can't." |
| *Why not?* | |
| | "Not on a first date . . ." |
| *Come on!* | |
| | ". . . even if it isn't a date." |
| *Tease.* | |
| | Déjà vu. "Not even." |
| *What then?* | |
| | "Try me on a second date?" |
| *And if I do?* | |
| | "No promises, but kiss me like that . . ." |
| *If I kiss you again now?* | |
| | "It's still our first date." |

*A girl with principles?*

"Most would argue with that."

*Maybe I like that.*

"Maybe I like you."

*Maybe I like you, too.*

"Well, then let me tell you a story. . . ."

# Twenty Minutes Later

He knows more about me
than anyone but Chase does.
In fact, he knows more about
me than Chase does, because
he knows exactly how I feel
about Chase. Adam. Heather.
Leigh. Jake. Scott. Mom.
And Brendan. He knows all
about Brendan.

Ten minutes later he could be
a total jerk, tell me my past
has nothing to do with him.
He could say, *Put out or get out.*
But he doesn't. He says,
*You weren't to blame. The meth
was not to blame. Only that
asshole was to blame. In a fairer
world, he would be dead.*

I'm crying now, crying because
I'm high. Crying because he
cares, or at least pretends to.
Crying because it fucking
feels good to cry. Trey takes
me solidly into his arms, tells
me, *No shame in crying. No
shame in hating. Go ahead, hate
him. He deserves that and more.*

Then he kisses me again.
Tender, this time. Soft.
Unexpectedly compassionate.
I kiss him back. Tearful. Needy.
Filled with questions. Hungry.
Finally, he pulls away. *I'll take
you back to your car now. And
I'll wait for our second date.
As long as it's tomorrow.*

# Not a Wink

Of sleep tonight.
I know that without
trying. Even if I wasn't
totally wired out of my tree,
thinking about Trey would
keep my mental wheels
turning. Churning.

I managed to
choke down dinner,
a major accomplishment.
Meth usually makes me yak.
But not tonight. Tonight, all
I could think about was
Trey. Trey. Trey.

After dinner I
played with Hunter,
watched TV with Mom,
Scott, and Jake, like nothing
was new, nothing different.
But everything's different.
And I'm scared.

I mean, yes, I'm
happy. Excited, even.
But nothing seems to go
right between me and a guy.
[Stop overthinking it,
would you please?]
I'm trying to!

I really like Trey
a lot. He's incredible.
So what does he want with
me? Besides the obvious, that
is, and he could get that
with pretty much any
girl. Why me?

One more thing
bothers me, but just a
little, because I'd probably
be doing it anyway. The meth.
Is it a requisite, a necessary part
of a relationship with Trey?
Which would come first?
The meth? Or me?

# I'm Glad

I have a little of my own stash
left this morning. I'd never make
it through work otherwise. It's
damn little, but enough to help me
shake off the no-sleep goofiness.
And hey, later today I'll have more
than enough to make up for it.

At least Hunter didn't need
attention before I got up, got
dressed, and left for work, three
whiffs of ice my only breakfast.

I know I should eat something.
Just don't know how to manage
that, with my stomach turning
cartwheels. The meth is only half
to blame. The other half is my
brain, which won't leave Trey at
the back of it. He's front row, center.

I'm in a pheromone fog
as I make coffee, stock rows
of cigarettes, mop up a customer's
mistake. Mindless work, and there's
always more when I'm finished
with what I'm doing. Except when
it gets busy, I leave the cash
register math to Midge, who's
unusually friendly today.

      Not a great thing on a day
      like today. She chatters
      about her grandkids, only half
      the time the apples of her eye.
      Today, to listen to her, they're
      angels with straight A's.

      Then she moves on to diss her
      retired husband, Al, who watches
      television all day, every day.
      *He loves those damn soaps,*
      she says. *Idiot TV. He won't*
      *even consider really good*
      *shows, like Oprah or Montel.*

Just before lunch, Kevin comes
in, payroll in hand. He gives
Midge her envelope, calls me
into the back room to offer mine.
Okay, that's a little weird,
but what am I going to do,
say no? As always, his eyes creep
up and down my body.
*Here it is, in all its glory,*
he says of my pitiful paycheck—
$329 and change.

        He pauses, assessing me in some
        way I can't put my arms around.
        Finally he says, *You're worth*
        *a lot more than minimum wage,*
        *but I can't offer a raise until*
        *you've been here six months.*

        Another, closer gawk. *Uh, some*
        *of my other girls work a side job,*
        *which pays extremely well.*
        *Would you be interested in*
        *something on the side?*
        Interesting choice of words.

Now it's my turn to study Kevin,
all wolf, on certain prowl. The way
he's looking at me makes me
very uncomfortable. But I can
handle him, can't I? [Probably not,
but I sure can!] Bolstered by Bree's
cheerful assurance, I answer, "Well,
maybe. Like, what kind of work?"

> *Customer service, of a sort.*
> *He reaches out, runs a hand*
> *softly down my arm. The crystal*
> *in my system responds, lifting*
> *a good crop of goose bumps,*
> *which Kevin is all too happy to*
> *misinterpret. He smiles a lupine smile.*

> *Ah, you just might be a good*
> *candidate after all. I thought*
> *you might. The job is easy work,*
> *really. Let's just say I've got*
> *a list of clients interested in*
> *videos starring young women*
> *of your caliber.*

He's a porn dealer! I knew it!
Okay, I didn't know that, specifically,
but it doesn't surprise me. Part of me
is revolted, part fascinated. What kind
of videos, exactly? Do I know any
of the girls? Would I ever stoop that
low? [How much does it pay, anyway?]

I formulate a careful answer.
"Uh, I don't really think so. Not now,
anyway. I'm still getting my figure
back, and I don't have a lot of spare
time, with the baby and all.
But I'll think about it, okay?"

# We Leave It at That

And it isn't until I run to
the bank on my lunch break
that it comes to me Kevin
thinks I'm some sort of whore.

I don't see myself that way at all.
Open-minded, yes. A druggie, sometimes.
An unwed teen mother, for sure. But
a sleep-around? No way. Never.

So why am I so hot for Trey?
Sex with him is definitely not
out of the question. Maybe even
tonight. So am I a whore?

[I am!] But I'm not. I want more
than just sex. I want a relationship—
someone to love and to love me.
Will Trey be that? I don't know.

The attraction between us is sexual,
yes. But I think there's something
more. I thought so the first time
we met, and yesterday confirmed it.

He could have played games. Didn't.
He could have played rough. Didn't.
He could have insisted all tweakers
are whores, one way or another.

The glass makes me brave, sends
waves of sensuality throughout my
body. I know being with Trey will
be incredible. But will it be only once?

Because once will not be enough.
Or maybe it will be way too much.
Either way, thinking about it makes
me believe I'm not a whore.

# The Rest of the Day

Goes fast. Goes incredibly slow.
Midafternoon, Trey calls.
*Hey, you. We still on for tonight?*
*Great. We're all set up, good to go.*
*Where and when can we meet?*

His voice sends chills through
my body. Good chills. "Give
me some time to run home
and clean up. How about five
thirty at the Starbucks on Mount Rose?"

*Five thirty it is. But I doubt*
*you'll need coffee.* He hesitates,
as if deciding what to say.
Finally, pay dirt. *Kristina? I can't*
*quit thinking about you.*

"The feeling is mutual. See you
tonight." I can't quit thinking
about him, don't for half a minute
as the workday dissolves. At
last the clock says four P.M.

I race to the house, rush through
the door. Hunter is in his infant
seat on the living room floor,
and from the corner of my eye
I see him smile at his mommy.

I should stop, pick him up, shower
him with love. But I can't slow down
or I'll be late. I run up to my room,
choose form-fitting jeans and cropped
crocheted sweater, decide to go braless.

Then I take a long steamy shower,
plenty of soap in all the necessary
places; shampoo with ginger spice;
shave my legs with a new razor blade;
dry off, apply plenty of lotion.

Finally, I put on more makeup than
I've used in a year—blush, shadow,
liner, mascara, even a smidge
of lip gloss. The person looking
back at me in the mirror isn't me.

[No, it's me. Thanks for letting
me out to play. And BTW, the no
bra decision? Good one!] Bree
and I are ready to go. We just
have to make our escape.

Mom is in the kitchen, working
on dinner. Jake is watching TV
in the living room. "Hey," I call
to him, "I've got something to do.
Will you watch Hunter for a few?"

                    He turns, assesses, understands
                    the gist of what he sees.
                    *Maybe. What's in it for me?*

He loves Hunter, often
babysits when Mom can't
play nanny. But it's only fair
I pay him something. "Ten
dollars?" I offer.

*Okay. But don't stay
out too late. And what should
I tell Mom?*

Mom. Oh, yeah. He'll have
to tell her something. Not
like the subject won't come
up before too very long.
"Tell her . . ."

What should he tell her?
Oh, what the hell. Why lie
about it? Not like I'm grounded,
and I did set up the babysitting.
"Tell her I've got a date."

# She'll Want to Know

Why I didn't tell her myself.
        Want to know who I've got
a date with. Want to know

                what we're doing on our
                    date. Where we're going.
                Exactly when I'll be home.
Sorry, Mom. Not in the mood
        for the third degree. Not
now, anyway. So we'll

                talk about it later. Hey,
                    maybe there won't be
                anything to lie about.
The Wedge Parkway
        Starbucks is a fifteen-
minute drive, with no

                traffic. This evening, lots
                    of traffic, it takes forever.
                Trey is already there.
I can see him through
        the frosted window,
sipping something

                        and watching for me.
                                  He stands when I go
                        inside. A gentleman?

Unusual, but I like it.
            He pulls me to him,
kisses me easily on
                        the mouth, eliciting
                                  jealous stares from
                        customers and salesgirls.

I inhale his masculine
            scent: Brut, tainted
slightly by a tinge
                        of ice.  But hey, I'll
                                  be tainted soon too.
                        [More ways than one!]

*You thirsty? Hungry?*
            he politely asks, and
it makes me feel
                        special that he bothers.
                                He *is* a gentleman!
                        [He's a player.]

# I Don't Care

If he's a player. He plays well,
and I'm ready for a challenge.
Besides, I know the rules of the game.

> We talk for a few minutes,
> about jobs and families and, yes,
> about Robyn, who's *only a friend*.

> Finally, Trey suggests, *Let's go.*
> *Why don't you leave your car*
> *here? We can take mine.*

He has washed his Mustang.
"Oh, I do love your car," I
say, "although I'd pick red."

> *Well, you know, the cops tend*
> *to home in on red cars. Red*
> *and yellow. Of course, I mostly*

> *drive the limit, especially*
> *on trips like this one. You*
> *ready for a party?*

I smile. "It's Friday. I don't
have to work tomorrow.
I'd say I'm ready to party."

> *My kind of woman.* He starts
> the car, puts it in reverse, but
> before he takes his foot off

> the brake, he turns, looks
> me right in the eye. *Did I tell
> you how great you look?*

"No, damnit, you didn't,
and I expect a sincere apology."
I love Bree's improv.

> Especially when Trey says,
> *Will this do?* And he kisses me—
> another long, delicious kiss.

I pull away, breathless. "Yeah
that will do," I whisper, hoarse
with heat. "For now, anyway."

He grins and kisses me again.
Even better than the first. About
the time my heart feels ready

to explode, he slams on the brakes.
*Holy shit.* We've been rolling
backward. He stops a split

second before taking out an SUV
at the drive-through window.
We both laugh, disturbing a very

tense moment. And we both know
we'll be back in each other's arms
very soon, expecting more than a kiss.

# We Merge onto the Freeway

Head north of town, and finally
I feel the need to ask, "Where
are we going, anyway?"
I let my fingers creep up
his thigh, feel an immediate
reaction. [Mmm. Long time.]

*To my cousin's house,* Trey
answers. *He's got a new
shipment of top-quality ice.
I had a taste earlier. Primo.*

"And I was going to give up
all my bad habits for Lent. Oh,
it's not Lent yet, is it? In fact,
I've got months! Right on."
Trey's right hand falls upon my
left, moves it higher up his leg.

*Actually, we're moving toward
Samhain,* he says. *Bonfires.
Sacrifices. Feasts. Those Celts
knew how to throw a party!*

Oh, yeah, he's smart. [Fine, too.]
And I am back in the game.
We drive north for twenty minutes,
turn east toward Red Rock.
The rural community is home to
commuters, dealers, and off-gridders.

As if reading my mind, Trey
says, *Brad doesn't live off-grid.*
*Good thing, since his wife walked*
*and left him with the kids.*

Raising kids with only solar power
could be tough. "How many does
he have?" Like I care. The voyeur in
me wants to know why his wife left
him. His dealing? Another man? Simple
boredom, locked up with kids all day?

*Two little girls, one of them*
*named after me—LaTreya.*
*Cute, huh? She's cute too.*
*Looks just like her mom.*

We turn off the main road, into
a relatively new neighborhood.
It's getting dark, but even so,
I can see that one house pretty
much resembles the next. "Glad
you know where you're going."

*Yeah, the houses are cookie-*
*cutter, okay. Main difference*
*is the colors. Incognito, that's*
*how Brad lives, and that's good.*

As we pull into the driveway,
I notice movement behind
a curtain. We climb out of the car,
into sweet high desert air and it
strikes me how normal we must
look to the neighbors. Family.

Trey slides his arm around
my shoulders and I love how
that makes me feel. *Here, now.*
*You're my new girlfriend, okay?*

I don't know if he means for real,
or for the benefit of the kids,
but either way, I'm fine with it.
I'm someone's new girlfriend, at least
for the moment. "Okay." I wrap
my arm around his waist. Seamless.

# A Little Girl

Opens the door. She's about six and looks
like an Irish doll—with bright green eyes
and soft red curls. *Daddy! It's Trey!*

Trey reaches down, scoops her up.
*How's my little Devon tonight?*
The affection between them is clear.

The doorway shadows. Brad is younger
than I pictured him, somewhere in his late
twenties, and there is a definite resemblance

to Trey. Okay, you get what I mean by
that. For an older guy, he's really cute.
LaTreya stands behind him, attached like a tail.

Trey pushes inside, reaches around
Brad to tickle LaTreya under the chin.
She can't help but giggle. *Stop it, Trey!*

Trey reaches for my hand, pulls me across
the threshold. *Hey, everyone, this is Kristina.*
He kisses my forehead. *Isn't she pretty?*

The kids give dubious looks, and I suspect
a fair amount of jealousy. *They* want to be
his girls. [Tell them to get in line.]

> Brad, however, gives me his instant stamp
> of approval. *She sure is. Lucky you. Go on*
> *upstairs. Ladies, you can watch TV, okay?*

Devon gives a little *Aw,* but LaTreya, who's
older, knows enough to take her into the other
room and turn on the oversize flat panel.

I trail Trey up the stairs to a studio over
the garage. Like the rest of the house, this
room is nicely kept, with a quilted bed beneath

the window and a fluffy futon against the opposite
wall. Apparently, this is the party room. A faint
scent of crystal lingers above vanilla air freshener.

> We settle onto the futon and Trey puts
> his arm around my shoulders, pulls me close.
> *Brad looked like he wanted to eat you.*

*I do too. And I've got first dibs. Don't
worry. I promise it won't hurt, unless you
want it to.* He nibbles my neck for effect.

Thankfully Brad's footsteps interrupt,
or I might have let Bree throw Trey
on the bed right then and there.

Brad can't help but notice the way
I'm blushing. *Wow, cuz. What did you
do to the girl, in only three minutes?*

Trey answers with a laugh. *Three
minutes is a long time to wait.
We were getting bored.*

*I can fix that,* says Brad. *I've got
just the thing right here.* He goes
into the bathroom, digs in a cabinet,

returns with a quart Tupperware
container. It's filled to the brim with
the same crystal Trey had yesterday.

My eyes go wide and my mouth
starts to water. Just call me Pavlov's
pooch. And within a few short minutes,

no way could we be bored. Despite
no sleep last night, I'm wide awake
and flying. And the higher I go,

the more I want more of the guy
sitting next to me. OMG. Maybe
Kevin is right about me, after all.

# We Make the Deal

Exchange our pooled cash
for a spectacular stash,

one-quarter ounce for me,
one-quarter ounce for Trey.

We smoke several bowls,
climb higher and higher,

until it feels like my heart
might explode, drown

me from the inside out
with iced-over blood.

Damn, it feels great and so
do I. [Me too, me too.]

Why does feeling like you
could die any moment

give you such an incredible
rush? [Who cares? Go with it.]

Finally Brad glances at his
watch. *Oops. Ten fifteen.*

*Better get the girls to bed.*
*You two make yourselves at home.*

Trey walks with him to the door,
pokes his head into the hall behind

him, says something I can't quite
make out, except for the words

"alone time." He closes the door,
dims the overhead light,

walks to me slowly. Oh, God,
he's so impossibly fine I can't

believe I'm here with him.
His hands cover mine, pull.

*I believe you said something*
*about our second date?*

I should say no, know I should
say no. But I don't. "Okay."

And then we're on the bed,
and our clothes are off and his

body is hard and smooth
and brown. He kisses me—

full on the mouth, hard
on the mouth, and when he moves

lower, I begin to tremble. Shiver.
Suddenly I start to cry.

He stops, rests his chin on my
belly, looks into my eyes. *You okay?*

I nod. "It's just . . . it's been a really
long time. I don't know if . . ."

He grins. *It's like riding a bike.*
*Don't worry. I won't let you fall.*

And then he does things no
one has ever done, takes me places

I've never been, and my tears
turn to cries of indescribable joy.

# After We're Through

He holds me, strokes
my damp hair, softly
kisses my face. And in

a moment

of weakness, I confess,
"That's the first time."
He doesn't understand.

"The first time

I ever had a . . . a . . ." I
can't bring myself to
say the word, so I try,

". . . you know."

Realization dawns and he
smiles, dimple to dimple.
*Really? Want another one?*

His touch

is like the perfect wave,
one you can surf but just
barely. It lifts me,

thrills

me, nearly engulfs me
as we crest together and
he knows I had another

"you know."

And he knows he'll never
have to take it by force,
never have to insist *You know*

                    *you want it,*

because he knows what
he has just given me
is something I'll lust for

                forever.

# We Drift for a While

Wired and tired and toasted.
We touch and kiss and talk
about where we've been,
where we might go
from here.

Back to work.
Back to the valley.
Back to freaky Kevin.
Back to my mom, Hunter.
Back to you . . . but when?

*Back to school.*
*Back to Stockton.*
*Back to freaky Robyn.*
*Back to my apartment.*
*Back to you...but when?*

I know it
won't be that long.
After all, I'm here, and
I'll be waiting. And if that's
not enough, his connect is here too.

# All Evidence of Our Tryst

Soaped and watered
        away, hair neatly combed,
        makeup completely gone,
Trey takes me [and a whole
        lot of crystal] back to my car.

        He kisses me one more time.
                *Careful driving home. It's pretty*
                *late. The cops will be on the prowl.*
        He guides me into my car.
                *I'll be in touch soon, okay?*

I look up into his eyes, hoping
        to find honesty. But I realize
        I'm not completely sure what
honesty is. Not honesty between
        a guy and a girl, anyway. "Okay."

I drive home, thinking about
        honesty. I drive home, thinking
        about possibilities. I drive home,
thinking about rediscovery. I drive
        home, sifting thoughts of Trey.

# Always, in the Past

I've measured the seasons by holidays,
how we spend them. This year, so close
on the heels of the birthday/baptism
fiasco, and with Hunter still too young
to care, Halloween was a non-event.
We stayed home, no trick-or-treaters
in sight. Never are up here on the hill.
Still, Mom always
buys candy, just
in case.

It's been a little over three weeks since Trey
and I were together, and I can't get him
out of my mind. At work, at home, amidst
Thanksgiving preparations, he's all I can
think about. Well, Trey and ice. Every
morning before work, I get high.
Every day after work before I go
home, I get high. Not too high, just
maintenance high. I'm at the point
where that's enough to stay semisane,
but not so much that I can't eat.
A little.
Sleep.

A little.

I know I've got to sleep a lot soon.
Suffer the crash-and-burn. Come down
all the way. But with a fabulous stash
within easy reach, I don't know how to
make myself do that. I've heard after
a while your body will just shut down,
speed or no speed. I'm almost looking
forward to that. Today is Thanksgiving.
I've got to work, so Mom is planning
the feast for after four. Turkey and all
the trimmings.
Ugh! How
will I do
that?

# At Least Kevin Won't Be in Today

Apparently even perverts
celebrate Thanksgiving.
And oh, is he ever

                        the pervert.

I hate when he comes
into the store, all steamy
and leering. Hate that he

                        won't leave me alone.

His back room "chats"
now include touchy-
feely games.

                        But I don't

know how to make
him back off. I need
the paycheck, don't

                        want to piss him off

by telling him he makes
me want to hurl. I think
he knows I'm high, think

                        he's high himself,

and that makes him even
more determined to back
me into a corner. Literally.

                        So far I've managed

to extricate myself without
getting physical, relying
on what's left of my brain

        to use a little humor,

crack jokes about my baby
fat or how Mom always warned
me against storeroom sex.

        So far, I've managed

not to let him kiss me or
touch me under my green
smock. So far I've managed

        to keep him at bay.

# It Being a Holiday

And the Sev actually being open,
we're getting a lot of customers.
Seems everyone forgot whipping
cream or cranberry sauce.

       We are currently out of both.

Personally, I am currently out
of cigarettes. I reach for hard
pack Marlboros, tell Midge,
"I'm taking a smoke break."

       It's arctic cold outside.

They say a storm is moving in.
With luck, we'll have snow
before Christmas. As I consider
hitting the slopes, my cell rings.

       The voice makes me shiver.

*Hey, you. You at work?*
*That sucks. Well, I'm in town*
*for Turkey Day. I want to see*
*you. When can we get together?*

Trey wants me, I'm there.

I know we should wait until
tomorrow. But I can't. "Will
you come pick me up after
dinner?" Mom will be livid.

But I couldn't care less.

# Livid Doesn't Cover It

I don't announce my plans until I choke
down the last bite of pumpkin pie.
I managed to eat a little of everything
Mom cooked, and even as "maintenance"
wired as I am, it tasted better than cardboard.

        I help with the dishes, then turn to leave
        the kitchen. *Where are you going?* asks
        Mom. *Hunter needs a diaper change.*

I lift him from his infant seat, sniff
his lavender-scented head. "Can you
watch him for me tonight? I've got
a date." I grit my teeth, anticipate the fall
of Mom's ax. It's a heavy swing.

        *You've got a* what? *Kristina, you can't*
        *be serious. It's Thanksgiving, for chrissake!*
        *This is supposed to be a family day.*

"Mom, you don't understand. Trey
is here for the holiday weekend. He has
to go back to Stockton soon. I have to see
him. I . . ." OMG! I'm ready to admit it
for the first time. ". . . I'm in love with him."

How can you love him, Kristina? You
hardly even know him. And what about
your baby? Don't you love him anymore?

Bam! Bam! That hurts, but not as much
as it should. "Of course I still love Hunter.
But I need the other kind of love too.
Anyway, I'm eighteen. I can do as I please.
You can't stop me from leaving."

She draws even, anger flickering in her
eyes. You have responsibilities, a child
who needs you. What if I refuse to babysit?

[Go ahead. Call her bluff. You know
she won't let you do it.] "Then I'll
just have to take him with me."
As if intuiting what that might mean,
Hunter puckers up, starts to cry.

Mom snatches him from my arms.
*Go on. Go out. Get out of my house.*
*But someday you'll regret this.*

# 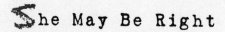She May Be Right

But I can't worry about that now.
I go upstairs, clean up, dress hot.
I've got to be hot for Trey.
I'm in love with him.

That scares the hell out of me.
Love is the first step toward
breaking up. [Come on. Love
makes making love better.]

Trey calls to tell me he's almost
here. I leave without saying
good-bye, wait for him outside,
feeling guilty. Anxious.

One thing's for certain. I may
be in love with Trey. But I'm
not going to tell him so. He
just might make a U-turn and run.

Headlights. He's here, and
I'm leaving, no turning back.
The Mustang purrs up the drive,
and the passenger door opens.

Trey leans toward me, smiles,
and there is no baby behind
me, no Mom, stepfather,
little brother. No leftovers.

There is only soft black leather,
classic rock on the radio (he
remembered!), the scent of crank-
tainted Brut, the taste of Trey.

# The Freeway Is Deserted

Everyone still at their tables,
      or catching a football game.
Trey drives over the limit
      to Red Rock today, chancing
the odd cop, who doesn't
      materialize. Brad and the girls
are still at the family shindig.
      We have the place all to ourselves.

      We're barely through the front
door and already kissing like
      there won't be a tomorrow, and
if there isn't, this time together
      will be worth every irate word
at home. Finally, Trey pulls away.
      *Do you know how much I want
you? Let's go upstairs, okay?*

And it's more than okay. It's
          necessary. We indulge in a taste
of the monster, losing our clothes
          before we're finished. Then I'm
back in his arms and he's doing
          those things to me again, those
things I've only read about before
          making love with Trey. They're real.

          He takes his time, shows me new
ways to make him feel good too.
          Fueled by ice, it all takes a very
long while, but finally we both
          ascend about as high as two people
can. Despite the glass, we float
          in a sea of exhaustion. Trey whispers,
*Please stay with me tonight.*

Cushioned by his arms, it occurs
        to me that I've never actually slept
with a guy before—never had
        the chance. But I love being knotted
together with him. "I'll stay. Wait.
        I have to work in the morning."
He stirs, disappointed. [Call in
        sick.] "Never mind. I'll call in sick."

# We Drift Toward Sleep

Never quite get all the way there,
but tangled in the warmth of Trey,
I'm glad I'm semiconscious.

At some point I hear noise downstairs,
so I know Brad and his daughters
have returned safely home.

Safe. That's how I feel. Safely home,
in Trey's arms. And some stupid
part of me mumbles, "I love you."

> He moves and I wonder if he'll
> get out of bed, make that wide U-ey.
> Instead, a rain of soft kisses falls
>
> over me. And suddenly, we're making
> love again. Sweaty, wonderful, don't-
> want-to-sleep-anyway love. When we
>
> finish, Trey props himself on one elbow,
> looks into my eyes, kisses my forehead
> and says, *I love you, too, Kristina.*

*I've only ever said that to one girl
before. Maryann Murphy. We were
twelve and I had this major crush on her.*

Still dazed by his declaration,
I smile at this confession. "And
what did Maryann say to you?"

He laughs. *She said, "Eyew! Gross!"
Damaged me for a long time.* He pulls
me back into his arms. *Fix me.*

# I Must Have Dozed Off

Because I wake to an assault
          of midmorning sun and,
                    somewhere close (outside?),
                              children's laughter. It takes
                    several long seconds to
          remember where I am, all
that happened last night.

          I was with Trey, slept here
                    with Trey, confessed to Trey
                              that I love him. And Trey told
                                        me he loves me, too. Me and
                              Maryann Murphy. Trey loves
                    me. Trey! Where is he, anyway?
          Beside me, the bed is empty.

I'd say it must have all
          been a dream, but this
                    is most definitely not
                              my bedroom. Suddenly
                    I notice, in the adjacent
          room, the sound of a shower.
I could definitely use one too.

I rouse myself, climb naked
            from bed, and am already
                    through the bathroom door
                            when it occurs to me it might
                    not be Trey in the shower.
            I take a quick peek. It's Trey,
all right, in all his soapy glory.

"Morning. Mind if I join
        you? I'll wash your back."
                Trey invites me to share
                        the hot water and after
                I wash his back, he says,
*Turnaround's fair play.* He
washes more than my back.

# 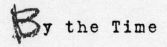y the Time

We're scrubbed and dressed,
the clock says 11:16
and I'm glad I called work
last night, even if I did have
to talk to Grade E.

*Sick, huh?* Grady's voice
dripped skepticism.
*Okay, I'll let Midge know.*

Thinking about it now,
however, I realize I didn't
call home. Mom was already
pissed. Now, most likely,
she's worried, too.

Before I can remedy that,
Trey says, *Come here.
Look out the window.*

I can't believe it! While
Trey and I were all wrapped
up in each other, it snowed.
And snowed. Inches of white
cover everything in sight.

Including Trey's car. *Hmm.
I don't have chains. Wonder how
the Mustang handles in snow.*

I slide my hand into his.
"I don't have to work today.
Might be a good excuse to
stay inside. If you can think
of something to do, that is."

*Doing nothing—with you—*
*might be nice. I don't have*
*anywhere I need to go.*

First things first. "I have
to call home. My mom
probably thinks we slid off
into a snowbank. Give me
a kiss for courage."

# Mom May Be Worried

But she chooses an entirely
different tack than I expected.

You think I don't know what's up
with you? Why you don't eat?
Why we catch you awake all
hours of the day? Why you stutter

your way through simple sentences?
How dense do you think we are?
You're using. I can smell
the speed, the tobacco, too.

Cigarettes aren't illegal, but
crystal meth is, and I won't have
that stuff in my house. Why would
you bring it around your baby?

You're right. You're eighteen now.
It's your life, so maybe I shouldn't
worry about how you live it. But
you're still my daughter and I love you.

*We'll get you help if you need it.*
*But you have to stop, and stop now.*
*You're a danger to your baby.*
*You're a danger to yourself.*

*So okay. Stay with this new guy.*
*Get him out of your system.*
*But don't ever bring him home.*
*And do not come back here stoned.*

*Oh. By the way. A Kevin from work*
*called you. He wants you to come*
*in Sunday to make up for today.*
*He left a number for you to call. . . .*

Click. She's gone. That was way
too easy. That was way too hard.

# They Know I'm Using

Want me to stop, and I know
I should. But I don't want to.
Don't even know if I could.

I want to use right now, in fact.
And guess what. I'm not home,
am I? "Can we catch a buzz?"

*Uh, sure. Hey, are you okay?*
*What did your mom say?*

I'm not going to tell him,
don't want him to know.
"She said work called."

*He looks into my eyes.*
*Nothing about snowbanks?*

Nothing about snow,
plenty about ice. I smile.
"Nope. Nothing at all."

*He senses something.*
*So . . . what's wrong?*

What can I tell him? That
everything has changed,
everything is changing still?

That even though I wanted
that change, initiated it, fueled
it, part of me wants to go back

to last summer, before Bree
reawakened, before I went
looking for the monster.

Before I met Trey. Should I
say that, even though he has assuaged
certain hungers, brought me

to a level of love I didn't believe
I would ever experience, fear
of losing him later makes me

think it might be better to lose
him now? [Don't even think it.You
don't want to lose him *ever*.]

"Nothing's wrong. Everything's perfect."

# It's Late Saturday Afternoon

Before Trey takes me home.
Two whole days, and two
whole nights, together.
We played in the snow
with the girls, watched
movies on Pay Per View.
Got high, talked with Brad.
Talked with each other. Kissed.
Talked. Kissed some more.

Last night was magical,
filled with monster-fed sensations,
sleepless hours in each other's
arms and declarations of love.
Night spilled well into morning.
I wanted it never to end.
But all great things must
end sooner or later. The plows
have been busy, the roads
cleared. Trey has to go
back to Stockton. And I
have to go home.

Before we leave, Trey and Brad
wander off for a private
conversation. Nosy me
eavesdrops as best I can.
I don't hear all the details, but
do understand that Brad is fronting
Trey a quantity above and beyond
his personal stash. What I learn
isn't surprising, but does make me
worry a little. Trey, it seems, buys
books and food by dealing at UOP.

I ask Trey to make a stop
on the way. I run into Target
for a lockbox, large enough
for a stash and some money,
small enough to fit under
the seat of my car. No way
will I bring anything in the
house. From now on, it will
reside in the LTD.

Trey pulls to a stop at the bottom
of our driveway. I told him it's
steep and icy, both true. Didn't
mention my mom's orders
never to bring him around.

*I'll be back at the semester
break,* he says. *We'll have lots
of time together then. You gonna
miss me, little girl?*

I'm going to go totally crazy
without him. "Of course
I'll miss you. More than
I can possibly tell you. Please
be careful, and promise you'll
call me!" At least I'll know he's
safe and thinking about me.

*I promise. But the phone*
*works both directions. You*
*can always call me. If I don't*
*pick up, leave a message.*
*I'll call you back.* He watches
me lock up my valuables,
then kisses a soft, sad good-bye.

# I've Got a Good Idea

What's waiting for me inside.
I'm strung. Tired. Scared
   I'll never see Trey again,
   despite his vows of love.
Mom is going to yell.
Scott is going to yell.
      Jake will watch, with some
      sort of bent satisfaction.
    Hunter will cry, and I'll bloat
    with guilt for not loving him better.

By the time I reach the front
door, I've built a barrier against
     all that. Don't want to hear
     it. Refuse to hear it. All I want
   to do is lie on my bed, listen
   to music through headphones,
       think about being with Trey,
       dream about the semester break.
    Suddenly I feel angry. Out-
    of-control pissed off at the world.

I yank open the door, slam
it shut behind me. Scott stomps
                in from the kitchen. *What the hell*
                *was that about? Did you have*
          *a fight with your boyfriend?*
The last word drips vitriol.
                        *If you think you can disrespect*
                        *my* house in this way, you'd
                    *better think about living*
                    *somewhere else. Understand?*

Obviously, they've been
discussing options. Like
                kicking me out of here. Mom
                comes up behind Scott, carrying
          a smiling Hunter, and it comes
to me that I have the means
                        to hurt her more than she can
                        hurt me. "Go ahead. Kick me
                    out. Hunter and I will go live
                    with Dad in Albuquerque."

Okay, that was semivicious.
The look on Mom's face
                    is indescribable—a mixture
                    of disbelief, panic, and rage.
          She tries to sputter an answer,
          but Scott interrupts her. *Over*
                              *my dead body will you take*
                              *this baby out of here. Have*
                    *you gone completely insane?*
                    *He would be dead in a week.*


What is he talking about?
The anger, hot and red inside
                    me, boils over completely.
                    "Do you really think I'd kill
          my fucking baby? What kind
          of a person do you think I am?"
                              I notice Jake, standing in the
                              archway, staring. "What the fuck
                    are you looking at, you
                    freaking little monster?"

Now Hunter *does* start to cry.
I reach toward him, but Mom
                          shakes her head. *No. Jake,*
                          *please take Hunter upstairs.*
              I expect a heated spew, but
              she stays completely calm.
                                    *Look at yourself, Kristina.*
                                    *You're incapable of caring*
                          *for a baby. You're off the deep*
                          *end. Do you want to drown him, too?*


Her words bring back a dream
I had when I was pregnant.
                          A dream about Hunter drowning.
                          Suddenly it's Bree I want to drown.
              Bree and the fucking monster.
              Tears well up, unbidden, and I
                                    have no chance at stopping
                                    them from falling. I want to die.
                          But all I can say at this moment
                          is, "I'm sorry. I'm so sorry."

# Not Exactly Forgiven

**S**
**E**
**M**
**I**
**C** On my big bed, swathed in mauve, almost catatonic,
**O** some part of me does understand that I have deserted
**N** my motherhood post, gone AWOL, at the urging of the
**S** the enemy——the monster. But I think, if I can only sleep,
**C** I'll find a way back to the company of my family. They
**I** *have* to forgive me, fold me in. Prodigal daughter, kill
**O** the fatted lamb. The image comforts me. But not as much
**U** as knowing I've still got a fat stash of ice in my car, safe
**S** inside its lockbox. And I've still got Trey, safe in memory.

# $\mathcal{N}$ovember Empties

Into December and life
has taken on a certain
rhythm.

                              Bumpy,

you might call it.
Work. Home. Work
again, all

                              up and down.

I've tried to keep
cool about my use.
But I can't not get

                              high,

especially in the early
A.M., have to get to work,
deal with that crap.

                              And

then I go home, deal
with that crap too.
That brings me down, way

                              low,

especially since I've only
heard from Trey twice
in two weeks.

                              Still,

Mom and Scott have tried
to leave me alone. In fact,
they've remained mostly

                              silent,

despite their assessing
stares, which must confirm
every suspicion. Hunter

                              cries

a lot, it seems. I do my best
to comfort him, but I'm
starting to think he

                              screams

because he sees me as a
stranger, like I'm the baby-
sitter. Guilt

                              rages

in me, but only when
I finally come down enough
to really think about it.

# Today I'm Coming Down

It will be a fast crash,
and for that I'm grateful.
My body aches. My brain
feels like mush. I need sleep,
even more than I need food.

Recognizing those needs,
I haven't played with
the monster for two days.
Work today was impossible.
I don't know how I made it through.

Now I'm home, and Mom
says, *I'm going to the gym
and then I've got some errands
to run. Jake is at practice.
You'll have to watch Hunter.*

"Sure. No problem," I say,
knowing full well that it might
be a problem. I give him a bottle,
lay him on a big quilt on the living
room floor, plop down beside him,

347

close my eyes. Tread a pool
of murky water, dreams gone
stagnant, or brewing dementia.
Somewhere I hear a baby gurgling,
giggling, cooing. Somewhere I hear

a baby fussing. Crying. Screeching . . .
But I can't wake up. Don't want
to leave this place so very near
sleep. I have to. Can't. Have to.
Won't. No, I'll deal with it

when I come up for air. Up from
this place I've finally settled into.
Sleep. Deep, deep sleep. What is
that noise? It won't stop, like an
alarm clock without a snooze button.

Suddenly I'm ratcheted awake,
roughly set on my feet, pushed
out the front door. Mom's
crazed face parts the cerebral mist.
*This is the last straw, Kristina.*

What's going on? My brain
feels like mush. Behind Mom,
I see Jake, holding Hunter,
who's howling like he's
just been bitten. "Wha . . . ?"

*You are leaving. And Hunter
is staying. Do not come back
here until you're completely
sober. And don't even think
about trying to take this baby.*

I don't get it. All I did was
take a nap. My head is thick,
my mouth unsure how to
work. "Wha . . . what d-did I do?
And where will I go?"

*While you were* sleeping, *Hunter
rolled under a chair, and got
stuck under there. He was screaming
and you couldn't be bothered to
wake up and find out why?*

Rolled? Hunter can roll?
Since when? He's only six
months old. Six-month-olds
can roll? Why didn't anyone
tell me he could roll?

*I don't care where you go.*
*Live on the street, sleep*
*in your car. Just don't come*
*back here. And don't ask*
*for money. Get help, Kristina.*

She won't even let me back
in the house to get my clothes.
Get my keys. She makes me
sit in my car while she gets
them for me. What do I do now?

# Help

I need help.
The first person
who comes to mind
is, of course, Trey. I dial
his cell. No answer but voice
mail. "Please call me. I need help."

Sleep.

I need sleep.
While I wait for
Trey's call, I'll catch
a little nap. I drive to an
out-of-the-way parking place,
climb over the seat into the back.

Warmth.

I need warmth.
Snow on the ground
outside, it's freezing in
here. No blanket in my car,
I burrow into my big overcoat,
tuck my face against my arm, catlike.

Buzz.

I need a buzz
to get me through
this time of trial. Sleep.
I'll sleep, then I'll catch a
buzz. It's under the seat in front
of me and that's a comforting thought.

# It's Dark

When I wake up, dark and bitter

        cold. My thoughts scatter

    like a swarm of mosquitoes.

I know I'm in the backseat

        of my car, but I can't remember

      exactly why. Hunter? Something

        about . . . Oh, now it all comes

back to me. I screwed up.

        I screwed up and Mom called

me on it. Called. Called?

      Did Trey call? I reach for my cell.

    No voice mail. He didn't call?

I punch my own call button.

On the other end, the phone

rings and rings, finally goes

to voice mail. "Would you *please*

call me?" I beg. "I need you."

Where the hell is he, anyway?

Then I glance at the clock

on my phone. Three A.M.

Most likely he's sleeping.

But is he sleeping alone?

# No More Sleep for Me

Now that I'm awake, I can feel the cold,
whittling my skin, worrying my bones.

I want to get high, but I need to eat first.
My belly is empty as a Mojave water hole.

Three A.M. I'll have to drive to Denny's
if I want to eat at this hour of the day.

I start the car, de-ice the windows, wonder
why Trey never called me back.

Fifteen minutes later, I'm in a pink
and orange booth, waiting for my Moons

Over My Hammy. Filling. Easy to eat.
Cheap. Guess I won't be eating at home

for a while. Maybe Mom was only jiving.
[Yeah, right. And I'm a prima ballerina.]

              The food comes, served by a stone-
              faced waitress. *Want anything else?*

Let me see. How about a place to go to
when I get off work later? "Not right now."

The sandwich is greasy and tasty and I eat
it slowly, not to savor the flavors, but to kill

time, three-plus hours until work. At least
it's warm in here. Safe. Warm. Safe. That reminds

me of a night, spent in Trey's arms, at his
cousin Brad's house. Brad! He has that big spare

room. It's kind of far from work, but hey,
there's a convenience store in Red Rock, too.

And guess what. Now I've got cash
register experience. Brad, who's cute.

Brad, who's cool. Brad, who has the best
connection this side of Mexico. [Give him a call.]

# Brad Is Home When I Call

I tell him what happened—that my
loving mother kicked me out
and kept my baby—omitting a little
information he doesn't need to know.

"So . . . any chance I might be able
to stay with you for a while?"
[Tell him you'll make it worth
his while.] I tell him exactly that.

He hesitates. *Uh, well, I never
really thought about taking in
a renter.* He thinks a bit. *First
off, you* are *over eighteen, right?*

"Eighteen and extra," I say,
giving him plenty of time to
think it over. It seems to take
a helluva lot more than plenty.

*Well, I can let you stay for a while,*
*I guess. I'm not sure I'm willing*
*to commit to a long-term thing,*
*so we'll have to play it by ear, okay?*

Whatever works. At least I won't
have to sleep in my car tonight.
"Okay. Thanks, Brad. Um, can
you remind me how to get there?"

# I Finish My Shift

About halfway
through, a distributor
comes in with a dolly
full of boxes.

*Where do you want
the candy canes?*

Candy canes.
Christmas is only
a few weeks away.

I have toys on
layaway for Hunter.
Will I get to play Santa?

Where will I be
Christmas morning?

# On the Way to Red Rock

I stop by the store, pick up the few
        things I know I can eat when I'm
walking with the monster—fruit,

light yogurt, several cans of soup.
        Probably rather impolite
to expect Brad to feed me too.

I also buy a toothbrush,
        toothpaste, and a hairbrush.
Mom neglected to pack mine.

She also forgot to include my
        makeup, but I can't afford more
than mascara, at least not until

my next paycheck. Paycheck
        to paycheck. Hey, I think I get
that now. It really *does* suck.

As I'm driving down Red
        Rock Road, my cell rings.
The caller ID makes me

happy. Pissed. Relieved. Pissed.
        I flip open the phone. "Where
the hell have you been?"

                Hey, you okay? What's wrong,
                        anyway? Are you hurt? In jail?
                What kind of help do you need?

I tell Trey what's up, but really,
        really want to know, "What took
you so fucking long to call?"

                I just got your message. My cell's
                        battery died and I couldn't find
                my charger. Just got another one.

I hate when someone has an
        unshakeable alibi. "Oh. Sorry.
It's just that I really needed you."

                Apology accepted. And I promise
                        to try to call more often, okay?
                Anyway, it's almost semester break.

Two weeks and counting down.
          Am I done being mad at him?
For now, I guess. Thinking

about being with him again
          has got me feeling a little
antsy. "Can't wait to see you."

                    *Me too. Hey, tell Brad everything's*
                              *jake, okay? And let me know how*
                    *you're doing. Love you, Kristina.*

I hope so. I need him
          more than ever right now.
"I love you, too, Trey."

# Life at Brad's

Isn't bad. I mean, I've got
this great room, utilities
included; easy access to
the best ice in Reno (not to
mention a cool place to smoke it);
and I'm pretty much free
to do exactly as I please.

Okay, I do need to work
because I promised Brad
fifty dollars a week—not bad.
I've been driving all the way
to the Sev, which has to change
very soon. I mean, with gas
at this price, and the LTD
rating a whopping nine miles
per gallon, I'm not netting
a mint from my paychecks.

There's another little problem.
And that is from time to time
my mom or Scott or Jake
happens in while I'm working.
It's awkward, to say the least,
especially if Mom has Hunter.
The Glacier Queen doesn't ignore
me, exactly. But she doesn't
act like more than a customer.

Mom and I, in fact, have not
exchanged more than a dozen
sentences since she pushed
me out the front door, almost
two weeks ago. I thought she
might invite me to share Christmas
with the family, but so far,
not one word.

At Brad's, preparation for
Santa is in full swing. I try
to participate (mostly because
I'm incredibly homesick), but
Devon and LaTreya have not
as yet identified me as "family."

I don't think they have a clue
why I'm here, and I'm pretty
sure they'd rather not have
me here, but such is life,
little girls. Still, I do my
best to be nice. Very nice.

That isn't always easy,
especially when the monster
insists their whining could
be dealt with by giving them
a good shake, or locking
them up in a closet. Okay,
not really viable options,
but kind of fun to think
about, when they go on and on
about cartoons and snacks and
*When is Mommy coming back?*

That one really gets to me.

# December Twenty-First

Last day of Trey's finals.
He says he'll be here tomorrow,
but the weather service is calling
for a major blizzard, so things might
not work out exactly as planned.
As my shift winds down, Kevin
comes in with the payroll.

He gestures for me to follow
him into the storeroom. I oblige
with a little smile, because I've got
a plan of action. Kevin looms in the
doorway, makes sure our bodies
touch as I pass by. I wait for
my check but before he

hands it to me, he says,
*I scheduled you to work on*
*Christmas. I know you asked for it*
*off, but Midge has seniority. She asked*
*first.* He measures my reaction, which
must disappoint him. No way would
I work Christmas, but I already

planned to quit today. "Sorry,
Kevin. You probably know I'm
living in the North Valleys now, and
the commute has become impossible.
I was going to give two weeks'
notice, but I'm not going to
work Christmas Day."

His face flares, one
shade lighter than purple.
Damn, it's scary! *You can't
just up and quit like that. What
am I supposed to do for help?*
He's actually waiting
for an answer.

"I don't know, Kevin.
Maybe you'll have to work
it yourself. Or call up one of
your little hos. I couldn't care
less. In fact, I may as well
leave right now. I think
it looks like snow."

He stalks closer, fists
clenched, eyes ablaze. This
guy is totally crazed. *You will
not get unemployment, you know,
and I won't give you a positive
reference. You might want
to rethink this decision.*

Come on, Bree, tell
me what to say. [You've
got a trump card. Play it.] "I
don't care about unemployment. But
I would like a positive reference. I
probably should tell you that
I've recorded a couple of

our conversations about
your entrepreneurial ventures.
I'd hate to see that information
fall into the uh . . . wrong hands, you
know?" (Total bullshit, but he has
no way of knowing that.) God,
this is totally great. Now

he's like plum purple.
*You little bitch. I should have
known. I'll have to think about
that reference, Kristina. Finish up
your shift, anyway. Do you want
me to mail your final check?*
He knows the answer.

# I Cash My Check

(Figure I'd better do it quick), then stop by

       Wal-Mart to pick up my Xmas layaway. It's a

freaking madhouse, four days till Christmas, no

       good stuff left, and what's left picked through.

Impossible lines zigzag toward the layaway desk.

       Might as well get comfortable. I'm lost in the shopping

diorama when someone taps my shoulder. *Kristina?*

       *Is that you? Wow, you sure have, um . . . changed.*

The voice is vaguely familiar, but somehow not right

       for this time and place. When I turn, my equilibrium

is threatened. It's Quade, my first crush, the one I

       couldn't quite find the courage to kiss. [Oh, man,

why the hell not?] "Quade? It can't be you. Talk about

changing!" His spiked hair is bleached on the ends,

and his eyebrows are pierced. Metal? I'm guessing

heavy. "You look great, though." [Understatement!

He's frigging fine.] "What are you up to nowadays?

Do you live in Reno?" [Like you could be so lucky.]

*No, actually, I still live at home, at least when*

*I quit moving around long enough to touch down*

*there. My band and I have a gig at Dr. Nasty's—*

*that new club on Fourth Street. Hey, you busy tonight?*

"Well, actually, no . . . but I'm not sure if they would

let me inside. I'm not quite twenty-one, you know."

Quade scans his memory banks. *Ah,*

*right. I can get you in, though.* He winks.

*You're with me.* He stands in line

with me awhile, and we talk about "the

good old days," as if we were ancient.

At least he helps me pass the time while

I crawl toward layaway. Finally I'm

just about there, and digging for my

layaway slip, which of course I can't

find. They'll have to use my phone

number. Oops. Mom's phone number.

*Well, let me know if you can make it,* Quade

says. *Here's my cell number. We fire up at nine.*

"Thanks. I'll definitely try. The only holdup

might be snow. They're calling for a killer storm."

*Cool. Let me know either way. And either*

*way, stay in touch.* He gives me a hug

and heads toward the monster checkout

lines. I watch him go as the lame layaway

girl says, *Picking up a layaway?* Unreal!

# Layaway Picked Up

And a couple of leftover baubles
bought for Brad and the girls,
I drive back to Red Rock.
Somehow it still doesn't feel like

home,

even if it is where my clothes reside;
where I go to sleep (sometimes)
at night; where I eat (sometimes);
where people (strangers) wait

for

me to come back to. No, "home"
is the other direction, in a protected
south valley, not here in a frigid
north valley Hades hole. [What

the

fuck is wrong with you? Remember
how much you wanted away from
home, only a few months ago?]
I do, but that was before the

holidays

intruded. I've never been away
from home on Christmas before.
Mom has transformed the house
into a Sugarplum Dreamland, only it

is

Hunter who she has transformed
it for.  [You're jealous of Hunter
now?] Yes. And of Mom [his
mommy] and Leigh, who is

where

I want to be—snug in front
of the fireplace, drinking hot
chocolate and munching popcorn
while trimming the tall fir tree.

I

want to hum along to carols, sneak
off to my room to wrap presents [and
do what else?]. Pipe down, Bree! Despite
your insistence otherwise, that is where I

really belong.

# It's Almost Eight

When I get to Brad's. The wind

has blown up, and it's north-pole
cold, but so far, not even a flurry.

Inside they're watching *A Charlie
Brown Christmas*. I can't see the TV,
but the music is unmistakable.

Brad looks my direction, smiles.

I wave him over and he follows
me into the kitchen, where I hand

him a crisp hundred. "This week
and next week," I explain. "I lost
my job today, so I'll have to find

another one. Didn't want you to

get shorted in the meantime."
[How adult of you, especially

considering you're just about broke.]

*Lost your job? What happened?*
I already figured this part out.
Might not be the best idea

to tell him I didn't want to work

Christmas. "The store manager
is a total letch. He won't keep

his hands off me. So I quit."
                    *That sucks. You could probably*
                    *sue him, you know.*

"Sure, if I could afford a lawyer.

Anyway, how would I prove it,
and would I really want *his* lawyer

to start digging up dirt on me?"

                    *Good point. Well, thanks for the money.*
                    *You're welcome to join the girls*

                    *and me for yet another encore*

*of* A Christmas Story. *They've seen*
*it three times already, but you know . . .*

"Thanks, Brad. But I ran into an old
friend whose band is playing at some
new club in town. He invited me to drop

by. I thought I'd go check it out."

Wow. He looks really disappointed.
*Be careful. They're calling for—*

"Snow. I know. I'll keep an eye out,
and if it starts to snow, I promise
I'll come straight home, okay?"

Did I just call this place home?

And why would I promise to
come straight here? Why

would I promise Brad anything?
He's not my dad. Not my boyfriend.
[But more than a landlord, no?]

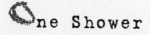

# One Shower

And three solid tokes later,
I'm off to Reno. The sky is dark,
            no moon, stars, or planets in sight.
A storm is definitely brewing.

            Trey is number one on my speed
dial. I give it a try but, as usual,
            fall into his voice mail basket.
God, that is so annoying! Oh, well,

            I feel pretty great, and I'm out
for the night, and isn't this what
            freedom is all about? I cruise
down Fourth, locate Dr. Nasty's.

            The name is perfect, the club
a dive. I dial Quade's number, tell
            him I'm here. He says to come
around back. He'll let me in.

            *Glad you could make it.* Quade
gives me another hug, and this
            time it's longer, warmer. *Come
on. It's just about showtime.*

I follow him backstage. Three
          guys, all dressed in personalized
leather and piercings, give Quade
          a nod. *You can hang here, okay?*

          "No problem." I grab a stool
as the band takes the stage,
          launches a hard metal song
guaranteed to blow eardrums.

Not my favorite music,
          but they play it well, one
song crashing into the next,
          Quade leading the charge

          with his bass. By the time
they take a break, my ears
          pound and my throat is parched.
Quade comes up, puts his arm

around my shoulder. *Thirsty?*
          The best I can do is nod.
*Me, too. I'll get us drinks.*
          *What's your pleasure?*

[Dangerous question.] "Um . . ." I've
never been much of a drinker,
        and I'm not even sure if he's offering
alcohol. "Whatever you're having."

He takes off in search of drinks.
        Meanwhile, one of his bandmates
comes up. *Hi. I'm Jeremy.*
        *You're Quade's old friend, huh?*

        I'm not sure why, but I smile
a come-on smile. [Way to go!]
        "Well, I'm not that old, but we've
known each other a long time."

That was a lot to say with
        cotton-mouth, and Jeremy
has a clue what that means.
        Now it's his turn to smile,

        and now I know where
this evening could go.
        Partying with the band? Isn't
that every girl's dream?

# It Was a Definite Party

And one that went way too late,
especially considering I was
the one donating most of the ice.

Quade didn't touch it, but his buds
all did. He watched, more than a tad
disapprovingly, but never said a word.

He drank. A little. Smoked pot. A little.
But no meth, and no tobacco. *Bad
for the vocal cords,* he claimed.

I did it all. Enjoyed doing it all,
surrounded by three decent-looking
dudes and one who resembled

a raccoon, with black circles
swallowing his eyes and pointy
(who knows why!) yellow teeth.

Anyway, it was fun. And I have to
admit, Trey or no Trey, my attraction
to Quade is stronger than ever.

Yeah, yeah, part of that's being
buzzed and wanting to be kissed. More
is wanting that missed-chance kiss.

As I was leaving, Damian (Raccoon
Man) pulled me aside. *Hey. Can you
score more of that crystal?*

"Maybe," I said. "But it isn't cheap,"
added Bree, recognizing the chance
to make a little on the deal.

*No problem. I'll take a ball, if you
can get it. And I'd rather pay more
than get one that's short.*

A man [raccoon] after my own
heart. I don't need to "borrow"
from his if I can come up with

some extra cash to apply to my own
account with Brad, who I'm
hoping will front me some.

Good thing I had plenty tonight,
to combat the alcohol. I had
half a dozen beers, something

I've never done before, and beyond
the high of the glass is a definite
three-point-eight low. That, plus

the pot, which I haven't smoked
since my days with Chase, have
combined to perhaps affect my driving.

# I'm Crawling Home

like an old woman, working hard
to stay centered in my lane.
The car wants to veer right, then left.

But whether that's because
of my condition, or weather conditions,
I'm not exactly sure.

It started to flurry before I left for Red
Rock. And now it's coming
down faster, starting to stick to the asphalt.

The LTD is heavy, its tires
fully treaded. But there's a long, steep
off-ramp ahead.

A nerve attack rattles my teeth. The hands
gripping the steering wheel
begin to shake, and when I try to stop them,

they don't respond to my
commands, as if they belong to someone else.
[Get it together. This isn't rocket

science. Remember what Scott told you about
driving in snow.]
Okay, stop sign ahead. Pump the brakes.

Wait! Was that don't
pump the brakes? Shit! I choose middle
ground, slide to a stop,

turn the corner gradually, head for Brad's.
Wow. That wasn't so bad.
Looks like it's been snowing longer here, though.

An inch or more of slick
white stuff covers the road. My headlights glare
off it, and off the falling snow,

falling heavier now, splatting the windshield
like giant wet bugs,
and it just keeps coming straight at me.

Oh my God, it wants me.
Slow down, Kristina! But this time when I semi-
pump the brakes, the LTD

has a mind of its own and it just keeps going,
wherever it wants, and I can't
slow it, can't steer it, and all of a sudden, *Wham!*

It stops, nose down, slamming
me forward, against the steering wheel. And I
can't move. Don't dare move.

# 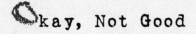kay, Not Good

I assess personal damage. Don't
think I'm hurt, at least not badly.
Beyond a likely steering-wheel-
shaped bruise, and having
the wind totally stolen from
me, I'm all in one piece, and
everything seems to work.

The car, however, is a different story.

It landed facedown in a drainage
ditch, one rear wheel tilted off
the ground. No way can I get it
out on my own. I'll have to walk,
and I'd better get going before a cop
happens along, not that many cops use
this road. Still, just my luck, tonight
will be the night one is visiting

his girlfriend out here or something.

I don't mind getting a ticket, if that's
the most that will happen. But any
cop trained as a DRE would definitely
know what's up. In fact, it probably
wouldn't take a drug recognition
expert to expertly recognize how fucked
up I am right now. I'll be a lot less
likely to go to jail in the morning. Oops.

It is morning, somewhere close to five.

It isn't too far, maybe a little over
a mile, but it's dumping snow, and I
didn't bring my coat. [Stupid.] My
feet slip and slide, and before very
long, my sweater and hair are frosted
white. The cold makes me shiver,
the meth makes me shake, and by the time
I jam my key into the lock,

my fingers barely work enough to turn it.

I tiptoe up to my room and into
a hot shower. By the time I dry
off, enveloped by warm scented
steam, a gray dawn illuminates
my window. Outside, the snow

keeps unfolding a canvas of white.

# I Sit by the French Doors

Dazed and sore, sorer by the minute,
watching the relentless storm. It hasn't
let up since I walked in the door. Trey
will never make it today. Guess
I'll have to call a tow truck,
unless Brad can pull me
out with his big ol'
Dodge four by four.
But he and the girls
are still sleeping off
their Christmas flicks.
Wonder when they'll
get up. Wonder if Trey
will call. Wonder if some
wayward cop discovered
the car, scraped snow
from the windows,
peeked inside,
hoping to find
something dead
past the frozen
glass. Wonder

just how close I
came to not ever
wondering about
anything again.

# After a While

The house crackles alive.
     Footsteps fall, weighted,
         on the stairs. I get up
           and trail them down
to the kitchen. Brad
     is at the sink, back
         toward me, wearing
           nothing but skimpy
briefs. I thought Trey
     was buff, but Brad's
         body is better. Whether
           that has to do with working
construction or only
     a matter of a few extra
         years, I don't know.
           [Who cares? Yummy!]
Anyway, ogling the hew
     of his shoulders and
         back is not why I'm
           here. "Brad, I, uh . . ."
He jumps and yanks
     in my direction. *Holy*
         *shit, Kristina. You*
           *scared the living*

*hell out of me! Your car*
            *isn't in the driveway,*
                        *so I figured you must*
                                    *have stayed in town.*
The quick move slightly
            parts the opening in his
                        BVDs, offering a glimpse
                                    of something rather private.
I can't help but smile.
            He glances down, but
                        doesn't make a move
                                    to rectify the situation.
All he does is shrug
            and return my smile.
                        Then it strikes him.
                                    *So where's your car?*
My turn to shrug.
            "I left it facedown
                        in a ditch, a mile
                                    or so from here."

*What? Hey, are you*
        *okay?* He moves
                closer, gives me
                        a concerned once-over.
He cares? "I'm fine,
        except for a giant
                bruise. Not sure
                        about the car, though."
*Give me a minute to*
        *get dressed, and I'll*
                *go check it out. Oh,*
                        *wait . . . the kids.*
"I can watch them,
        unless you need me
                to come too." I hope
                        he says no, in case
there happen to be cops
        around. I'm still pretty
                buzzed. Brad, on the
                        other hand, looks fine.

He thinks for a minute,
        finally shakes his head.
                *I'll assess the damage.*
                        *If I can pull it out, I'll*
*come get you. If not,*
        *we'll call my buddy*
                *at Reno Tow. He owes*
                        *me, anyway.* Telltale wink.
Brad takes off to find
        some jeans, and I find
                a growing affection for
                        the guy who took me in.

# Brad Takes Off

And I go upstairs, seriously in
need of a smoke. When I reach
for my Marlboros, my cell tells
me I have two new voice mails.

The first is from Trey.
*Hey, babe. It's about nine*
*on Saturday and it's raining*
*like insanity, which means*
*it's seriously blizzarding up*
*in the mountains. I'm not*
*going to chance it until it*
*stops and they plow the roads.*
*I'll get there soon as I can, okay?*

I knew he was going to say
that. But was there another—
definitely female—voice
in the background?

The second message is from
Mom. *Kristina? Where are
you? Are you okay? I just
got a call from Deputy Freed.
He found your car and had it
towed to impound. But he had
no idea what happened to you.
Will you please call and let us
know you're okay? Please?*

Guess the snow filled in my
tracks. Guess Brad's off
the hook. Guess Mom might
care about me after all.

# But What About Trey?

I step out onto the back step
to smoke and fret about that.
Snow falls, insistent, intent.
I watch it tumble

                down.

Was he with a girl when he
called, or only somewhere
where there was a girl? Am
I paranoid? I know,

                deep down,

that falling hard for the first
guy to take interest in over
a year was not the best idea.
But how do you tell

                your heart,

No, don't swell with magic,
you'll only burst? How do
you tell it to clamp itself off
from possibilities? God

                knows

I don't need more pain in
life. Why did I invite it in?
Do I have to feel pain to
believe I feel anything at all?

# I Guess I Should Call Mom

She answers on the first ring.
*Kristina? Thank God you're*
*all right. What happened?*

I omit most of the story—
the band, the booze, the monster.
I do mention running into Quade

at Wal-Mart. "We got to talking
and by the time I left, there was
too much snow on the road."

Her voice has relaxed. *I'll*
*have to tell his mother you saw*
*him. What about your car?*

"Impound won't be open until
Monday, so I don't know how
much they'll want, or how

much damage there is to my car.
But Brad's friend has a tow service.
We can bring it back here."

*Sounds like you're not too*
*worried about getting to work.*
Fishing. Definitely fishing.

No use not copping. "Actually,
I quit my job. It was a long drive,
especially with gas so high."

I consider mentioning the pervert
excuse, but decide to save it
in case I need it in the future.

Mom pauses, and I know she's
considering what to say next.
*What about Christmas?*

I knew it! Knew she couldn't
do Christmas without everyone
home. That's my mom. Everything

has to be perfect. And how could
it be perfect without me? [You're
kidding, right?] "What about it?"

*Are you going to spend it at*
*home? Do you need me*
*to come out there and get you?*

I've got a couple of choices
here. I could play smart-ass—
ask why she wants me to come

home, when she knows I'll
only spoil the party. I could play
coy—tell her I'm not sure

of my holiday plans, could I let
her know? But the truth is, I want
to spend Christmas with my family.

Still, I don't want to sound too
anxious. After all, *she* kicked *me*
out. "Let's play it by ear. If my car

is okay and the roads are clear,
I can drive down there. If not,
we can figure out something."

We leave it there, and it isn't
until after I hang up that I realize
I didn't even ask about Hunter.

# I Sit at the Kitchen Table

Sketching Hunter from a recent photo.
Every now and then I look up to watch
the snow. I'm lost in a silvery view
when a little hand taps my shoulder.

*Whatcha doin'?* asks Devon.
*Who's that?* referring to the portrait
becoming flesh on my sketch pad.

The girls don't know about Hunter,
and I don't want them to know
I left my child in my shadow.
"That's Hunter. Isn't he cute?"

*Uh-huh. Will you draw my picture
too?* Self-absorbed, but what can
you expect from a six-year-old?

"Sure. But how about if I make
you breakfast first? What do you
like?" I expect a simple answer
like cereal or cinnamon toast.

*Bacon and eggs and pancakes.*
*Mommy used to cook those.*
*Can you?* Some sort of a challenge?

"Of course I can cook them,
and you can help, if we have
the ingredients. Let's go look."
I push back from the table,

and am surprised to feel a little
hand slip into mine. *The eggs*
*is in the 'frigerator.* She tugs gently.

It's the first time I've really
realized how much she misses her
mother, and she tugs more than my
hand. She tugs at my heart.

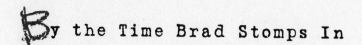

# By the Time Brad Stomps In

Tracking wet snow,
LaTreya has joined the party.

  Devon runs over, jumps up
  and down. *I'm cooking, Daddy.*

    LaTreya keeps stirring a thick,
    creamy batter. *Me too. Pancakes.*

      Brad takes in the domestic
      scene. *Good thing. I'm hungry.*

      Then he turns to me. *I drove all
      the way to the freeway, but couldn't*

      *find your car anywhere. It's either
      buried or they towed it.*

405

"Mom called. They towed it.
I tried your cell, but no answer."

Devon happily interrupts,
*'Tina's gonna draw my picture.*

LaTreya shoots an envious look.
*How come? What about me?*

Before I can answer, Brad does.
*I'm sure she'll draw you, too.*

*But first let's eat. I haven't had
pancakes in a really long time.*

I smile at him and he silently
mouths, *I need to talk to you.*

# After Breakfast

The girls go upstairs to play
dress-up while Brad and I wash
the dishes. He waits for them
to leave the room, then says,

*I've been thinking. Day care takes*
*a big chunk of my paychecks.*
                    *How would you like to play nanny?*
                    *Room, board, and a hun' a week.*

I make a few quick calculations.
A hundred a week isn't much,
                    but it's under the table, and hey,
                    I'll also have food, a place to stay,

                    and nowhere I have to be but here,
                    so gas is not a concern. Just one little
thing. "That's Monday through Friday,
right?" I still want my weekends free.

                    He grins. *Monday through Friday*
                    *works fine, party girl. And speaking*
                    *of parties, we can have one later.*
                    *I just got a delivery last night.*

407

"Are you buying my cooperation?"
Fresh stash, works every time. Which
reminds me. "Oh, one of the guys
in the band wants an eight ball.


"I told him I'd check on it. But no
way can I deliver it to him now."
Brad grows serious. *How well
do you know the guy?* It's the first


hint of paranoia I've seen. "Not well.
But I've known Quade since we were
kids and Damian looks like more than
a casual user. I don't think they're narcs."


Tension falls from his shoulders
like boulders off a cliff. *If you're
sure, no problem. Maybe Trey can
take you when he finally gets here.*


My turn for tension. "If he gets
here. He says not till the roads clear."
Brad's eyes travel the contours
of my body. *I promise. He'll get here.*

# Monday Morning

It has snowed all weekend,
and several feet of the sticky
wet white stuff cover everything.
Still, the day dawned critical
blue and the plows are busy.

Damian got his eight ball. We
met at the convenience store,
made a quick trade—awesome
ice for a pile of cash, including
fifty extra for me. Dealer me.

Quade didn't come along. Part of
me hoped he would. Most of me
knew he wouldn't. He definitely
doesn't like the idea of his buddies—
or me—dancing with the monster.

Brad is home today. Not much
in the way of construction
jobs when you need a sleigh
to deliver nails. Wonder if Santa
could contract with the Home Depot.

Probably too busy today, it being
Christmas Eve and all. I put in
a call to the impound yard, but
the phone message says to try
back on Wednesday. Tick, tick.

Higher and higher go those
impound fees. Brad says
they're twenty dollars a day, plus
the initial fifty for paperwork,
plus a hundred for the tow. Tick.

Around one P.M. Trey calls.
*I'm on my way. Can't wait*
*to see you. I've got something*
*special for you too. Hope*
*you like the way I play Santa.*

# Santa Is Coming

I can't
believe I
will finally get
to see him in the flesh.
Touch his flesh. Taste his
flesh, and beg him to taste mine.
I want to be in his arms again, sleep
in his arms again, and wake, skin to skin.
Just thinking about it breaks me out in a cold
sweat, sends quivers through me, all the way to the
very center of me. How long has it been? Only a few
weeks? It seems an eternity. They say the best things in life
are worth waiting for, but patience is not my best thing. Still,
he's coming, and will be here in just a few short hours. So I'll do

my best to sit here,
arms crossed. Yes,
it's going to be an
extremely merry
Christmas after all.

# Around Four P.M.

The phone rings and I rush
to answer. It has to be Trey, and
I need to hear his voice, closer now.

> *Kristina?* It's only Mom. *What's*
> *the game plan? Should I come pick you*
> *up for Christmas Eve services?*

Christmas Eve services? A yearly
family ritual. But I can't leave.
Not now. "Uh, sorry, Mom. I have to

take care of the girls." A lie. A big
fat lie, and on Christmas Eve! "Oh,
did I tell you I'm their nanny now?"

> Hugely pregnant pause. *No, I*
> *guess you forgot to mention that.*
> *Well, what about tomorrow?*

Tomorrow? Christmas. Presents
and dinner with the family. And Hunter.
[He's too little to care this year, anyway.]

I have to make a decision. Family.
Or Trey. Spending Christmas making
love with Trey. Easy decision.

> Mom's still waiting to hear it.
> *Kristina? Do you need a ride?*
> *I can pick you up in the morning.*

Okay, I can't tell her I'm playing
nanny tomorrow. What kind of excuse
would placate her? Hard answer: none.

"No, no. Don't pick me up. I'll try
to get a ride from a friend. What
time are you planning dinner?"

> *The same time it's been your*
> *entire life. You do remember*
> *what time that is, don't you?*

# Snippy?

No doubt, and she
has every right to snip.
Only problem is, right now
I'm unsnippable, shielded by glass-

plated armor. Another choice: Try
to find peace in the twilight zone,
or climb into the monster's
rocket and lift off.

Plenty of time
to get buzzed anon. I'll
try to slide into some manner
of sleep, to make up for what I'll

miss later. "I love you," I murmur,
knowing Trey's not here, but
feeling him next to me
anyway. Next to . . .

Voices. Where
are the voices? I want
to find them. Need to find them,
can't say why. But it's dark here.

I run, searching, until some foreign
vine wraps itself around my
ankles, stopping my feet
cold, strapping

my body in
place while the rest
of me flies. Insane! It's so
easy to fly, and I rise over ever-

green spires, granite cathedrals,
slip into the troposphere,
surf vertical winds,
still seeking . . .

# oices

Voices, again. The same,
but not. Little voices.
Girls. Little girls.

Can't find them now. I'm

                                        flying.

Male voices, bigger.
One voice. Two.
Two men.

Not now. I'm

                                        flying toward

Andromeda. Cassiopeia.
Pisces. Orion.
But the voices pull me back.

The interior me—the one
that flies—slips back inside
its shell, a turtle returning

                                        home.

Home. That word again.
The one that makes me
want to release tethers,

            fly away.

Don't fly.
Must find the voices

            instead.

Girls. Devon. LaTreya.
Men. Brad.
Trey.

Trey? I'm

            flying again,

but not away.
Flying from bed.

            Flying from dreams

into awake, aware.
Flying from dreams

            toward love in the flesh.

# Halfway to the Door

I realize I must look like crap.
[Not to mention how you must taste.]
Quick detour to the bathroom,

and I do mean quick, to brush

teeth and hair, dab some perfume.
Screw the makeup, except to rinse
off what has puddled under my eyes.

Through the door, down the hall,
down the stairs and yes, while I flew,
Santa delivered my gift safe

and sound. He stands, moves toward
me, catches me in his arms, cinches
them around my waist, lifts me off
the ground. And now we're kissing.

And I don't ever want to stop kissing
him, even though the girls are squealing.
*Ooooo! Cooties! Gross! Oooooo!*

And we can't help but laugh around

our kiss. And suddenly everything
is right. Everything forgiven. Every
minute apart and alone, forgotten.

# We Spend Christmas Eve

Like a normal family—eating
and drinking and laughing together

like we're a mom, dad, and uncle, plus a couple
of kids, instead of a father with two children

missing their mom and trying not
to resent their "nanny," who has stolen

their uncle's affection. Not that Trey
doesn't play with them. He gets down

on the floor, helps them build a puzzle.
I watch, thinking what a great dad

he'll make one day. I wonder if he could
ever become Hunter's dad. [Stop it. Wishful

thinking will get you exactly nowhere.]
Brad builds a fire and lights the Christmas

tree, and if I were six again, I'd be chirping
"We Wish You a Merry Christmas" right along

with Devon and LaTreya. Finally, Brad
tells the girls they have to go to bed.

*Santa won't come if you're awake, you
know,* he says. *Come on. I'll tuck you in.*

The girls run ahead, and he turns to Trey
and me. *Hang on. I'll break out the new stuff.*

When he leaves the room, Trey pulls me into
his lap. *God I've missed you. I can't wait*

*to give you your present.* He kisses me, hotter
this time, and beneath me, through his denim

and mine, I can feel the promise
of his Christmas gift soon to come.

# 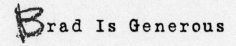rad Is Generous

With his personal stash.
[He can afford to be. Have
you ever seen so much uncut
meth in one place at one time?]

Once we're sure the girls
are asleep, we help him play
Santa, filling the empty
space beneath the tree.

> Gifts spill across the floor.
> *I wanted to make it up to*
> *them for their mother not*
> *being here,* he explains.

> We share yet another
> bowl, then Trey says,
> *It's after one. We should*
> *probably call it a night.*

He pulls me to my feet,
and as we start upstairs,
I turn to say good night.
Brad's looking at us

in an odd way. He smiles
and waves, but not before
I can interpret the look
on his face—envy.

We tiptoe upstairs, past
the pink bedroom where two
little girls dream of eight
tiny reindeer. My first Christmas

away from home. My first
Christmas in my new home.
My first Christmas with Trey,
and I pray it isn't my last.

# Especially as He Gently Peels

My clothes from my body, picks
me up, carries me naked to the bed,
like we're on our honeymoon.

As he takes off his own clothes,
I tell him, "I think your cousin
is just a wee bit jealous."

       *Can't blame him a bit.*
       *If the situation was reversed,*
       *I'd be jealous too. Jealous*

       *that he could do this. . . .*

[Can you believe he can do that?]

       *And this. . . .*

[OMG. No one can do that!]
But Trey can. And he does.
And I learn something new.
Something dark. Perverse,
even. But the monster [and me!]
embrace it, beg him for more.

*Oh, you like that, do*
*you, you nasty little girl?*
*If Brad were here, doing this*
*to you, I might have to kill him.*
*Either that, or ask him to share.*

I wonder if they've ever
done that—shared a girl.
For about half a second
I consider asking.

Better not. Odds are good
I won't like the answer.

# Before It's Possibly Possible

The eastern window silvers,
       the earliest hints of sun crisp
upon an awesome white landscape.

A white Christmas, something
       all northern Nevadans hold
their collective breath over.

It's the same question every
       year—will we or won't we
celebrate a white Christmas?

This year we will, and despite
       the fact that it's just beyond
dawn, the celebration downstairs

has already begun. Devon:
       *Santa was here! Santa was*
*here! He ate up all the cookies.*

LaTreya, more pragmatic:
        *Holy cow. Look at the presents!*
*How can we ever open them all?*

Trey pulls me into his arms
        for one last kiss. *Santa was here.*
*Guess we'd better get up.*

We made love, off and on, most
        of the night, but he has not said
the words I've waited to hear.

Should I say them now? I'm
        almost afraid to, like if I do it will
make him vanish into thin air.

# I Have To

Have to tell him
how I feel, how
much I miss him
when he's not
here. So I snug
my face against
the pulse in his
neck. "I love you."
I wait, barely
able to breathe.

He tightens
his arms around
me. *I know, and
I know how lucky
that makes me.
Come on. Let's
take a shower.*
He rolls out of
bed, heads for
the bathroom.

I watch him go,
wondering just
what the fuck
that meant to me.

# My First Reaction

Is anger. I want to jump up, run
into the bathroom behind him, demand
a reciprocal declaration. [Don't be stupid.
Demands are the best way to lose someone.]

      Now hurt gulps at me. Even
      if he doesn't love me, after all
      we just shared, the least he could
      do is lie. [You'd rather hear lies?]

           If he doesn't love me, I'm mortified
           for giving myself in the ways I just
           did. Those things can only be justified
           by loving someone heart and soul.

[Men are clods. Maybe he thinks
what he said qualifies as "I love you."]
What did he say? That he's lucky because
I love him. Nope, not the same thing at all.

Now I'm pissed again. I stomp into the
bathroom, clear a spot on the steamed-
up mirror, stare at the girl staring back
at me, eyes harboring confusion.

Trey throws back the shower curtain.
*Are you getting in here or what?*
He moves to the back, helps me climb
in past his soapy body. Hot, soothing

water falls all around me, and the herbal
scent of shampoo fills my nostrils. Trey
snakes my body with slick, lathered arms.
*Merry Christmas, Kristina. I love you, too.*

# 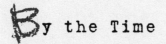y the Time

We reach the living room, ribbons and wrapping

      paper litter every square inch of floor, red and green

and gold. *Lookie, Trey,* shouts Devon. *Look at the million*

      *presents Santa Claus brung. There's even some for you.*

Trey grins, reaches down and scoops her up.

      *Santa brought a present for me? Where? Show me!*

We spend the next hour opening packages and watching

      the girls play with their "million" new toys. My own

contributions to the pile are a Barbie for Devon and

      a unicorn for LaTreya, who insists dolls are dumb.

For Brad, I made a pretty card. Inside is a "gift

      certificate" worth *One Family Portrait by Kristina.*

He smiles and offers a thank-you kiss, and it's more

       than just a friendly kiss. Trey can't help but notice.

*Hang on there, cuz. Don't be kissing my girl like that.*

       Despite all the kissing Trey and I did last night,

I have to admit some part of me really enjoyed Brad's

       kiss. Maybe I'm turning into a pervert. [Join the club!]

Now Brad hands me a present, small and cheerful

       in its shiny purple foil wrapper. Inside is a music box,

handcrafted of cherrywood, intricately inlaid with gold

       leaf hearts. It plays "Für Elise," my favorite Beethoven.

My eyes lock with his, and what I find glittering

       there makes me slightly uncomfortable. "Thank you.

It's beautiful. How did you know I love this song?"

Brad shrugs. *It reminded me of you.* He unhooks his eyes

from mine, and his looking away draws a tinge of regret.

Trey clears his throat. *Don't you want my present?*

"You mean there's more?" I smile. "Of course I do."

He hands me a plain brown sack. *Sorry. Didn't have time

to wrap it.* Inside is a pipe—blown glass, milky blue swirls.

Luckily, the girls are distracted by toys. I drop the pipe

back in the bag. "Maybe we should break this in?"

Trey looks at Brad. *What time are we supposed to be at

your mom's for dinner? I probably shouldn't smoke first.*

I glance back and forth between Trey and Brad. "You're going somewhere for dinner?" [Well, duh. Isn't that what families do?]

Brad nods. *Uh-huh. My mom always does Christmas dinner for*

*the entire family. We're supposed to get there around one.*

I look at Trey, waiting for an invitation to join them. But he

just says, *I hope she made pecan pie. I love that shit.*

# Keep Waiting

But it's almost noon, and still
no invitation. We go upstairs
so Trey can put on a button-up
shirt. Finally, I get brave enough
to ask, "So, can I come along?"

> He looks at me like I'm insane.
> *No way. Sorry, Kristina, but*
> *that isn't a good idea.*

"I don't get it. You say you
love me, but you won't take
me to Christmas dinner? Are
you ashamed of me, or what?"
Ashamed of his tweaker girlfriend?

> *You don't know our family.*
> *The only way I could bring a girl*
> *is if we were getting married.*

We're not getting married.
But I still don't get it.
"You'd be wel . . ." Okay, he
wouldn't be welcome at my
home. But that's different.

*See?* He comes over, puts
his arms around me. *We
won't be gone that long.*

I push him away. "Don't
you understand? I gave
up spending Christmas
with my own family so
I could be with you."

Uncertainty flashes in his
eyes, but only for a second.
*I never asked you to.*

# Twelve Thirty-Five

And he leaves me
alone in my room,

simmering,

one click of the burner away from
a hard boil, in a big red pot of

anger.

Okay, true he never asked
me to snub my own family,

never

promised to spend this day
with me. Never

expected

I might choose time with
him over time with them, but

to be

honest, I never would have
believed I could be

rejected

in such a way by someone
who's supposed to love me.

So what

does that say about the way
I rejected those who love me?

Do I

call Mom, tell her I'm sorry,
I couldn't find a ride?

Do

I ask her to come get me, please
come and get me right

now,

two hours until the big feast?
She would. But she'd also be

angry,

and I really don't want to spend
Christmas day arguing. I'm

mad

at Trey and, for some stupid
reason, at Brad, too. I'm

mad

at Mom for not being more
insistent. Mostly, I'm

mad

at myself for being such an idiot.
I guess I deserve to be lonely.

# I Do Call Home

Find myself glad when Jake
answers the phone. "It's me.
Merry Christmas. How's it going?"

*Great! I got a new computer.
Hey, Mom, it's Kristina.*

No, no, I don't want to talk
to Mom. But it's Leigh
who comes to the phone.

*Where are you? Dinner's
starting to smell really good.*

Just hearing her voice comforts
me. [You can still change your
mind.] "Uh . . . I'm not coming. . . ."

*What? But you have to. Do
I have to come get you myself?*

[Just say yes.] "No. It's just, uh . . .
I'm not feeling well. I've been
throwing up all morning."

*Extremely long pause. Throwing
up? Kristina, you're not . . .*

Pregnant? No. Can't be. Can I?
[You're not really throwing up.]
"No, not that. Food poisoning."

Concern turns to concern. *Do you need to go to the hospital?*

"No, I'll be fine. I'm just weak
and wouldn't be good company.
Tell Mom I'm sorry about dinner."

*Heather and I will be here until
Thursday. I hope we can see you.*

"I hope so too. I've got presents
for you. I'll call tomorrow,
okay? Tell everyone I love them."

*We love you, too. Christmas
isn't the same without you.*

I hang up the phone and halfway through my miserable weep
session I realize that once again

I never even asked about Hunter.
Do I miss him at all? Does he miss
me? Does he even remember me?

440

# What Is Wrong with Me?

Surely I don't really want
to spend Christmas alone.
So why didn't I let Leigh
come and get me? Why?

Instead I chose to sit here,
stressing over Trey and his
family. Stressing over why
I don't qualify to share their

table. Is it really any girl
that wouldn't make the cut?
Or is it just me? Exactly what
is wrong with me? What?

Well, I'm not entirely alone.
I can share what's left of
this day with my Christmas
presents. I wind the music

box, open the lid. The sweet
melody offers familiarity,
and there's solace in that.
But there's more solace in

the pipe and what goes inside
it. Getting tweaked alone is
not what I'd have chosen.
But it's better than being

alone and not getting tweaked.
How long until they get back?
How long will I sit here, staring
out the window, listening to

my favorite Beethoven, all by
myself? How long will I hit
my new milky blue pipe, all
alone? How much can I do?

# Turns Out

More
than I thought.
possible. Turns out

         more

than I wanted to.
Turns out I've
gone through a lot

         more

of that quarter
ounce than I
realized. It's

         almost

gone and so is
my car and most
of my money,

         gone

just like Christmas,
spent mostly alone,
like a downtown wino,

         nothing

much to live for, no
better place to go,
too many hours
                              left

before tomorrow
arrives, bringing with
it, . . . what?

                    Nothing.

# When They Finally

Come through the door,
          one little girl fast asleep on
the shoulder of each guy,
          I am very high. And also
a little bit out of my mind.

With the kids in bed, the guys
          want to party. I've partied
solo for hours. Can I party
          more, just because I have
company? [No-brainer. Ha!]

Smoking ice is the weirdest
          thing. I mean, one minute
you're totally pissed at the world
          (not to mention the people
who populate the place).

The next, all is forgiven,
              everything right, and you
can't really remember why
              you were so mad in the first
place. It's irritating because one

of life's true joys is being
              righteously angry about
something. But load the pipe
              and the "righteous" part
vanishes in a puff of smoke.

# moke

There's been a lot of that,
in and out of my lungs,
in and out of my room,
in and out of my life, for
the past two-point-five weeks.

It's Friday, the eleventh
of January. Trey and I have
been together the entire

time, a long, spectacular
semester break, almost over.

My car is out of impound,
thanks to a generous loan
from Brad. I asked Mom,

but she was still pissed
about Christmas and told
me to come up with the two
hundred sixty bucks on my

own. I tried Leigh, too, but
she's tapped out from her
trip. Airfare isn't cheap.

Brad's tow buddy brought
the LTD home. It's in the garage,
in need of a new radiator.
The nose-down gig sent the fan
smack through the old one.

That will have to wait until
I come up with a few hundred
dollars. The car can use a little

bodywork, too, but not much.
Those classic Fords are tough.

And anyway, Old Man Winter
has seriously arrived. More than
five feet of snow have fallen.

Not enough plows to go around,
even the streets are piled high.
No way could I maneuver icy
avenues. Trey's Mustang isn't

exactly a snow-country car either.
He finally broke down and bought
tire chains so we could go somewhere.

Mostly we've stayed inside,
watching Pay Per View, pulling
domestic duty, playing with the girls—
and each other. *Just like an old
married couple,* Brad observed.

Trey begged to differ. *Except
we're not old, and I don't think
too many married couples stay*

*up half the night, smoking glass
and playing kinky games.*

That piqued Brad's interest.
*Oh, do tell me more. I'm living
vicariously through the two*

*of you, I hope you know.
Please feed my imagination.*
Trey looked at me, and Kristina
flinched but Bree knew just what

449

to say. "Maybe someday we'll let
you watch. Until then, your
imagination will have to go hungry."

Damn, she is brave! I still can't
believe she and Kristina share
a brain—or a mouth. And now
that Trey has to leave, I hope she
can show me how to stay strong.

# Highlights of the Last
## Two Weeks

One:
Sledding with the girls on a long, wide
track down a
nearby hill. Towing them up, pushing
them off, watching
them laugh—really laugh—for
the first time,
according to Brad, since their
mommy went away.

Bonus:
Hauling out-of-control
down that hill, safe in Trey's arms.

Two:
New Year's Eve with Trey and Brad,
after having made
ourselves eat and sleep for a couple
of days. Feeling
hopeful, like the resolutions I made
(less meth, more
family, and all the Trey I can get)
are within reach.

Bonus:
Staying up after
midnight without feeling sleepy.


Three:
Introducing Trey to Leigh and Heather.
Okay, Heather
didn't really much matter, but it meant
everything for Leigh
to have met the guy I'm in love with.
I'm glad she agreed
to hook up with us, even though
Mom was livid.


Bonus:
She brought Hunter
along. And yes, he remembered me.

# Every High

Has an equal, measurable low:
One:
Baking cookies with the girls. Slice-
and-bake dough,
a brand-new oven, and spotless
Teflon cookie sheets,
and no matter how hard I tried,
how diligently
I watched them, I burned every
single batch.

Bonus:
LaTreya's observation:
*Mommy never burned the cookies.*

Two:
My first real argument with Trey,
after a three-day
bender, both of us booming toward
a major crash.
He had the nerve to mention this
girl in Stockton
who has a thing for him, and tell
me she's cute.

Bonus:
This fabulous information:
*If I wasn't with you, I'd be with her.*

Three:
That schizoid, blank-brain state
that accompanies
every total crash. Forcing yourself
into that state
because you know you have to
crash or die.
Sweating. Shaking. Running
to the bathroom.

Bonus:
Remembering Leigh's words:
*Throwing up? Kristina, you're not . . .*

# I Haven't Mentioned the Possibility

To Trey, because I don't really believe
it's possible. I mean, I haven't even
had a period yet, not since giving birth.
Think, Kristina, back to eighth-grade sex ed.

How long after having a baby until you're
fertile? Doesn't breast-feeding delay that?
[Yeah, like you breast-fed so long!]
Maybe it is possible. But not probable.

I guess I should go on the pill. But those
ob-gyn visits . . . I haven't even gone in
for my postpartum checkup, and I wasn't
supposed to have sex again until after

some icky doctor with plastered-on
concern put his gooey latex gloves
in unmentionable places; pushed
here, poked there, manipulated

internal organs, assessing any damage;
and finally, like the act could be a gift,
checking mammary glands for signs
of blockage. [Whose gift—his or mine?]

Nope, I didn't exactly hurry in for that.
Too late now. [Hopefully not too, too late.]
Shut up. I can't be pregnant because I won't
be pregnant. There, I've made up my mind.

# But Lying Here

Next to Trey, who has somehow
managed to attain sleep on our
last night together, possibility
piles on possibility.

Possibly,

I'm pregnant.

Possibly,

I've damaged the baby.

Possibly,

I will choose to abort.

Possibly,

Trey won't support me,
won't even come back to me.

Possibly,

he'll settle down with the pretty
girl in Stockton.

Possibly,

he'll settle down with some
other pretty girl in Stockton.

Probably,

        he'll break my heart because

definitely,

        I am totally in love with him.

        I listen to the shallow in-and-out
        of his breathing, reach
        for the warmth of him,
        draw it into the bitter cold
        well in the pit of my stomach.

        I will not sleep tonight.

I will cry.

# In the White Shadow of Morning

He reaches for
    me. Rains down
        on me, showers
            me with ecstasy.
My tears fall
    upon the pillow,
        fall upon his skin.
            It drinks them in.
*Don't cry,* he
    soothes. *You know*
        *I love you, will*
            *never hurt you.*
But hurt pounds
    against me now,
        a hammer of pain
            beating my heart.
I crawl into his
    arms, lay my head
        against his shoulder,
            a fearful child.
"I know you have
    to go. But I don't
        know how to let
            you. So just go."

# The Door Closes

behind him.
I pretend he's
just gone to
the kitchen.
I worried all
last night. I'm
all worried out.
All smoked out.
All talked out.

Sleep hovers,
just there, and
I reach for it so
I won't hear the
girls' good-byes,
the Mustang's rev,
the *tink-tink* of its
chains against
the pavement.

Chains against
the icy pavement.
Chains against
the snow. It's
snowing, I think.
Snowing in my
brain. I close my
eyes, give myself
up to the blizzard.

# A Kiss Falls Softly

On my forehead, coaxes
me awake. A kiss? Trey?
Did Trey come back already?
How long have I slept?

    *Wake up, Kristina. No, not*
    *Trey. I open my eyes.*
    Brad smiles. *I was starting*
    *to worry. You've been asleep*

    *since yesterday. Trey called*
    *to let you know he made*
    *it back okay. I asked if I should*
    *wake you, but he said no.*

The blizzard has cleared,
but I'm still pretty fuzzy.
The light is soft, secretive.
"What time is it, anyway?"

    *After three. You've been*
    *out for almost thirty hours.*
    *Even the girls were starting*
    *to ask where you were.*

*I'm making a pot roast*
*for dinner. You could probably*
*use some food too. Do you*
*think you can eat?*

"I'm starving!" I look into
his eyes, find a stew of concern
and humor, which I tap into. "In
fact, I could probably eat you."

He laughs. *I'll keep that*
*in mind. Maybe for dessert?*
*Anyway, we're watching*
Harry Potter. *Come on down*

*and join us, if you want.*
*Meanwhile, I'll let the girls*
*know you haven't left like*
*their mother, after all.*

# I Still Haven't Left

Five weeks since Trey went
back to school, and life as a nanny
has become the status quo.

It isn't really hard most
of the time. LaTreya leaves
for school at eight A.M.

Devon is in P.M. kindergarten.
She catches the bus at eleven.
The two ride home together.

So I have several hours each day
to myself. Funny thing is, except
for the easy supply of meth,

life isn't much different here
than it was at home. I still get up,
have breakfast [or not], study

for my GED, which I plan to take
next month. Only now I care for
for a stranger's children instead

of my own baby. Okay, that's not
fair. Brad hardly qualifies as
a stranger. He's become a real

friend, not to mention an ear for
my semi-demented ramblings,
mostly about Trey, who still

hasn't learned to call. When he
first left, it was easy to believe
he was just too busy with settling

into the new semester. But now
I'm starting to think he has settled
into his pretty new girlfriend.

> *Don't worry* is Brad's learned
> council. *Trey has never been*
> *a master communicator.*

But the fact is, I'm lonely, way
out here in Red Rock, still no
transportation, and no company

during the day but a couple of kids.
They've warmed up to me some,
but I will never be Mommy.

Trey manages to touch base
maybe once or twice a week.
Not enough. Not enough.

And there's not enough crystal
between here and Mexico to combat
my growing sense of isolation.

lone

Everything changes.
You might call it
distorted

reality

and as much as I once
might have disagreed,
now the silence

closes in,

like in those B
scary movies where
a crypt forms around you,

walls you in,

brick by invisible
brick, regret the mortar
sealing the chinks,

until

there's only a tiny hole
left, one pinhole
between you and

suffocation.

# 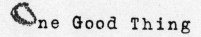ne Good Thing

I finally started my period,
        the bad part of that being that it
was a doozy. I bled like a butchered

pig for over a week. Don't
        know if that means I miscarried
or my body just jumped back

in, balls out. Either way, I'm not
        pregnant. And that is a very good
thing, especially now that it's over.

I'm marking the date on my
        calendar so I have some idea
when to start being careful.

Oops. Don't have to be careful.
        Trey won't be home until spring
break, and that's still weeks away.

[Remember that ob-gyn thing?]
        Yeah, yeah. I'll get around to it,
maybe even before spring break.

Jeez, maybe I can't get pregnant.
        Maybe having a baby at seventeen
screwed up my uterus, confused

my hormones. [Wishful thinker,
        aren't you?] Anyway, I'm safe
for now. A couple fewer possibilities.

# Brad Is a Little
## Late Tonight

*Stopped to see my Mexican amigo,*
*he explains. Es muy bueno!*

The new batch is really good.
Why is it I don't doubt that?

As we eat dinner, my stomach
churns in anticipation. I can't

afford to buy much, but I hope—
no, I know—he'll be generous.

*Homework, baths, then bed!*
*Spoken like a true dad.*

We help the girls with their
assignments, hustle them off

to the tub and sweet dreams.
I even read them a bedtime story.

*Once they've dozed off, Brad*
*knocks on my door. In the mood?*

I know he means for a couple
of tokes, but something else

creeps into my warped brain.
"I'm always in the mood."

He smiles, and shows off his new
stash, as good as or better than the last.

I've been thinking things
through for a while. After

several very smooth hits,
I say, "You know I'm tight

on cash. I was hoping maybe
I could off a little for you, in

exchange for some personal."
His response is long, slow.

*Do you know people who you*
*can trust? I mean, you've been*

*out of the loop for a while now,*
*and I have to be very careful.*

He is very careful, has to be because
of his kids, and I understand that.

"Yeah, I know a couple of guys
who'd go ballistic if they saw

meth of this quality. Don't worry.
I'd keep you my bestest secret."

> He grins. *I trust you, Kristina.*
> *I just want you to be careful too.*
>
> *You're the best nanny in Reno.*
> *I can't imagine being without you.*

We share a couple more bowls,
then he stands, kisses me on the cheek.

> *Better go. My mind is going places*
> *it shouldn't. See you in the morning.*

The door snaps shut behind him.
My mind is going places

it shouldn't too. I call Trey,
before my body follows.

# The Downside

About counting on someone else
        to help you do the right thing
        is they're not always available.
In Trey's case, that's often.

The downside of smoking ice
        is when you can't get hold of
        someone, sometimes you get mad.
In my case, that's tonight.

        As usual, I get Trey's message center.
Tonight, I need to hear his voice,
live in my ear. Where are you, damn
        it all? Can't you just once pick up?

        Buzzed, antsy, I try TV for company.
But late-night tripe won't backfill
the gaping hole inside me. The longer
        I sit here, the more cavernous it grows.

I go into the bathroom, turn on the
        shower, hot enough to redden my
        skin, scrub away the building desire
in a release of sandalwood steam.

No such luck. All it does is remind
            me of sharing this small, encapsulated
            place with the person I love, the one who's
supposed to love me, but doesn't call.

            I brush my teeth with the same energy
I used on my body, notice a streak of blood
in the spit that spirals down the drain.
            No worries. That's normal, right?

            Cleansed, scented, hair wet and cool
down the length of my spine, I feel like
a goddess, jailed in her Olympus. Little
            wonder, how the gods toyed with humans.

Toyed with women, to watch
            them squirm, pollinate the seeds
            of despair; toyed with men, to
satiate their Seven Deadly Sins.

I know it's not right, that I have
            no right at all to do what I'm about
            to do. Maybe he'll say no, send me
back here to swim in emptiness.

# Wearing Nothing

But a thigh-length button-up shirt,
barely buttoned, I creep down the hall.
Stop outside the girls' door, poke
my head inside. Lights out. Totally.

One step at a time, silent as night,
I keep going until I reach Brad's room.
One ear to the door. Not a sound.
I knock softly and he says, *Come in.*

He's lying in bed, alone in the dark,
only moonlight to let me know.
I hesitate, but Bree gives me a shove.
[Go on. It's only between the two of us.]

Brad draws back the quilt and I slither
beneath it, into his arms. *I was hoping
you'd come.* Now he's kissing me, and
it's nothing like how Trey kisses at all.

But it's good. Great. And his strength
becomes mine. But before we do
more, I have to tell him, "I know
this isn't right, but I need you."

And he says, *We need each other.*
*How can that be wrong? I still love*
*Angela, and I know you love Trey.*
*Can't you and I love each other too?*

I haven't thought past loving Trey,
never considered loving someone else,
especially not at the same time.
Can I love more than one person?

Would that make me love Trey less?
I have no answers now, need no
answers now. Except one.
"Are you saying you love me?"

# He Doesn't Answer

Not with words, as if
vocalizing his response
would give it too much
weight. His silent reply
is heavy enough.

Silent, but for the *shush*
of skin against skin;
the sigh of heightened
senses; the exclamation
of bodies, no longer
strangers.

# The Problem with Sex

Is that it changes everything.
Brad and I are still friends.
But we're a different kind
of friends. More than pals.
More, even, than fuck buddies.
It's like we're stand-ins
for the true loves of our lives.
And the only way to be that
is to let ourselves love
each other.

When you love someone,
you don't want to hurt
them, even if they deserve
to be hurt. When you love
someone, you want to hurt
them, even when they don't
deserve to be hurt. It's totally
messed up, and so are Brad
and I. Totally messed up
because of—and over—
each other.

We don't talk about the future.
Don't talk about what will
happen when Trey comes
back, or if Angela decides
her husband and children
mean something to her,
after all. We're taking things
one day at a time. One night
at a time.

# The Problem with Meth

Is similar. It changes
everything. The monster
and I are still friends.
But we're a different
kind of friends. More
than pals, fuck buddies.

Six months since we met up
again, we are inseparable,
an intricate weave.
No longer do I believe
this is a temporary fling.
More like total commitment.
More like I have walked
down the aisle, holding
hands with the monster.

I don't think about the future,
or what life would be like
without crystal. It's almost
always here, within easy
reach. I don't think about
what it might be doing to
my brain, or my heart.

I know people die from doing
too much. But I'm in control.
Okay, mostly in control.

I am thin. But that's how
guys want girls to be, right?
I do grind my teeth, and
every now and then I lose
a chip from one. But those
can be fixed, right? Probably
the worst thing is how I'm
kind of edgy. Sometimes
I lose it completely. Once
in a while, I even scream
at the girls. But kids can
be obnoxious and a nanny
should keep them in line.

Right?

# Relax

It's not like I hit them. I can stop myself

before things get that out of hand. The most

physical I've gotten is giving Devon a good shake.

She deserved it. I mean, she was crying—

freaking out—because I said no to ice cream

after she got home from school. Ice cream?

I told her to go watch TV while LaTreya did

her homework. Devon screamed, *Mommy*

*would give me ice cream* and then she just

stood there, yowling like a dying cat. Nerves

frayed, I stomped across the kitchen,

grabbed her cheeks in one hand, squeezed.

484

"Shut the hell up." But would she? No!

She looked me right in the eye. *I'm gonna*

*tell my daddy.* Definitely not the right

thing to say. I took her by the shoulders,

shook until her head snapped back and forth.

"I wouldn't do that if I were you." Her eyes

went wide and snot flew everywhere. But

she finally shut up and went to watch TV.

Okay, it wasn't nice. Blame it on the monster.

# Part of My Snappish
## Behavior

Is being stuck here, no way to go
anywhere unless I walk, or wait

until Brad can take me. It's like
being stuck in childhood again.

Fixing the LTD will make life
easier, and everyone happier.

I called around, and Pick 'n' Pull
has a used radiator and fan I can afford.

I just have to find a way to get them,
then talk someone into installing

them for me. I happen to know someone
who's tool-friendly, and Brad is cooperative.

*I'll pick them up on my way home.*
*It will give me something to do*

*this weekend. Oh, I'm getting a new*
*shipment, so if you still think you*

*know someone you can off some to,*
*you might want to give them a call.*

My car is getting fixed, and so
is my dwindled stash. Life is good.

# I Know Exactly Two People

In Reno who would be interested
in scoring some killer ice. Well,
I might know more, but two for sure.
Both, however, are problematic.

I'll have to get hold of Grade E
at the Sev. And I can't do that until
after eleven. And if he wants some,
I'm not sure how to arrange a meet.

The second person is one I hate
with every ounce of my being. One
I swore never to talk to again. Can
I get past all that to make a deal?

[Why not get back at him the only
way you can—make a bundle
off his greed.] It's a delicate dance,
but using him has a certain appeal.

Despite whatever brain cells
the monster has eaten, I remember
his number. Dial it? Don't? God,
I hate indecision. Kick me, Bree!

[If you don't deal with him, Grady
will. Why not be your own middle-
man?] All it takes is a glance in my
lockbox. Empty, but for a few bucks.

Fine. I'll call. But he'd better not
get the wrong idea. The phone rings
and rings, and I'm starting to think
that's the way it should be, when

he finally answers. The sound
of his voice sends chills through
my body. And not good chills.
*Your dime. Start talking.*

And I'm trying to, really I am,
but my own voice sticks in my
throat like a big wad of taffy.
At last I manage, "Hello, Brendan?"

# I've Tried to Get Over

What happened that night.
    Tried to blame the meth.
        The booze. The situation.
            I even tried to forgive him
                because Hunter is an angel.
But I can't forgive him.
    Can't forgive that he forced
        himself on me, inside me.
            If he'd only been patient,
                I probably would have
said yes. Okay. Let's.
    But I was scared, and
        he knew it, and my
            being afraid pushed
                some kind of on button.

And it seems to me
        if that happened once,
                it will likely happen
                        again. I should have
                                called the cops. Turned
him in, seen to it he'd
        never get the chance
                to flip that on button
                        again. And if it wasn't
                                for the monster, I would
have. So who is really
        to blame? Brendan?
                The monster? Or me?
                        Hey, guess what. It
                                doesn't matter, anyway.

# We Set Up a Tentative Meet

For tomorrow evening. Barring
complications, my car should
be running by then. I guess
I should be a little scared,
but I'm not. It's not like he can
rip off my virginity twice.

Later I'll call Grady, who'd
jump in front of a moving
train to score glass like this.
Hmm. Maybe I should have
arranged to meet Brendan
down by the railroad trench.

Next time. Meanwhile, looks
like I've gone into business
for myself. Entrepreneurship,
the American Way. Although
I doubt Warren Buffett ever had
anything like this in mind.

It's simple. [If not exactly legal,
but then neither is that insider
trading shit.] It doesn't take a
college degree. [Or even a GED.]
And it's lucrative. [Only if you're
not dipping into the profit margin.]

Therein lies a major problem
for me. Wonder, if I quit using
and kept the profit, if I could
actually make some money, save
it up, even. Wonder if I could
quit. [Don't make me laugh.]

# Have You Ever Tried

To quit

        a bad habit, one
        that has come to
        define you?

To cease

        using a substance—
        any substance—
        that you not only
        need but enjoy?

To stop

        yourself from
        lighting up that
        cigarette? It's going
        to kill you, but hey,

you're going
to die

        someday anyway,
        why not die happy,
        why not die buzzed,

why not die

        satisfied? Why not
        die sooner, with
        fewer regrets, than

later?

# Sooner Than Later, Brad
## Follows Through

He picked up the radiator on
his way home last night, and
        he's already out in the garage
        working. Okay, we were up
all night, so he got an early start.
The new stash is all it should be.

        Good thing Brad is handy with
        tools, and the LTD presents few
                surprises. Bolt this here, screw
                that there, new hoses, new fluid.
        Voila. The car is ready to go by
        noon. He comes into the kitchen,

                all greasy. I smile at the black
                gunk smeared across his forehead
                        and dotted at the end of his nose.
                        "I owe you one. I mean, another
                one." And he just looks so cute
                I can't help but go over and kiss

him. We're lip-locked, temps
rising, when all of a sudden,
             *Hey! What are you doing?*
             *You can't do that with Daddy!*
We jerk apart, and there's
LaTreya, hands on hips.

Okay, this one isn't nanny
material. It's up to the daddy
             in question to assuage her ire.
             But he sputters, helpless, so
I offer, "I'm just thanking him
for fixing my car. Okay, honey?"

             *No! It's not okay. He's my*
             *daddy, and daddies are only*
                     *supposed to kiss mommies.*
                     *You're not my mommy, so you*
             *better not kiss him anymore!*
She storms into the other room.

Brad smiles apologetically.
*Sorry bout that. Jeez, she's*
        *more like her mother than I*
        *imagined. Who knew such*
*a little girl could have such*
*a big temper—or opinions?*

   I've never really asked
   about Angela before. This
        seems like as good a time as
        any. "Tell me about Angela.
   What happened between
   you? Why did she leave?"

He shakes his head. *Not*
*much to say. We got married*
        *and had kids, right out of high*
        *school. One day she said she*
*needed some space. Guess*
*she found some she likes.*

# He Drops It

And so do I, but thinking
about leaving kids behind
has made me want to see
Hunter. I pick up the phone.

"Hey, Mom. My car's on
the road again. I thought I'd
drop by this afternoon. Uh,
maybe around three?"

I'm meeting Grady at five,
Brendan a half hour later.
That should give me plenty of
time to reconnect with my baby.

Brad weighs out an ounce
into eight balls. I'm not exactly
sure how much they'll want,
or how much they can pay.

He is rightly concerned.
*Promise you'll be extra careful.*
*An ounce is trafficking—*
*definitely heavy jail time.*

"Hey, no worries. I'll drive
like an old woman. The last
thing I want is to get popped.
I'm too busy to spend time in jail."

Brad walks me to my car,
looks right and left before
bending down to kiss me.
*Call if you'll be late, okay?*

*I'm going to worry until*
*you get home.* He'd probably
worry a lot more if he knew
just who I'd lined up to score.

# The Roads Are Dry

The car's running great, and I feel no
sense of fear, despite the large quantity

of fine Mexican methamphetamine
beneath the front seat. It's a forty-

minute drive home, at the speed limit,
and I have to admit getting away

from Red Rock, Brad, and the girls feels
like freedom. Guess I'm finding space I like.

On a lark, I hit Trey's number on my speed
dial. I about drop the phone when he actually

answers, and on the second ring. *Hey, you.
Must be ESP. I was just thinking about you.*

My first thought is, He's thinking about
me! [My first thought is, Yeah, right.]

We talk for ten minutes and every doubt
about what he feels for me dissolves.

There are a few uncomfortable moments,
like when he asks, *So, what's up with Brad?*

The Bree in me has a ready smart-ass answer,
which I quickly squelch in favor of telling him

Brad fixed my car. [Oh, he fixed more than
that, didn't he?] But Trey's next query, about

"availability," elicits an "Oh, duh" moment.
When I tell him, "No problem," he says,

*Cool. I'm thinking about a quick trip over
the mountain. You'll be around, won't you?*

Well, where else would I be, especially with
him coming? My heart hammers, blood

pumping wildly until I pull into Mom's driveway
and realize he's coming more for glass than for me.

# That's What's on My Mind

When Scott opens the door.
*Hello, Kristina.* Cool as sleet.
He gives me a noticeable up-
down-and-sideways, and if he's
half as savvy as he thinks he is,
he has to know the score.

Regardless, he steps aside, lets
me in. Jake comes out of the
kitchen, carrying Hunter. How
long since I've seen him? Two
months—just after Christmas—
and he's grown. Changed.

His hair falls in long dark waves,
almost to the bottom of his neck.
His coos and gurgles sound
suspiciously like words: *M-m-m-a.*
When he spots me, he smiles, and
beyond his lips are two little teeth.

I reach for him and he draws
back, seeking safety in Jake's
arms. Anger flares, but only
briefly. After all, thanks to Mom,
he knows Jake better, trusts
Jake more than he trusts me.

*Your mother had to run into Reno,*
says Scott. *Jake, why don't you
put Hunter in his walker?* I
follow them into the family room.
Comfortable in his baby bumper
car, Hunter rises up on his tiptoes.

He scoots across the hardwood,
laughing. Finds the TV, punches
at buttons without success.
He's determined. Determined,
like the person he so resembles,
the one I'll see much too soon.

# 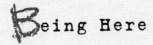eing Here

At home
seems kind
of surreal. Okay,
maybe that's partly
because I'm two-days
buzzed, brain a little fuzzy.
Beyond that, I know the room
upstairs still has purple butterflies,
fluttering on mauve walls. [Are you
sure? Maybe it's an office, with turquoise
angelfish on blue walls.] No, I don't think so.

Being here with Hunter
synthetic state of mother-
being a nanny, because I
no matter how fucked up
really my responsibility.
my responsibility. But
to usurp the mommy role,
lesson. But who's really
[Huh. Really? Well, you

is weird too. Kind of a
hood, not so different from
know no matter what I do,
I am or become, he's not
Okay, morally, Hunter is
Mom took it upon herself
so great. She taught me a
getting hurt here? Not me.
sure could have fooled me.]

# I Leave Without Seeing Mom

And that's fine by me. Nothing
    to say to her, anyway.

            Nothing.

Next stop, Grade E. We set up
    the meet at his house.

            Not far.

He opens the door and his eyes
    practically pop

            clear out

of his skull. *Wow. You look
    great.* See? What

            did I tell you?

Guys like girls thin. "Uh, can
    I come in?" He steps

            out of my way,

ushers me back to his bedroom.
    *Mom won't be home*

            *till later,*

*so we're cool.* We sit on his bed,
    and that makes me

            slightly uncomfortable.

When I open the baggie,
    give him a taste, he

            just about

goes ape shit. *That's what*
      *I'm talking about.*

                    *Where*

*did this come from? Local?*
      He's right where

                  I need him to be.

So I say, "I can get more.
      But it isn't cheap."

                  He makes a buy.

A half ounce. And he says,
      *I'll be calling for more.*

# 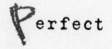erfect

I made a nice little profit,
plan to make a bigger
profit at my next stop.
Brendan and I hook
up around back
at the Sev.

Can't do
the deal here.
*Get in,* he says, but
I insist "No, we'll take
my car." It's bigger. Safer.
And, behind the wheel, I've got

the power. We drive in silence
a mile or so up Virginia Grade.
Despite being gravel,
the road is icy, the
shoulders piled
with snow.

It will be
tough to turn
around, so I keep
driving until I find a place
where I can do that. I want to
be parked in the direction of quick

escape. Just in case. Finally Brendan
says, *I was surprised you called.*
Yeah, me too. "Water
under the bridge," I
answer. What
else can I

say—*I*
*want your cash?*
But it's really hard to
look at him, especially after
just being with my baby. His
baby. Our baby. God, that stings.

# He Wants a Sample

I'm generous with that.
We smoke three bowls,
and as the ice does what
it's supposed to do, his

> eyes take on the glow
> of the monster. Major
> déjà vu. Have I made
> an irreversible mistake?

> *Not bad,* he says. *You*
> *fucking the guy you*
> *got it from?* There's
> the Brendan I know

and hate. The worst
part is, he's right. "No,
he's fucking me. So,
are you in or what?"

> A slip of the tongue,
> and he pounces on it.
> *It might be a little tight,*
> *with the steering wheel*

*and all, but I'm game*
*if you are.* He's a nervy
bastard, I'll give him that.
He smiles a *Yeah, so?*

Stay cool. He brought
money. "Thanks for
the offer, but I've got
someone waiting."

Then he says something
completely unexpected.
*I saw your mom with your*
*baby the other day.*

*I knew it was your mom*
*because she looks like you.*
*I knew it was your baby*
*because he looks . . .*

He can't know. I won't
let him. I'll deny it until
the day I die—or he does.
I hold my breath.

*. . . like you, too.*

# Too Close for Comfort

Time to go before we get any closer.
"So, how much do you want?
Uh, how much *ice* do you want?"

> He smiles. *I'll take a ball,*
> *if you'll front it to me.*

Okay, now I'm just pissed. "Sorry,
cash and carry. Godammit, I
ain't the Bank of America."

> *I'm just a little short and I*
> *don't get paid until Friday.*

"So why did you say you were
interested? It's not like we're friends.
You expect me to trust you?"

> *Why not? We were friends once, weren't*
> *we?* He dares put a hand on my knee.

[Stay calm. He could bust you.] Calmly
I push his hand off my knee. "How
much money do you have on you?"

*Seventy or eighty dollars. Is that*
*enough for a down payment?*

"On a gram. But all I have weighed
out are eight balls, and they're three
fifty." I can't afford stupidity.

He counts the contents of his wallet.
Eighty-six dollars. *The rest on Friday?*

If he actually calls with the money,
I'll have to see him twice in one week.
He'll probably rip me off. So why

do I say okay?

# At Least He Didn't Try

To steal the stuff.

At least he didn't try
to rape me.

[Give him time.]

At least he didn't decide
Hunter was his baby.

[Ditto.]

Sometimes the little things
in life mean the most.

[Double ditto.]

[Everything in your
life is little.]

Would you get the fuck
out of here? I can't double-
think everything.

[Split personalities
are indeed a bitch.]

Am I totally schizo?

[Close. But there's
a bigger question.]

Oh, yeah?
Like what?

[Which half is the real you?]

513

# Wired (Weird) Out of
##   My Tree

I won't eat tonight.
Won't sleep tonight.
Won't want to deal
with inane questions,
prime-time TV, or Barbie.

Luckily, Brad has fed
the girls, bathed the girls,
and they're playing
quietly in their room.

Perfect.

What I'm focused on
now is Trey, and when
[if] he'll arrive. I sit in
my room, waiting.

Smoking.
          Waiting.
Toking.
          Waiting.
                    Waiting.

# Finally, There's a Knock

"Come in," I call softly.
(The girls must be asleep
by now—almost midnight.)

My heart stutters. Crow
hops. Bucks wildly. But
it isn't Trey. [Told you.]

Brad's head pops through
the door. *You've been awfully
quiet. Everything go okay?*

I'm disappointed. But at
least I'm not alone. "Like
clockwork. Come on in."

We do what you do when
you're wasting an evening,
playing with the monster.

Finally, the clock betrays
that it's well after two A.M.
Trey isn't coming after all.

*Guess I should at least*
*pretend to sleep.* Brad stands,
pauses by the door.

Choices. Choices. This
choice is all mine to make.
"Want some company?"

# Long About the Time

The sun shows its face, I am spent,
woozy, not quite asleep. Brad has
managed to slip into dreams and I
listen to his shallow breathing.

It's hypnotic, and I steal lower
and lower toward the nowhere
place between consciousness
and blessed sleep. Somewhere

there's a noise. A door closes.
Footsteps? On the stairs? I can't
move. I'm weighted, shackled.
I should. I must. But I'm close

to oblivion. My door creaks open.
The long, silent pause tells me
it isn't one of the girls. Footsteps
across the floor. I'm afraid.

Rooted. Not even the sound of
fabric falling against the carpeting
convinces me to move. Somehow,
this person is familiar.

Behind me, the sheets part.
*Move over,* Trey whispers, and
I do and it makes no difference
that Brad is semisoundly sleeping

beside us. Trey pulls me to him
and I stiffen, terrified of what he
must be thinking. *It's okay,* he
whispers, and we're making love.

# Two Guys, One Bed

It's really too weird.
[Yeah, but kind of nice.]
What has happened to my

                  morals,

my sense of right, wrong?
[Way overrated.] Shit, I'm
a one-woman Sodom and
Gomorrah, awaiting

                  transformation.

I hope Trey [and/or Brad]
likes salt, 'cause I'll soon
be a regular pillar, in
exchange for this brand of

                  sin.

Trey definitely must like
salt. It's bad enough that I
felt like it was okay to be
jam between slices of

                  bread.

But why doesn't Trey care
about finding me in bed
with Brad? His cousin, yet.
Two separate trusts,

                              broken.

I mean, Brad accepts that
I've got a major thing for
Trey. But will Brad accept
the fact that Trey has climbed

                              into

the bed we shared last night?
Will sharing a bed, sharing
someone they love, blow
their closeness into distant

                              pieces?

# Brad Stirs

I'm not sure I'm ready to test
his reaction, so I push back against
Trey, shove him gently out of bed.

He goes into the bathroom and I
follow, turn on the shower, climb
inside, hoping the noise doesn't

wake Brad, but knowing it will.
At least we won't be a sandwich.
I'm shaky. Scared. Is this the end?

I put my arms around Trey's neck,
lean my head into his chest. "I'm
sorry. I didn't mean . . ."

*It's okay, Kristina. We never*
*made any promises. Anyway,*
*I know Brad's lonely.*

I look up, hook his eyes. "I'm
lonely too. And that's all this is.
I love you. But you aren't here."

I want to ask if he's been with other
girls. [Don't.] Need to ask. [No.]
Have to know. [No, you don't.]

He tells me anyway. *I love you,
too. But I can't tell you I haven't
been with other girls.*

[See? You didn't want to know.]
Anger scalds, hot and white. But
why? And what can I say?

Now I want to know who. [No,
you don't.] Need to know if it's
Robyn. [No, damnit, you don't.]

He tells me anyway. *Not Robyn,
in case you're wondering. Guess she
left school. Her apartment is empty.*

"So who is it, then?" [Not that it's
any of your business.] "That girl
you told me about?"

*She's one. But there have been*
*others. Nothing serious. Sex*
*only. I love you. No one else.*

White heat stings my eyes. Not fair!
[Sure it is.] Shut up! [What comes
around goes around.] Shut up!

My heart does wind sprints. My
brain somersaults. The tub is slippery
and I start to fall. Fall. Fa . . .

# Where Am I?

Everything is dark. Mostly dark.
There's light somewhere,
like at the end of a tunnel.

Am I dead?

Someone is talking. Calling.
Calling my name.
*Kristina? Kristina!*

Trey? Is he dead too?

My head hurts. There's a
thumping. A noisy thrumming
against the lining of my skull.

Can you hurt
when you're dead?

Wait! I don't want to be dead.
Don't want to walk in darkness—
semidarkness—alone.

Death is lonely.

Lonely? Lonely. Why is lonely
familiar? *I know Brad is lonely.*
It's getting lighter. Light.

Maybe I'm not dead.

But I still can't move. Don't
dare move because it hurts.
My head hurts. My back hurts.


Are my eyes open? It's light
but I still can't see. *Kristina?*
*Look at me, Kristina.*

Maybe I do wish I
were dead.


I don't want to look at Trey.
If I do, I'll really wish
I was dead.

# His Face

Materializes, wraithlike.
"What happened? Am I dead?"

*Don't even say that. You
slipped and fell, that's all.*

No wonder my head hurts. I reach
up, touch the gestating lump.

I start to sit up, but my head spins
and I fumble back against the floor.

Trey strokes my cheek, moves
my hair from my eyes. *Stay still.*

Stay? Like a dog? Monstrous
anger grips me, shakes me.

*Are you cold?* He jumps to his
feet, runs into the bedroom.

I use the time to try my legs,
which refuse to cooperate.

Back comes Trey, blanket in hand.
*Please don't move, Kristina.*

I reach down inside, find Bree,
grab her strength. "Leave me alone."

Flip onto my belly. Push to my knees.
I'm shaky. But damnit, I'll stand.

Trey steadies me best as he can.
*You are so fucking stubborn.*

Stubborn. Aching. Straight out
pissed and the worst thing is,

I have zero reason to be. Well,
other than the fact that the monster

coldcocked me and I feel like
a steaming pile of manure.

# Brad Has Vacated the Room

Trey helps me across the

stretch of carpet, to the

tousled bed. A soft

of pillow lures me toward

sleep. As I sink closer to

I breathe Trey in, desperate

I want him beneath my skin,

fast by my bones,

by my body like

"Please don't go." A slow

*I won't.* He is tender,

And I believe him.

endless

empty,

cloud

dreamless

oblivion

inhalation.

held

absorbed

oxygen.

exhalation.

warm.

# But of Course

I wake, knowing this.

He has to go.

"I don't want you to go."

He is sitting by the bed.

I have to think why.
Oh yes, spring break.

*I know. But I'll be back
in a couple of weeks.*

I'm not okay with any
of it. "Why is it okay?"

*I talked to Brad and told
him I'm okay with you two.*

"I can wait three months
for you, if you just tell
me you want me to."

*Because it has to be.
School will be out in less
than three months. . . .*

He takes my hand, kisses
it gently. *Let's play it by
ear, okay? No worries.*

No worries? "How can
I not worry about you?
I love you, remember?"

Now he pulls me from bed,
into his lap, cinches me with
his arms. *Kristina, I love you,
too, really I do . . .*

Okay, there's a major
"but" coming. [Yeah, like,
*But I'm a major player,
and want to play around.*]

*. . . but this is totally new
territory. I've always loved
girls for what they could give
me, not for who they are.*

I understand what he
means, but still don't get
where this is headed. "So,
what are you saying?"

*I'm asking for some time*
*to figure out if I love you*
*for what you're giving me,*
*or for who you are.*

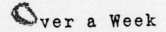

# Over a Week

Since Trey went off
to decide why [you mean if]
he loves me. Messed up!

Brad and I have kept
our thoughts regarding that
night to ourselves, not

easy to do when you're
spun, and we have been spun
on an ongoing basis.

It's maintenance spun
now, not really enjoyable spun.
I can nibble soft foods,

sleep fitfully, brain
begging to shut all the way
down. But I'm scared

to shut all the way
down. Scared I might dream.
Scared I might not

wake back up.

# It's About Noon

On Thursday. I'm fumbling
             around in the kitchen, trying
to figure out what to make

             for dinner. My head is in
the freezer when the phone
             bellows. It takes four rings

to find it, and I'm totally
             surprised at who's on the other
end. *Hi, Kristina? It's Robyn.*

             Okay, she's after something,
and I can guess what. *I don't
             know if you heard, but I left*

*UOP. I'm working out here
             in Moundhouse, and was
hoping you could hook me up.*

             Moundhouse = whorehouse.
There are several in the little
             community, not far from

533

Nevada's capital, Carson
          City. One was even featured
on a prime-time cable show.


          Now, it doesn't necessarily
surprise me that Robyn is
          whoring for the monster, but


I never would have guessed
          she'd sink so low as to whore
for truck drivers and tourists.


          "Well, maybe I can help you
out." Don't want to give it all
          up the first time we talk.


"I'll have to check on it.
          But if it's doable, it will
be on the pricey side."


          *Very cool. Some other girls*
*are interested, too. Can you*
          *and I work out a quantity?*

Just like that, I move from low-
            to midlevel dealer. Good thing
Brad's connect is bottomless.

            *Can you come out to the ranch?*
*I'll tell them you're my sister.*
            *Oh, you have to ask for Aphrodite.*

# If You've Never

Been to a fancy whorehouse
(and believe me, I never have

before!), you might be surprised.
I'm nervous, thinking the Pink

Pussycat will be scary—dark, sweaty,
with lots of peepholes, maybe. But a

better word to describe the place
is gaudy, with plush pink carpeting

and silver and gold brocade covering
the walls. If there are peepholes, they're

hidden behind paintings of busty
naked women, like in an Old West

saloon. Only pinker. Pink. How
appropriate. It's early for truckers.

Only a few haunt the "parlor," perusing
a menu of services and a couple of girls.

Neither men nor girls are what you'd call
attractive. This is no place for romance.

*Hey, sis. Long time no see.* Robyn escorts
me to her room, much like she did several

times in the past, only this time she's dressed
in a purple silk teddy. Her legs are too thin,

her own chest flatter than I remember, and
a thick layer of makeup barely disguises

sores. Monster sores. I chide myself
to slow down before I end up with sores.

Or here.

# Unlike Her Apartment

Robyn's room is neat.
Guess perverts dislike
having paid-for sex
amidst piles of clutter.
Like everything else
here, it's pink and gold
and sparsely furnished.

It smells of old sweat
and cheap perfume.

Robyn locks the door
and we sit on her bed,
just like in the good ol'
days. *I'm pulling grave-*
*yard so we don't have*
*to hurry. Anyway, the*
*manager is a friend.*

*That's how I wound*
*up here, in fact.*

She tells me how she
met the guy, how he
talked her into "easy"
money, working in the
"entertainment industry."
As she talks, I notice
the way her eyes beg.

"You sure it's okay to
do the deal in here?"

Her head bobs. *No
problem. I told them
you have some private
news about our mother
and not to interrupt us.
They probably think she
has cancer or something.*

*Sweet. A little sympathy
goes a long way here.*

I can only imagine. I
produce a quarter ounce
of excellent glass and
immediately Robyn's
hands begin to shake.
She doesn't only want
the meth. She needs it.

"You can try some if you
want. Where can we go?"

In answer, she opens the
window, turns on a fan
that sits on a small table
by the door. *Right here
is the safest place. I'll
get the pipe.* I watch her
inhale, eyes popping

pleasure. *Thank God
it's not street crank.*

She talks about the last
crank she snorted, a tip
from a customer. Oh
yeah, truckers love their
crank. And when they're
all cranked up, they love
other stuff too. The ice

opens her mouth and
she tells me all about it.

*Some of 'em are really*
*gross. I always make*
*them shower first. No*
*way will I let something*
*dirty up inside of me.*
*Condoms? Yeah, they're*
*supposed to wear them.*

*But they pay a lot extra*
*if you don't make them.*

They also pay extra for
oral sex and unusual sex,
including threesomes
with other girls. Robyn
claims she's judicious.
But I know how your
caution can slip, when

you have a threesome
with our pal, the monster.

# I Leave

Feeling slightly better about
        myself and a whole lot better
                about my own client list, which
        has just grown exponentially.
Robyn knows girls at some

of the other ranches too.
        Meth is one way they handle
                what they do. I guess you could
        say it isn't much different from
trading sex for companionship.

Okay, it's a helluva lot damn
        different. I mean, screwing nasty,
                smelly men [without a condom,
        yet] to feed your meth habit [no
worries about feeding your face].

The word "condom" reminds
            me again that I need to get
                        in and get on the pill. I'll
            call tomorrow and make
the appointment. And that

reminds me that Trey should
            head my way next week. No
                        calls to confirm, as yet. Anxiety
            swims up like a giant squid, snakes
tentacles around my throat. Squeezes.

# Easter Sunday

Brad took the girls to

an Easter egg hunt.

I thought about taking

Hunter, but it's cold

and he's just a baby,

anyway. Like he'd

know the Easter bunny

from some giant rodent.

Anyway, it's a long

drive and I think I'll

use my time alone to

crash and experience

the snooze of the dead.

Brad traded speed for

some downers. Guess

I'll have to borrow a

couple. I want to be

good and rested by

the time Trey arrives.

Not that I know exactly

when that might be.

Not that I have a freaking

clue what he might be

up to in the meantime.

I pop an Ambien and
wait, thinking about Trey

and what he might be
doing at this moment. My

head starts to spin, like
riding a Tilt-A-Whirl.

I close my eyes, hang
on tight against loop

the loop in my head.
I'm over the edge. . . .

# It's Gray

I rise
        up out        of the
                        depths        into flat
Where                                          pale light.
        am    I?
                Is it        morning
Why                                  or night?
        are my
                legs        sticky?
Did                              Sticky red.
        I    hurt
                myself    in sleep?
What                              On  purpose?
        is wrong
                    with me?     My brain
There                                is mud.
        goes the  Tilt
                    -A-      Whirl
I'm                            again.
        spinning
                out of     control
Stepping                     again.
        over
                the edge    again.

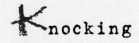

# Knocking

Pounding. Little fists
falling against the wood
of my bedroom door.

*Wake up, sleepyhead!*
*Daddy has to go to work.*
Devon's voice is bright

as the sunshine, painting
streaks on the walls.
I throw back the sheets.

Blood. Lots of it. Great.
My monthly visitor. At
least I don't have to feel

so bad about not calling
the doctor. No need for
the pill today, anyway.

I clean up, strip the sheets
from the bed and take
them down to the washer.

The girls are in the kitchen,
munching cereal. No school
this week, they're all mine.

I put in a call to Trey. No
answer. No surprise. I'm
getting ready to leave a

voice mail when the door-
bell rings. He's here!
LaTreya beats me to the door

and flings it open. *Mommy!*
she screams, throwing her arms
around the slender redhead.

Angela steps through the door,
levels me with a shot of green
eyes. *Who the hell are you?*

# Standing There

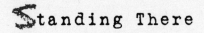

Wearing zip but a long T-shirt
and underwear, I
introduce myself,
"I'm Kristina, the girls' nanny."

         Angela is unimpressed. [Angela
         is totally irritated.]
         *Well, I happen to*
         *be the girls' mother. Where's Brad?*

She's pissing me off. "I figured
that's who you
were when LaTreya
called you 'Mommy.' Brad's at work."

         Another evil blink of snake green eyes.
         *I thought I'd take*
         *the kids shopping.*
         *Girls, go put on your shoes, please.*

The kids hustle upstairs, which is good.
Trying to take them could
come down to blows.
"Not without Brad's permission."

The cobra strikes quickly. *I don't
know who you
think you are, but
I'll do as I please with my daughters.*

"No, I don't think you will. You lost that
privilege when you
walked out the door.
Now let's give Brad a call, okay?"

*You are awfully possessive of someone
else's children.* She
looks me up and
down. *And you don't dress like hired help.*

My face heats, but I stand my
ground. "One call
will settle this.
Let's go into the kitchen and make it."

# It's a Short Conversation

Brad is on his way home.
Angela sits at the kitchen
table, waiting. The girls
bound into the room, all
giggles. I think I'm jealous.

I know I'm jealous when
Brad walks through the
door. The look on his face
is unmistakable. He loves
Angela, through the pain.

*Daddy!* cries Devon. *Mommy's
home.* She jumps into Angela's
lap and LaTreya moves to her
side, protective. They love her
unconditionally, pain all gone.

I excuse myself so they can talk,
knowing my life has veered,
suddenly, surely. But exactly
which direction it has veered
in remains to be discovered.

# Four Cigarettes

And two bowls later,
Brad calls me downstairs.
      Without his saying a single
word, I know I'm leaving.

      Angela has already left,
and she took the kids with
      her. Not a good sign for me.
But what about for Brad?

          *Angela wants to try again.*
*He pauses to let it sink in.*
      *I don't know if it's the*
*right thing to do, Kristina.*

          *But the girls miss her so*
*much. I have to think about*
          *what's best for them, right?*
His eyes hold massive hope.

      I want him to be happy.
"I don't guess she wants
      a live-in nanny, huh?" I
reach for an honest smile.

He shakes his head. *I'll help*
*you find a place, okay? Oh.*
*There's more. I have to give*
*up the ice. I don't know if I can.*


Wow. He really does love her.
Could I give up the monster
for Trey? I don't know either.
Luckily, it isn't an issue.


*I'll make you a deal. Take*
*my stash. Pay me when you can.*
*And I'll introduce you to my*
*connection. You'll be okay.*


I feel like I swallowed
a plate of mercury. Still, I go
over to Brad, look up into
his eyes. "Sure. I'll be fine."

# 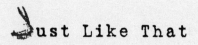ust Like That

Everything's different.
Just like that, everything's

                  changed.

Just like that, every
vestige of imagined

                  stability,

like a time-worried
weave, has come

                  unraveled.

Not long ago, I believed
I wanted complete

                  independence.

But living here with
a borrowed family

                  demolished

that idea. I don't
want to be without

                  companionship.

And the monster
doesn't count.

# 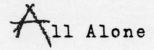ll Alone

In a weekly
motel, in a
not-real-nice
part of Reno,      I look at my
                   possessions,
                   every damn
                   thing I own,        contained in
                                       one medium-
                                       size suitcase
At least the                           and one box.
place is clean,
no noteworthy
bugs or stains.    I sit in the red
                   vinyl chair, flip
                   on the twelve-
                   inch TV, stare      mindlessly at
                                       whatever's on.
                                       And only now
                                       do I let myself

                           cry.

# No Word from Trey

Despite the desperate voice
mails I left. I can't stand
sitting here, alone. No one
to talk to. No one to laugh
with. Only the monster for
company. What fun is that?

I'm going crazy. Fucking
crazy. Even hanging with
Mom and Scott would be
better than this. At least
I'd have Hunter to play
with. A sudden wave of

guilt rolls over me. With
it comes a thought. Would
they let me move back in?
I dial the house, but get
the machine. Aagh! Maybe
I should just get in my car.

and drive out there. [No
one's home, idiot.] I've
got to talk to someone.
Who can I call? Robyn?
[She's yanking off some
guy from Toledo.] I know.

I open the address book
on my cell, punch some
numbers, cross my fingers
that a real, living being will
actually answer. He does,
first ring. "Hello, Quade?"

# We Talk for Half an Hour

He's kind, but not overly
sympathetic. *You've made
some rotten choices. They
caught up with you is all.*

The meth makes me want to do
more than talk. I want to confess.
"Have you ever slept with
two women at the same time?"

*You mean "every guy's
fantasy"? I had the chance
several times but no, I never
took advantage of it.*

He *is* lead singer in a band.
He describes a couple of
times he had the chance
to play sandwich meat.

*But for me sex is more
than just about feeling good.
It's about feeling something
special for someone.*

"You mean love." It's
a statement, not a question.
Loveless sex is meaningless.
Has Trey concluded that?

> Exactly. The other guys
> in the band don't feel
> the same way, but singing
> for sex negates the art.

Okay, he's a little strange.
But I really, really like him.
And I really need a friend.
"Is it okay if I call again?"

> Anytime, little sister.
> Anytime at all. You know
> I've always cared for you.
> That hasn't changed a bit.

Intense. He cares for me.
But does he care for me
as a friend? Potential lover?
Or—heaven forbid—little sister?

# uzzed

Bleeding. Bored out of my tree, I decide
to take a walk. This part of town is run

down, with cracked sidewalks and pot-
holed streets and dirty people, huddled

against weary buildings. A few yellow
streetlights buzz with effort, but don't do

much against the moonless night. Still, downtown is only a few blocks away, and there's

plenty of light there——neon light, in rainbow
colors, fountaining up casino towers. It's spring

break, so even though it's very late, a lot of
people flow along the main avenues. Strangers.

They're strangers, but I don't care. I want to be
among them. Flow with them. Bodies. Faces.

Most from any place but here. I like looking
at the faces. All races. Expressions. Joyful (winners).

Hateful (losers). Confused (users). Suddenly
a single face falls into focus. Familiar. Loved.

"Chase!" I run toward him, parting the crowd.
He sees me. Smiles. Frowns. Half-waves.

I see now he's walking with someone. Holding her
hand. She's prettier than me. And she's pregnant.

# What Do I Do Now?

I want to turn. Flee.
Act cowardly. But we're
practically touching.

[Play the game.] "Hey,
Chase. Long time, no see."

        He drops the girl's hand,
        dares to reach out and hug
        me. *God, it's good to see*

        *you.* He backs away. *Oh,*
        *this is my wife, Amanda.*

Wife? Yep. Matching
gold bands. [Don't you
dare cry. Suck it up.]

"Hi, Amanda. I'm Kristina.
Chase and I . . . are friends."

        Amanda tosses her long
        blond hair. Smiles. *Good*
        *to meet you. I've heard*

*a lot about you. You were*
*a hard act to follow.*

Chase told her about me?
Yes, I guess that's like
him. Honest till it hurts.

I don't know what to say
except, "Home for a visit?"

Chase nods. *We eloped,*
*so my mom hadn't met*
*Amanda yet. Thought*

*we should fix that*
*before the baby's born.*

We make small talk
for a few minutes, my
end of the conversation

minuscule, compared
to all of Chase's news.

Finally he decides,
*It's pretty late. We'd*
*better go before Mom*

*decides we skipped*
*town. Take care.*

"You too. And let me
know when the baby
comes, okay?" I watch

them walk hip-to-hip
down the street. And

despite all the people—
bodies, faces—swarming
around me like pissed

yellow jackets, I have
never felt so abandoned.

# I Sit for a While

On a bench along
the River Walk,

                    listen to

the opera of
the Truckee
River at night.

                    The water

is high, after our
massive winter.
It rushes past,

                    calling

over the rocks,
*You're not alone.*
*I'm here, aren't I?*

                    Coaxing,

*Oh, the places I*
*can take you. Ride*
*along with me.*

                    Cajoling,

*Come on. It's easy.*
*Just walk to the railing.*
*One quick step over . . .*

                    Chanting,

*Easy. It's easy. One*
*quick step. It's easy.*
*I'll sing you to sleep.*

                        *One quick step.*

I go to the railing,
tilt my face over, into
a cold, black breeze.

                        *Into death,*

reaching out for me.
It touches my face,
tempting me,

                        *It's easy.*

No! Not yet. I throw
myself into reverse,
head back to the motel.

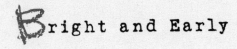

# Bright and Early

The next morning, Brad
calls on his way to work.

*Glad you're up. Is
everything okay?*

"I've been up since day
before yesterday. And
everything's fucked,

like anyone gives a shit."
Okay, I'm kind of bitchy.
Several reasons for that.

Brad ignores the jab. *I talked
to Cesar. He's good with
meeting you. After work?*

"Sure. Pick me up? You
know where to find me."
For the second time I'm

about to become intertwined
with La Eme. Mexican Mafia.
Some totally tough Latinos.

Definitely not the kind of
guys you want to mess over.
No problem. I'll play straight

with them. Cash and carry.
That's the only way to deal
with Cesar and La Eme.

# Brad Picks Me Up

Right on time. I figured we'd
head for the projects. Instead,
> he drives well east of the city,
> to the little bedroom community
of Fernley. It's a silent twenty-
minute drive. What's left to say?

> Cesar lives in a well-kept
> mobile home on a ten-acre
>> piece of high desert ground.
>> When we pull through the gate,
> we are greeted by a rottweiler
> the size of a Shetland pony.

>> The animal woofs like a bear,
>> and drool slides from his jowls.
>>> The commotion brings Cesar
>>> (I assume) to the front door.
>> León! Abajo! he commands.
>> The dog drops to the ground.

*He'll expect us to stay at*
*least a half hour,* Brad says.
                    *But he doesn't use, so don't*
                    *even go there.* He opens the
door, slips from beneath the
wheel, and I follow him inside.

Furnishings are sparse. We
sit around a small card table.
          Brad handles the introductions,
          and Cesar regards me carefully.
After a few tense moments, he
nods, deciding I'm not the heat.

          *I don't deal less than quarter*
          *pounds, and won't front until*
                    *I know you're a regular. Then*
                    *we can talk. How much today?*
          His eyes travel back and forth
          between Brad and me.

A quarter pound? Holy shit.
Brad never mentioned that.
            I don't have that kind of money.
            Do my eyes reflect the terror I
feel? *We'll take a quarter.*
Brad produces a wad of cash.


Apparently, we're now partners.
Cesar shrugs and goes into the
            other room. *We'll split the
            profit, okay?* says Brad.
*Move the quarter, you'll
have plenty of cash to score.*


I hope he's willing to share
his customer list too. I need
            to off the stuff as quickly as
            possible, for several reasons.
Four ounces? I have graduated
again—to the major league.

# Brad Drops Me Off

I half-expect him to ask
to come inside, smoke
a little, make love a little.

Instead, he turns to me.
*I know you're mad at me.*
*But please understand . . .*

"I do understand. Not
your job to babysit me."
Kind of mean, but oh well.

*Okay. Right. But please*
*be careful. This is a major*
*quantity. Don't leave it . . .*

His money. I understand
that, too. "I'll be careful. I
want to off this right away

and pay you back. Will you
let your people know how
to get hold of me?"

*No problem. I trust you to pay
me back.* He pauses. *I just
want you to know I never*

*expected Angela to come
home or I wouldn't have . . .
I still care for you, you know.*

That phrase again. Everyone
cares for me. They just don't
know how to love me.

# I Left My Cell

On the charger. When I turn
it on to check messages,
there are two.

Mom: *Sorry I missed
your call yesterday. We
were out celebrating my
birthday. Are you okay?*

Trey: *Where are you?
I know Angela moved
back home. I'll be there
tonight. Are you okay?*

They both sound totally
stressed. Guess Mom
doesn't like the idea
of chalking up
another year.

But what's
up with Trey?
Probably hungry for
meth. Guess what. Now
he'll have to get it from me.

# Why Am I Not More Excited

About Trey coming tonight?
        I still love him. But I can't
        seem to find that high-
blood-pressure anticipation.
        Maybe it's knowing some
        other girl has sent him on
his way. Maybe it's because
        I'm on my period and can't
        make love to him, anyway.
Is it because I'm not buzzed?

Regardless, I dial his number,
        with the usual result, leave
        him directions to the motel,
sans an "I love you" addendum.
        Wonder if he'll even notice.
        Wonder if he'll even care.
Wonder if he'll drop in, score,
        drop back out of my life again
        until he needs to restock.
Maybe I should get buzzed.

Next, I call Mom. "Sorry I
            missed your birthday, but I
            had to move out of the Red
Rock house. . . . No, the guy's
            wife came back and they
            don't need a nanny anymore. . . .
I'm in a weekly for now. Can I
            come out tomorrow and bring your
            birthday present? See you then."
Maybe I shouldn't get buzzed.

Who knows if or when Trey
            will get here? I flip on the TV,
            debating whether or not to get
buzzed. An hour passes. Two,
            with nothing but reality shows
            to keep me company. Who needs
that kind of reality? I pick
            up the phone and call Quade.
            We talk for a long while, and
after we hang up, I get buzzed.

# By the Time Trey Knocks

On the door, I am very buzzed
and almost beyond caring
that he has finally arrived.

One look at him and all that
changes. He's shaken, pale.
He stumbles through the door

and I lock it behind him,
invite him into my arms.
"What's wrong?" I guide

him into a chair. *I, uh . . . just
had a major blowout with
Brad.* He catches his breath,

chooses his words. *I went out
there first, looking for ice.
Angela was over the top.*

*How was I supposed to know
she'd gone to Narcotics Anonymous
and made Brad go too?*

How was I supposed to know
she'd fucking freak out and
threaten to call the cops?

I mean, standing on the door-
step, screaming. Damn, she's
crashing hard. Then, when I

told her to shut the hell up, Brad
went off the deep end. I thought
he was going to haul off and hit me.

I can picture it all clearly. But
there's a puzzle piece missing.
And it has something to do with,

"Crashing?" How did he know
she was using, let alone crashing?
I never noticed it, not even

sitting across the table from
her. What hasn't he told me?
"What haven't you told me?"

He stops ranting, studies me,
trying to decide how much
information I can handle.

*Promise you won't get mad?*
*I don't want to fight with you,*
*too.* He looks like he could break.

This can't be good. But
what the hell? I'd almost
given up on ever seeing

him again, anyway. If this
is the last straw, I don't have
to get mad, do I? "Promise."

*You know the girl in Stockton,*
*the one I told you about?*
*Truth is, it was Angela.*

Bang! Everything falls
right into place. I do get
mad. Jealous. Insanely so.

My mouth tries to open.
But I won't let it. Not yet.
Not until I've had enough

time to completely digest
his confession, consider
its implications. I did promise.

# Waiting for Digestion

I figure we might as well
ingest a little crystal.
Maybe not the best idea,
but I can't just sit here
staring at him like a fool.
Anyway, I need more
information and this is
the best way to get it.

The monster knows
the right questions to
ask. Finally, it pries
my mouth open. "Did she
leave Brad for you?"

The monster supplies
answers. *Not exactly.*
*I mean, we flirted a little.*
*I think that convinced*
*her she wanted to see*
*other men. But she didn't*
*come directly to Stockton.*
*And when she did, she*
*dated other guys too.*

A bigger question looms,
one I don't want to ask
because I might hate
the answer. "Are you
in love with her?" Is
that really why he went
over there tonight?

> He comes over, kneels
> in front of me, looks up
> into my eyes. *No. I told
> you it was sex only. In
> fact, I was relieved when
> she informed me she was
> going back to Brad.*
>
> *The guilt, believe it or
> not, was incredible. Not
> only because of Brad,
> but because of you.
> I love you. And I don't
> ever want to hurt you.*

Kristina wants to kiss him
with every fiber of her
being. But Bree wants
him to pay, or at least
sweat it a little. We
reach a compromise.
"Does that mean you'll
quit sleeping around?"

　　　　His immediate answer
　　　　surprises me. No, it
　　　　shocks me. *Only if
　　　　you ask me to.*

"I'm asking."

　　　　*Okay.* He tilts his face
　　　　up toward mine, requesting
　　　　a meeting of lips.

"One more thing."

　　　　*What?*

"Answer your damn phone."

# 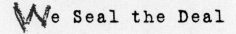We Seal the Deal

With a kiss—and more.
Yeah, I'm still on my
period. But you'd
be surprised at
all the things
you can do,
anyway.

Trey is full of surprises,
and not just sexy
ones. We make
love, but even
as our bodies
work, my
brain is
busy.

Two months till school
is out for summer,
two months till
Trey can be
mine full-
time. I
can't
stay

here, alone in this flea-
bag motel. I need
another place.
A place with
people. One
comes to
mind.

Home. I want to go
home. Tomorrow
when I'm there,
I'll push Mom
to please let
me come
home.

But only until summer.

# Clean, Maintenance-Buzzed

We take my car home.
Mom and Scott didn't
meet Trey before, but
they might recognize

the Mustang. I want
them to like him. Need
them to love him, one-
tenth as much as I do.

I hold a dozen supermarket
roses in my lap. Scentless.
What happened to red rose
perfume? Has the monster

stolen my sense of smell?
No, I smell tobacco, too
strong in my hair and
clothes. I smell deodorant,

his and mine. I smell
leather seats and a faint
aura of crystal. But still
no red rose perfume.

Frustrated, nervous, I
decide confession is
in order. "Remember
a few months ago when

you dropped me off at
home? Mom told me
never to bring you there.
That's why I wanted

us to come in this car.
I want them to get to
know you without thinking
you're a meth fiend."

*Well, I'll do my best to make
them think otherwise.* Then
he poses an interesting question.
*But what if that's what I am?*

# Mom Greets Us

With a frosty *Hello.* The Queen
of Cool assesses Trey. Finally
she offers, *I'm Marie.*

*And you are . . .*

Trey does his best to be
pleasant. *Pleased to meet
you. I'm Trey, Kristina's . . .*

He crash-lands on *fiancé.*

Mom's mouth drops wide,
in perfect unison with mine.
*Is that a fact? Kristina*

*forgot to mention it.*

Unfazed, Trey trumps
Mom's clichéd hand. *We
only decided last night.*

*She wanted to surprise you.*

I interrupt the uneasy
introduction with a bouquet
of scentless red roses.

"Happy birthday, Mom."

Trey, as already noted,
is a major player. *Yes,
happy birthday . . . Mom.*

He gifts her with his great smile.

Mom is not appreciative.
*Ahem. Let's go inside . . .* Her
unfinished sentence hangs midair:

*before anyone notices you here.*

# 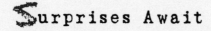urprises Await

The first is Hunter, who
can now not only crawl
but also pull himself up
and walk, holding on to
the coffee table. He'll be
off and running soon.

Where has the time
gone?

The second is Jake, whose
voice has lowered into
bass range. I guess we
haven't spoken enough
the last few months for
me to notice the shift.

Where has my little brother
gone?

His girlfriend is inside
too. They wade patiently
through the obligatory
introductions, disappear
upstairs to spend time
alone in Jake's room.

Where has propriety
gone?

Despite Mom's clear
disapproval of Trey,
Scott seems to accept
him. They talk sports.
Talk college. Talk me.
Mom remains aloof.

Where has solidarity
gone?

# While the Guys Talk

Mom draws me into the kitchen,
sits me down at the table.

*So what are your plans now?*

Can't tell her about my new
career, dealing to hookers.

*New job? School? Uh . . . marriage?*

[Quick, think up a lie.]
"I signed up for classes."

*Did you get your GED?*

[Go ahead, lie bigger.]
"I did, in fact. Last month."

*Where are you going to school?*

[She won't believe a university.]
"Up at the community college."

*Good choice, all things considered.*

[What does that mean?]
"Trey thought it was a good idea."

*You're not really going to marry him?*

[You're not, are you?]
"What's wrong with him?"

*Kristina, he's a total loser.*

Blood pressure rising.
"He is not! And I love him."

*You don't know what love is.*

And rising. "I suppose no
one knows that but you?"

*You're too young to get married.*

Not that old line. Answer:
"You got married at eighteen."

*To a total loser. Look what happened.*

Ears burning. "I don't care!
Your life isn't mine."

*Lower your voice this instant.*

Up. Up. Up goes my voice.
"You can't make me."

*I'm still your mother . . .*

"Yeah, you're my mother,
and a cold-hearted bitch."

*Don't ever talk to me like that!*

"What are you going to do?
Ground me until further notice?"

*I think it's time for you to leave.*

So much for moving home.

# Halfway Back

To the motel, Trey
drops another surprise
smack in my lap.

*What would you say
if I told you I'm not going
back to school?*

Weird, but Bree sides
with Mom. [She's right.
He's a loser.]

Kristina, however,
is all for it. "Really? Since
when? Are you sure?"

*I totally screwed up this
semester, anyway. I can
always go back and*

*finish up, or maybe I'll
transfer to UNR. Meanwhile,
we'll be together.*

        A ton of questions pop
into my head. Did he
screw up because of

        the meth? Angela? Me?
What will this mean to his
dream of becoming

        an electrical engineer?
Does this translate to we're
living together? Was

        the word "fiancé" just
for my mom's benefit? I'm
afraid to ask any of that.

                *I was thinking we could
                get an apartment together.
                I mean, if you want . . .*

        Well, of course I want.
Being with Trey twenty-
four, seven? A dream.

*I could get a job. And*
*your baby could live with*
*us too, if you want. . . .*

Trey, Hunter, and me, like
a real family? This is starting
to sound pretty serious.

*We'll need some money*
*for furniture and stuff.*
*Maybe we could sell*

*this car. We'll only need*
*one, right? I think mine is*
*probably more reliable. . . .*

He talks all the way back
to the motel about how we
can make it all work out.

By the time we park the
car and go upstairs, my life
has shifted gears, again.

# It All Sounded So Easy

But a number of obstacles
popped up right away.

Getting an apartment

when you don't have a job
is tough. I guess they want
to know the rent will happen.

Getting a job

when all you want to do
is get high isn't exactly
a priority. Anyway, dealing
is much easier than

working for a living.

But you can't really put
"dealer" under "occupation"
on the rental application.

Convincing a manager

took a fair amount of lying,
and Brad's cooperation.
And, with Angela squarely
in the way, that

wasn't easy either.

But blood is thicker than
marriage. Brad didn't

really give Trey a job.
He just said he did.

Selling an old LTD,

classic or not, took a little
time too. And now that it's gone,
I feel bad. It was all I had
that was really my own. But

with gas so expensive,

it's probably best. So now
Trey and I have a place,
garage-sale furniture, his
Mustang. Each other.

And a bottomless supply
of the monster.

# May I Just Say

That moving in with someone
isn't as easy as it sounds either.

You both have habits, good
and not-so. Sometimes those

habits grate on each other's
nerves, especially when you're

wired. Especially, especially
when you're coming down.

You have different tastes,
in TV shows, music, and food.

Compromise can be difficult
to reach, especially when you're

wired. Especially, especially
when you're coming down.

I do love Trey, and being with
him is exponentially better than

being alone. Especially when
I'm wired. But not so much

when I'm coming down. That's
when those little differences

really get on my nerves. Then we
argue. Sometimes we fight.

Always, we make up with heart
felt apologies and great sex.

So maybe the compromise
is worth it, after all.

# The Scariest Thing

I'm facing now is trying to get
Hunter out of my mother's grasp.
But he is *my* baby, damnit.

Finally, I find the courage to call.
"Hi, Mom. Trey and I are all set
up in our own apartment.

We want to bring Hunter for
a visit. Can we come pick him
up?" How will this go?

Mom is silent for several
seconds. *Do you really
think that's a good idea?*

I've rehearsed this. I know
what to say. "I appreciate
that you've taken such good

care of him. But he needs
to get used to being around
his mom . . . and stepfather."

Was it the wrong card
to play? *Kristina, I hate
to say this, but Hunter*

*barely recognizes you. Do
you think it's fair to
leave him with a stranger?*

[Stay in control. Temper
in check.] "There's only one
way to change that, Mom."

[Choose words carefully.]
"Or were you planning on
keeping my baby for yourself?"

# Ultimately, She Agrees

I'm glad, because the last
thing I need is to get
the courts involved.
Social Services frowns
on the crystal scene.

Trey drives me out,
moves the baby seat
into his car while I go
inside to collect my
baby and his things.

Mom holds Hunter,
kisses him gently,
hands him off to me.
*Call me right away*
*if anything goes wrong.*

Hunter waves bye-
bye, and as we turn,
I notice Mom start
to cry. She loves him.
But I love him too.

On the way back
to the apartment,
Trey detours east,
to the Pink Pussycat.
One quick delivery and

we're on our way,
two hundred dollars
in the black, plenty
to buy formula and
diapers for a week.

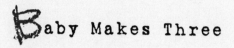

# Baby Makes Three

And even though he's
    little, his presence in this
        cramped one-bedroom
            makes the place even
                more claustrophobic.
Seems he's always
    underfoot, unless he's
        in his porta-crib. And
            unless he's sleeping,
                he's not happy there.
Trey says we'll have
    to get a bigger place,
        and to do that he
            needs to get a job,
                one he can list on
an application. He's
    out looking right now.
        Which means it's just
            Hunter, me, and the
                monster, killing time.

It's nice outside.
      Maybe Hunter
            and I could walk
                  to the park. Only
                        thing is, I'm tired.
I do have a way to
      fix that, don't I?
            I prop Hunter in a
                  chair, in front of
                        *Sesame Street.*
"Stay there with Elmo.
      Mommy will be
            right back." I go
                  into the bathroom,
                      open the window,
so the smoke won't
      taint the living room
            air. I'm halfway
                  through my second hit
                      when Hunter screams.

I run into the other
          room. He's crumpled
                    on the floor in front
                              of the chair, trickling
                                        blood from his mouth.
"Oh, God." I scoop
          him up, hug him
                    close, and see he's
                              okay, except for
                                        biting through his
bottom lip. He stops
          crying, looks up at
                    me with big dark
                              eyes, as if to say,
                                        *You let me fall. How*
*could you let me fall?*
          *That's not what a*
                    *mother should do.*
                              And it hits me. Maybe
                                        Mom was right, after all.

# Trey Is Gone

A very long time. Daylight
fades to darkness, and still

no word. I call his cell. Nothing.
I put Hunter to bed, worry

prickling my senses. I could
get high. Instead, I let myself

doze on the love seat. By the time
the creak of the door wakes me,

my neck is stiff from tilting so
long at an odd angle. That is not

conducive to a quiet discussion.
"Where the fuck have you been?"

    *Spent all day job hunting.*
    *I figured I deserved a couple*

    *of beers. You don't have a*
    *problem with that, do you?*

I do, actually. Leaving me
here, alone, while he's out

who-knows-where? But I'm
not going to say that. "Why

didn't you call? Didn't it occur
to you I might get worried?"

                                 *I'm okay, Kristina. I'm okay,*
                                 *you're okay. Everything's okay.*

                                 *I'm a big boy. I know what I'm*
                                 *doing. And you don't have to*

                                 *worry about where I am or what*
                                 *I'm up to. You're not my mommy.*

No way for this to go but from bad
to worse. I could fall silent.

Ballistic will feel better. "No, I'm not
your mommy. But I *am* a mommy,

and we had an emergency here today.
I couldn't get hold of you. Why won't

you just answer your fucking phone
when I call? What's wrong with you?"

*If I answer, I'll just have to listen*
*to this kind of shit. . . .* His voice is almost

as loud as mine, and now Hunter wakes
up. His crying makes my words sink in.

As I go to give him a comfort bottle,
Trey asks, *What kind of emergency?*

I don't tell him everything, just
that Hunter bit through his lip.

Trey is contrite. *I'm sorry. I should*
*have called. I'll do better, okay?*

# For a Few Days

He does do better. He
even answers his phone.
But he's spending more
and more time away.

Job hunting, he claims.
Seems to me anyone
searching that diligently
would have found one

by now. Maybe playing
house isn't his thing after
all. I'm afraid to ask.
Afraid he'll say I'm right.

Without a vehicle, I can't
very well make deliveries,
so when people call looking,
they have to come to me.

Grady is here when Trey
gets home this evening.
We're just about to take
a little test drive when

Trey bangs through
the door. He takes one
look at Grady. *Who
the fuck are you?*

"This is Grady, an old
friend. He's here to b—"
Apparently I should
have said "customer."

*Old friend, huh? Like
a real good friend?*
Trey's eyes are glazed.
He's wired out of his skull.

"No, not that kind of
friend. What's wrong
with you? And how
come you're fucked up?"

*I'm fucked up? Heh-heh.
Guess I am. While you
were getting high with an
old friend, hey, so was I.*

Grady looks more than
slightly uncomfortable
as things heat up. "I don't
suppose her name was Angela?"

*Damn, you are psychic.*
*Poor Brad has no idea*
*she's using again.* He stops,
waits for my response.

It isn't verbal. Before
he can possibly react,
I'm across the room, in
his face, slapping. He puts

up his arm, moves into
me, and now we're on
the floor. As we roll
around, I notice the pipe

and its contents have
spilled into the soiled
carpeting. Grady doesn't
think twice, rooting

around like a hog in
the mud. Fine. Let him
have it. I wouldn't smoke
that dirty stuff now.

We bump heavily against
the bedroom door. Instantly,
Hunter is crying. Bellowing.
It's enough to end the battle.

# Trey Rolls Off Me

Away from me, onto his feet.
*Take care of your baby.*
He vanishes into the night.

Close behind is Grade E,
with a sizeable buy and
a pilfered rock. I glance

around the cluttered room.
An ash tray overflows on
the coffee table. A glass

pipe lies on the floor, midst
papers, knocked off a chair.
A raft of papers, floating

on a swamp of nasty carpet,
a place no baby should crawl.
The sink cannot possibly

hold another crusty dish.
Clothing, dirty and clean,
decorates the furniture.

I should straighten up.
Scrub. Make the place
presentable. Habitable.

A place I want to be in.
But I'm exhausted. Sore.
Sore. Too sore to pick up

my stuttering baby. I warm
a bottle. Similac pacifier.
Then I locate the phone.

"Mom? I know it's late,
and I'm sorry. But I need
you to come get Hunter."

# They Say a Picture

Is worth a thousand words.
Mom studies the picture
that is my apartment, says
not one word except, *This
is the right decision.*

I kiss Hunter good-bye,
knowing this is the right
decision, knowing too
that I probably won't see
him again for a while.

He goes to Mom with
enthusiasm, gooing a hello.
Poor baby should be fast
asleep. He's going home
now. Home to sleep.

I will not sleep tonight.
I sit in the dark, staring
out at the stars. Where
is Trey? I want to tell
him I'm sorry.

Want to have "make-
up sex." Want to make
everything okay again.
Stable again. More stable.
Minus baby makes two.

# I Am Still by the Window

When he stumbles in. Wasted.
Like me. We don't bother with
words, instead collapse into bed,
shedding clothes as we go.
Finally, sweaty and shaking,
I whisper, "I'm sorry. Oh, God.
I don't want to be without you."

> The same hands that only hours
> ago hurt me now caress me. *I'm
> sorry too.* He lays his fingers into
> finger-shaped bruises. Perfect fits.
> *I can't believe I did this to you.*
> *Why do I hurt you when I love*
> *you so much? Am I crazy?*

We both know why, but we
don't dare admit it. What would
we be if we did? "We're both
crazy. I don't care, as long
as you're with me. Kiss me.
Make love to me, hard. Don't
think about it. Hurt me more."

# Afterward

We lie, knotted together,
as if to undo this macramé
would unravel us altogether.

> After a while, Trey sighs.
> *I have to tell you something.*

Every muscle tenses. He's
leaving. Or he's been with
Angela. Or he wants to be.

> *I haven't been job hunting*
> *all the time I've been away. . . .*

I don't want to hear this.
I don't want to lose him.
I don't want to share him.

> *I've been going to the casinos.*
> *I . . . I'm not lucky at gambling.*

He's not leaving. I don't have
to share him. Wait. Gambling?
He's been gambling? And losing?

*I'm sorry. I thought I could make*
*a little profit, to get a nicer place.*

My body stiffens and bends
in half, like a mannequin, sitting.
"Where did you get the money?"

> *From the lockbox. I know some*
> *of it was to get more speed. . . .*

Yes, and for rent. Electricity. Phone.
Gasoline. And, until a few hours ago,
baby food. "How much is left?"

> *I don't know. Not much. But there's*
> *still a little glass. We can sell it . . .*

Lockbox. I spring from bed, rush
to its hiding place, line up the numbers
on the lock. One hundred sixteen dollars.

Trey is still talking. *We just have to stay
out of it until we make our money back.*

Stay out of what? Oh, the stash. Right.
We're so very good at that. I sit back
in the chair beneath the window, stare

at the same stars in the same night sky.
Inside, everything is different. Again.

# I Still Love Trey

But I can't trust him,
and so the love feels

          different.

I still love Hunter,
but know he's better
off away from me,
and so the love is

          distant.

I still love Brad, in
some warped way,
even though I was

          discarded,

used then tossed
aside, like a once-
favorite toy,

          outgrown.

Funny, but I still love
Chase. Seeing him,
married and

          moved on,

stuffed me with pain.
It throbs, stabs.
But that isn't so bad.
At least I know I'm

          still alive.

# Alive and Throbbing

I've formulated a plan.
First I put in a call to Cesar, who tells
me to stop by anytime.
Code words for *There's plenty around.*
Next we have to sell what
little is left in the lockbox. I put Trey
on that. Anyone but Angela
is fair game. He'd better leave that ho
alone or start packing.

I stash a couple of pipes
full, just in case everything goes to shit.
I mean more to shit. I've
avoided doing what I'm going to do,
because if we screw this up,
we'll have Mexican Mafia on our ass.
Not a good thing. No, not
at all. So I guess the message is:
Do not screw this up!

Trey returns with a couple
hundred bucks and we head for Fernley.
León lets us out of the car,
a good omen. Cesar greets us with his
usual not-quite-smile.
That doesn't change as I tell him we
want to up our regular.
Holding this much meth halfway
scares the crap out of me.

I offer Cesar three bills,
which leaves us with sixteen whole
dollars until we manage.
to off a great deal of glass. "I know
we're really short, but
we had to change apartments. Can
you front us the rest?
We'll get you the money by next
week. We've got buys

lined up." Major lie.
Better to call it a bluff. Makes it
sound more like a game.
Cesar shrugs. *You been a pretty*
*good customer. No reason*
*to think you won't make good. But*
*fuck wit' me, you ain'*
*gonna like what happens. You know?*
Oh yeah, we know.

# The Plan Has Flaws

Like, the rent is due and we're
        out of cash. I give the manager
        a sob story about the baby getting
sick. Since the baby isn't here,
        she buys it, gives us a few days
        *to catch up, with a little interest.*
Translation: twenty-five for her.

Like, we really need to sell some
        ice right now, and everyone seems
        to be *a little short on cash* or set
for the foreseeable future. Trey
        actually goes downtown to peddle
        small quantities to tourists and card
dealers—an inspired way to play.

Like, because we're not selling it
        very quickly, we're tempted to go
        ahead and smoke it. First the profit
goes up in a cloud of exhaled ice.
        Next goes the investment capital,
        or it would be investment capital,
but it wasn't our capital to invest.

Like, by the time we're supposed
          to pay Cesar what we owe him, we're
          even further behind than when I
concocted that ridiculous plan.
          We don't have close to what he's
          expecting, and wouldn't, even if
we sold everything that's left.

Anyway, we can't sell everything
          that's left, or we won't have any
          personal, or any way to get more.
Which leaves us pretty well
          screwed. Like 100 percent
          screwed, unless I can, with lightning
speed, concoct a workable Plan B.

# 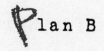lan B

Revolves around that we need
money. Lots of it and fast.
Three possible ways to
come up with it.

Beg.

Not really my style. I mean,
I suppose I could call Mom,
tell her I can't even afford food.
But would she believe me,
and would she care even if she did?

Borrow.

I could maybe call Leigh, ask for
a loan until payday, lie and tell
her there really is a payday
coming up soon. But she's not
exactly rolling in money herself.

Or steal.

I've never considered this option
before. Course, I never had to.
Would I even be good at it?
Who would I steal from?
And afterward, would I feel

no remorse?

# One Thing's for Sure

If I'm going to steal, Trey has to be
in on it. This is his fault to begin with.
"So, any ideas how we might come
up with some cash, uh, illegally?"

> *You mean like counterfeiting?*

Huh. That thought never crossed
my mind. We couldn't do that, could
we? "No. I meant more like . . . hmm,
borrowing. With no intent to repay."

> *You aren't serious, are you?*

"Far as I can see, we don't have
much of a choice. We're almost dry,
and we've got to make good with Cesar
to get more . . . and stay in one piece."

> *Well, I'm not about to snatch purses.*

Sheesh. Never thought of that, either.
"What if I could get hold of some checks.
Think we could get away with cashing
them?" I have an idea where to get some.

*Probably. At least with a fake ID.*

Fake ID. Good idea. It could, in fact,
come in handy in a number of ways.
But I have no idea how to get one.
"How could I get one of those?"

*I do happen to know this guy. . . .*

A guy who makes them for college
students. A guy who once helped
Trey himself out. A guy who isn't
the least bit difficult to get hold of.

That must be some kind of sign.

# The Guy Lives

In a little brick house, with a white
picket fence and flowers in the yard,
a few blocks from the university.

He greets Trey with a nod, says
to me, *Hi. I'm Frank. Come in.*

Frank doesn't look like a crook.
He looks like a computer nerd,
which he most definitely is.

His turn to check me out. *So,
you want to get into the clubs?*

"Uh, yeah. Can you help me out?
Guess I don't quite look twenty-
one." Perfect. Just perfect.

*No problem. Come on. Let's
take your picture.*

Digital this. Special program
that, my new ID is almost ready
to go. Just one thing missing.

       *What name did you want here?*
       *Most people use someone else's.*

Well, duh. Of course I want to
use someone else's, the someone
whose name will be on the checks.

"Put Marie Springer."

# Now All I Have to Do

Is figure out how to get the checks.
        Best if no one is home. I give Mom
        a call. A bit of small talk, then I ask,

"When is Jake's next baseball game?
        Trey and I thought we might stop by."
        I'm turning into an experienced liar.

I listen for a tone of suspicion, but can
        find not a trace when Mom informs me,
        *Friday at three. He's starting pitcher.*

"Very cool. Are you bringing Hunter?"
        Like she would leave him with a baby-
        sitter. If she's going, he's going too.

Her voice totally cools. *Of course.*
        *We're going out to dinner afterward.*
        *You're welcome to come with us.*

Everything clicks completely into
        place. Unreal. *Maybe we'll take*
        *you up on that. See you Friday.*

# Who Knew Burglary

Could be such a piece of cake?

A major dose of the monster
provides plenty of courage.

Trey parks his car well away
from the house, and we hoof
it from there. I could use my

key, but we want this to look
like the real deal, so we go around
back, trying windows as we go.
We're in luck with the laundry room.

It's a small window, but I shimmy
through, then unlock the sliding
glass door, just like real burglars
might do. Wait. We're real burglars,
and getting caught would mean jail.

Getting caught doing any of this
would mean major jail time.
Why worry about it now? Mom
keeps her checks in her desk.
I locate the box, dig down for

the bottom batch. *Let's go!*
insists Trey. But I want to make
this look real, so I go into Mom's
bedroom, empty her jewelry box

and, for good measure, grab
the digital camera, too. Out the
door, no one the wiser. For now.

We even stop by the game. Fifth
inning, Jake has been replaced.

And we're too wired for dinner.

# Mom Can't Have a Clue

About what we just did,
where we just came from.
But she definitely knows we're high.

She gives Hunter to Scott, pulls me down
the steps, behind the bleachers.
Trey stays behind.

Mom puts her hands on my
cheeks, squeezes as she looks
into my eyes. I can imagine how they look.

*God, Kristina. Look at you. If you keep*
*this up, you're going to die.*
*Are you trying to die?*

I can't look that bad, can
I? [You can. Do. But play
the game. Deny.] "What do you mean?"

Concern becomes anger. *You know what*
*I mean. Jesus. How stupid*
*do you think I am? I know*

*fucked up when I see it, and*
*you're fucked up every time*
*I see you. You've got to stop. Or die.*

"Don't you get it, Mom? I really don't
give a shit if I die. What,
exactly, is there to live for?"

Holy crap. Did I just say
that? And did I mean it?
Damn, maybe I did. Maybe I really did.

Mom's eyes tear up. *There's not a lot*
*more to say, is there?*
*I'm your mother, and*

*I'll always love you. But*
*I can't watch this any-*
*more. Clean up. Or don't call again.*

# Locate the Ladies' Room

Luckily, it's empty, no
one to see the vacant-
eyed girl, staring
in the mirror.
Staring at a stranger
who doesn't care
if she dies. Maybe
wants to die.

Who would care
if I died?

My face is hollow-
cheeked, spiced with sores—
the places where I stab
at bugs. Tiny bugs,
almost invisible,
but irritating.
Usually they come out
at night, when I'm lying
there, begging for sleep.
I've been meaning
to tell the manager
that the apartment needs to be

sprayed. Sprayed. Steam
cleaned. Deodorized.

My hair looks odd too.
It used to be darker.
Shinier. Prettier.
Can hair lose color
when you're only eighteen?
What if I go all the way
gray? Will Trey still
love me? Will anyone?

That is, if I fool
them all and don't die.

# Trey Is Waiting

Outside. One look tells him
more than he wants to know.
                    He opens his arms, reels me in.
                    *What's the matter? Mom, again?*
I can't even address that.
"Would you care if I died?"

He pushes me back, eyes
netting mine like a difficult
                    catch. *What the fuck are you talking*
                    *about? Who said you were going*
*to die? Never mind. Don't*
*tell me. Your loving mother.*

"Forget about my mother.
Do I look like I'm going
                    to die? I feel good, but I look rough.
                    Don't I? Tell me the truth, okay?"
That's what I say. But he
knows what I need to hear.

*Kristina, I don't know what*
*your mom had to say to you,*
                    *but you are beautiful. Incredible. If*
                    *you died, it would break me in two.*
*You taught me what love is.*
*How could I live without you?*

He kisses me, and it's better
than our very first kiss because
                    I know it means more than his just
                    wanting to get into my pants. It's
affirmation. After all these
months, all the good and bad,

he really does love me.
As much—or more—as
                    I love him. That makes everything
                    worth it—the lying. The stealing.
The leaving others in my
dust. The inseparable guilt.

# Guilty

Ka-ching! Guilty? You betcha. Fact
is, I'm going to get guiltier, soon
as I can figure out how to cash a few
checks. Checks,
with my mom's
name on them.
Cash 'em, with
a fake ID, with
Mom's name
forged on it.
Paid for with
owed-for ice.       So what now? Do I
cash one big       check, hope the bank
doesn't ask       just why do you need
so much cash       right this
minute? Or do       I cash one
here, cash one       there, till
they add up just right. Oh, here you go,
Cesar dearest, and oh, could you front
us please, one more time, thank you! **UILTY!**

# Trey Counsels

Me to write several smaller checks,
cash them at different locations.
In similar fashion, we hock
the jewelry at three pawnshops,
in three towns. All ask for a name.
None requires an ID. Go figure.

I do feel kind of bad about offing
a couple of Grandma's rings. One
is Mom's favorite. But hey, if
she liked it that much, she shouldn't
have kept it where some stupid burglar
could find it. Steal it. Pawn it.

Take the money and pay off her debt
to La Eme, ask for another front.
Perhaps not the best move, but I'm
no longer worried about making those.
I'm just trying to stay high and survive,
whatever that takes. I have no plans

for the future. Any future. As Cesar
might say, *Qué será, será.* What will
be, will be. No one lives forever, do
they? For some, living longer, slower,
less complicated lives is their only
goal. Personally, I need to live faster,

even if it means dying younger. Don't
ask me why. As for the guilt, it comes
and goes. Mostly, it's gone, right along
with Mom's jewelry and a chunk of her
money. Part of me thinks she deserves
it. Another part doesn't know why.

# I Consider That in the Shower

Scrubbing off yesterday's sweat,
          last night's sex. All of a sudden,
the front door throbs with noise.
          Knocking. Pounding. Thumping.
Whoever it is wants a reaction.
          But who? The manager? Cops?
Shaking, I wrap a towel around
          myself, wishing Trey was here
instead of making a delivery.

A glimpse out the peephole gives
          no definitive answers. It's a guy
in a suit. Detective? If I don't answer,
          he'll go away, but I'm guessing
he'll be back. At least my semi-
          naked state will give me the excuse
to go into the other room, dispose
          of evidence if need be. I crack
the door around the chain. "Yes?"

*Kristina Georgia Snow?* He slides
            a sheaf of papers through the opening.
*Consider yourself served.* The man
            turns on his heel, leaves without
threatening to come inside. Not
            a detective. Only a process server.
Relieved but still shaking, I force
            myself to look at what's written on
the papers. Something about Hunter?

I read further. Despite the hefty
            legalese, I understand the gist
of the six-page document. Mom
            and Scott have filed for custody.
They claim I'm an unfit mother,
            cite drug abuse and several instances
of observed "unstable behavior."
            They're asking to be appointed
legal guardians. Immediately.

# If I Want to Fight Them

I'll have to pass a drug test.

Go to court.

Talk to a judge.

Tell him why I'm more

fit to raise Hunter than

Mom and Scott are.

Convince him those instances

of unstable behavior were justified.

Or aberrances.

Do I want to fight?

Am I more fit to raise him?

Am I fit to raise him at all?

Do I want to raise him?

Am I ready for full-time motherhood?

The answer to all these questions:

"How the fuck

do I know?"

# When Trey Gets Back

I show him the papers.
He is kind. Reasonable.

*It's up to you. I'll support
you, whatever you decide.*

But I've already pretty
much made up my mind.

*They'll take good care of
him. And it's only temporary.*

That's right. I can always
go to court for him later.

*Meanwhile, we'll find a nicer
place. Get our feet under us.*

A bigger place, in a better
neighborhood. Good schools.

*Please don't cry. Come here.
I'll make you feel better.*

We get high. Make love.
Lie softly folded together.

*We're good together, aren't we?
And this is just the beginning.*

The beginning of what?
And why does it feel so much

like an ending?

# 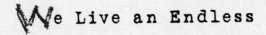We Live an Endless

Mindless cycling.

        Buzzed.
        Barely buzzed.
        Crash.
        Buzzed again.

Recycling.

        Buzzed.
        Barely buzzed.
        Crash.
        Buzzed again.


Augmented by
a different cycling.

        Score.
        Pay up.
        Deal.
        Score more.

Or, depending on
what's due when,

        Score.
        Forge checks.
        Pay up.
        Score more.

I don't worry about
getting caught. I don't

worry about me at all,
although I could
worry about

> Kristina and Mom.
> Kristina and Hunter.
> Kristina and Trey.
> Kristina and the monster.

Call me stupid, but I do,
in fact, worry about

> Trey and Angela.
> Trey and casinos.
> Trey, helping himself
> to the contents of the lockbox.

# 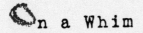On a Whim

I pick up a newspaper.
Maybe I'll get a job.
A new direction.

A way out.

Why do I think I
need that? Doesn't
matter. I already

spent

the fifty cents for
the paper. And hey,
since I bought it,

might

as well read it.
What's going on
in the world?

Perhaps

a new war? New
president? Not that
either event would

affect me.

Anyway, Section B,
page three, I come
across a photo.

Definitely

[an ugly] me, cashing
a check at a local bank.
The caption reads:

        *Does*

*anyone know this*
*woman?* Fuck me.
Someone out there

        definitely does.

# First Things First

Trey and I decide our abode is no longer
a safe place to stay. Not only does the greed-

fed manager know us, but a process server
has lately been by. I'm not real sure he got

a good look at me, but you never know.
That guy is no doubt always on the prowl

for an easy buck. Secret Witness is painless
pickings. The major bummer is, we just paid

the rent. But such is the not-pretty life of
a dealer/burglar/forger. What a mouthful!

An ugly mouthful of crap, defining me. But
no worries. We toss most of our belongings

into suitcases and boxes. Two suitcases.
Three boxes. Trey plus me equals: not

a whole lot more shit. We have to write off
most of the furniture. Garage-sale, oh well.

The best thing to do would be to go far, far
away. But we're glass-heavy, cash-light.

Trey has the solution. *We'll sleep in the car*
*until we're off the meth. Then we'll score one*

*more time. A big one, before we take off.*
*I hear ice is a big commodity in the Midwest.*

Good plan. One we settle on. We move into
the Mustang. Sell a shitload of crystal.

Go to Fernley for one final score. A major
one. Cesar is happy to front us a half pound.

After all, we've always made good on his fronts.
Always come back for more. Always . . .

# But This Time

We have no plans to come back.
No plans to pay up. No plans
to stay in this place. The only
place I've ever known as home.

An ending.


But we won't head east. We'll
go west, to California, where
meth was first invented and
remains the drug of choice. Is this

a beginning?


I wish I could feel. Or maybe
not. If I could, I would feel loss.
Hunter. Mom. Jake. Leigh. Even
Scott, who has always been there

for me.


They say meth affects the brain.
Destroys the pleasure center.
Could it smash the pain center too?
Would feeling pain be better than

feeling numb?

# Homeless

Out of Nevada, we touch down
in California. Unsure of where to go
from here, we decide we need food.

> *McD's okay? We should*
> *probably eat cheap for a while.*

We're on a downswing.
Sleepy. Hungry. Empty. "Cheap
is good, as long as there's a lot of it."

> *Ronald would be proud.*
> *Big Macs and fries, times two?*

"Times two, twice." Fuck it.
I can invest a few calories. Not
like I've eaten a whole lot lately.

> *Okay. But you know I'm not*
> *real fond of Two-Ton-Tessies.*

"Love me fat, love me skinny.
Just keep loving me. Hey,
sounds like a song. Love me—"

*You might want to work on it*
*before you try out for* American Idol.

We locate a McDonald's off
the freeway, go inside to pee,
order our fifteen-dollar feast.

*Let's eat in the car. Looks like*
*they're getting ready to close.*

It is pretty late. Trey pulls
the Mustang back into a dark
corner of the parking lot.

*No one will bother us here.*
*Oh, man, this shit tastes great.*

He's right. It does. And as
my belly fills with greasy
food, my eyes grow heavy.

*We shouldn't swing for a room.*
*Let's sleep in the car, okay?*

It's not the comfiest bed. But
it is free. And we don't dare
drive anywhere this tired.

We'll make L.A. tomorrow. We
can bunk with a buddy then.

Cool. Whatever. Meanwhile
I'm just going to close my
eyes, slip into Dreamville.

# Tap-Tap-Tap

Tapping on the glass. Glass?
Where am I? And who's knocking?

*Come on. Wake up!*

Car. I'm in a car. Trey's car.
And he's here too, arms around

me, trying to wake up, just like I am.
I don't want to. I want to sleep.

*Hello? Open the window!*

Just a minute. Just a freaking
minute. I manage to open my eyes.

The guy outside the window, the one
who's been knocking, wears a uniform.

His flashlight parts the darkness,
seeks immediate information.

*Good evening. May I see some ID?*

Trey politely offers his license.
*Something wrong, Officer?*

*Don't you know you can't sleep here?*

*Sorry. We had no idea. It's just
that we got off the freeway . . .*

The cop shines his light in our eyes.
Then he speaks directly to me.

*How 'bout you, miss? ID?*

The cop takes our licenses back
to his car. I'm getting a very bad

feeling. Trey notices. *Don't panic.*
Eventually, the uniform returns.

*Please step out of the vehicle.*

Holy shit. There can't be an APB
out for me already, can there?

Someone would have had to identify
me, right? Could it happen this fast?

*You say you're just passing through?*

Okay, maybe it isn't an all points
bulletin. Maybe he's just being nosy—

doing his job. "That's right." I give him
my best smile. "We can just be on our way. . . ."

*Mind if I take a quick look inside?*

He wants to search the Mustang.
The meth is in the lockbox, under

the front seat. It would take a warrant
to unlock that. Maybe he won't bother.

Maybe he won't even see it. Trey
must be thinking the same thing.

He looks over at me, gives a small
shrug. "Sure," I say. "Why not?"

# A Second Patrol Car

Joins the party as Cop
Number One leans inside
the Mustang, flashlight
at the ready. It takes
about two seconds for
him to find the lockbox,
extract it, place it on the seat.

Surprise! It isn't locked.

And talk about surprised.
One of Sacramento's finest
has just discovered a half
pound of 90 percent pure
crystal methamphetamine.
You should see the look
on his face. He'll be the talk
of the locker room for days.

No surprise. We're fucked.

# Cuffed

Totally busted.
We are stuffed
into separate cars,
hauled off to city
jail. It's a short ride,
not even long enough
to think about what
will happen next.

Poked. Prodded.
Grilled. Well done.
Through it all I stay
calm. Silent. The ball
is in—ha-ha-ha—
their court now.

I'm allowed a call.
Need to call some-
one, let them know
where I am. What's
happened. But who?
Mom? Don't think
so—like she needs
more ammunition.
Brad? Uh-uh. He
never bothered to
check up on me.

One person might
actually care. One
person might
actually answer
his phone.
"Hello, Quade . . . ?"

# Jail Regulars Will Tell You

Not to get busted on Friday
night. Law demands arraignment
within forty-eight hours. But
weekends don't count.

Four days    before we might
be granted bail. (Highly
doubtful. We're not only
flight risks, but mostly broke.)

Four days    before we can get a feel
for our future. Four days to
come to grips with the thought
we might be here awhile.

Four days    without a cigarette.
Smoke-free lockup. Whose
stupid idea was that? Inmates
in deep withdrawal. Idiotic!

Four days   without the monster,
               and that withdrawal doubles
               me over. Makes me sweat. Shiver.
               Puke, in and out of the toilet.

Four days   wishing I were dead, instead
               of screaming back at the monster.
               Dead, instead of running from
               the demons. Demons, rampant

in this
Godless
place.

# The Officers on Duty

Do keep an eye on things.
But they don't exactly
come rushing to my rescue.

> *Don't worry. You'll survive,*
> *says one, a woman about*
> *the size of a steer.*
>
> *Frigging tweakers are all*
> *alike. Whiners. Sweat that*
> *shit out of your system,*
>
> *you'll be good as new, 'cept*
> *for lacking a few brain cells.*
> *You wanna see ugly, watch*
>
> *a wino in lockup, fighting*
> *d.t.'s. Oh, mama, now that*
> *is some scary shit.*

I've heard hard-core alkies
can die without booze. That
they bring 'em fixes, so they

don't croak in custody. I call
that out-and-out prejudice.
Injustice. Maybe I should sue.

# I Don't See Trey

Until the arraignment.
We share the defendants' table,
the public defender who stands
with us. Share a "not guilty" plea
to several charges, including
possession of and trafficking
methamphetamine, importing
it across the state line.

The only other thing we'll
share for quite a while is our
fate. Already indexed
in that mostly unwritten
book is extradition.
Nevada wants us also.
Serious charges there, too.

No longer will Trey and I share
an apartment, a car, a bed. Won't
share a pipe. A cigarette. A kiss.
Won't share promises.
Dreams.
Vows.

We will, however, share one
very special thing, in the not-
too-distant future. A baby. All
that poking, prodding, and analysis,
in search of AIDS or Hep C, netted
that information. Guess it's too
late to make that appointment
with Planned Parenthood.

I only hope I'm out of jail
before that big day comes.

# 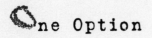ne Option

Can shorten my stay.
It's not only distasteful
but dangerous. Maybe
even life-threatening.

My public defender,
a rat-faced little man
with a squeaky voice,
brings me the offer.

*The Feds want to disrupt*
*the flow of Mexican meth*
*into the continental U.S. If*
*you'll turn state's evidence . . .*

I don't really hear all
the details, through
the whir in my brain.
But the message comes

across loud and clear:
Turn in Cesar, pull
a lot less time. Some-
thing to think about.

We will have to convince courts in two states that your cooperation will benefit society at large.

Now, there's something to put down on a future résumé. Right after "felony convictions."

# 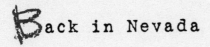ack in Nevada

Behind home-state bars,
I have a ton to think about
while awaiting sentencing.

                                Hopefully

the Feds won't rescind their
offer. I'll only have to spend
six months in jail. Not so long.

                                Hopefully,

they will arrest Cesar, put him
away for much longer than that.
I'll have to testify against him,
but I won't have to pay him.

                                Hopefully,

his people will tuck tail, sprint
back across the border. If not,
they shouldn't be able
to get me in here.

                                Hopefully,

the Department of Corrections
can safeguard me—and those
I love—against La Eme–style
retribution.

                                        Hopefully,

Trey and I will hook up again
after we get out. Hook up and
raise our baby together,
or at least share the parenting.

                                        Hopefully,

he'll write me. If not, Quade
has promised to. And I believe
him. *You're a complete mess,*
he said. *So why do I love you?*

                                        Hopefully,

one day I'll be worthy of his
love. Anyone's love. Trey's.
Our baby's. Hunter's. Mom's.

                                        Hopefully,

she can forgive me for betraying
her trust. She knows about
everything. She saw the bank
photo too. Turned me in.

                                                    Hopefully,

my dance with the monster hasn't
caused irreparable harm to me,
or to my just-forming baby.

                                                    Hopefully,

it will be a girl, a beautiful
perfect daughter, with hair
like Trey's, eyes like mine.

                                                    Hopefully,

I will love every hour of being
her mother, even late-night
feedings, diaper changings,
the whole experience.

                                                    Hopefully,

most hopefully of all, by
the time I get out of here,
the monster will be nothing
more than a distant memory.

An unforgettable nightmare.

# Yeah, Yeah

I realize that's an awful
lot of hoping. But hey,
I've always been
an optimist . . .

. . . don't ask me why.

## author's note

This book continues the story begun in my first novel, *Crank*. Both books, while fiction, are loosely based on the very real story of my daughter's walk with "the monster" drug crystal meth. Our family is healing, but will always wear the scars of the monster. I hope that by opening our windows and letting you peek inside, you will gain some insight about the nature of addiction.

# A Reading Group Guide to GLASS
# by Ellen Hopkins

## PREREADING ACTIVITY

Ask students one of the following: 1) What do you know about the drug meth? 2) Why might a seemingly "perfect" teen turn to meth? 3) To what extent would you be willing to support an immediate family member who is addicted to meth?

## DISCUSSION QUESTIONS

In the opening of *Glass*, Hopkins reminds the reader of Kristina Snow's fall "into the lair of the monster," a metaphor for meth. How is the word *monster* an appropriate metaphor for meth?

Kristina's alter ego, Bree, takes over when she is high on meth. What does Kristina mean when she says she made a "conscious decision" to turn into Bree?

Kristina meets Trey, a user and drug dealer, and falls head over heels for him. A year previously she had fallen for Adam, who introduced her to meth. After their relationship, why does Kristina fall for Trey, another drug dealer? What characteristics does he have that draw her in? Why does she maintain this relationship even though she knows Trey has other girlfriends?

Kristina knows that she should resist the monster. Why do you think she lacks the strength? Why might recovering addicts believe they can use again but control their drug habit?

Chase, a boyfriend from *Crank*, has a minor role in this novel. When Kristina encounters him, she is somewhat tentative. What feelings does she have for him? Why do you think Hopkins develops the scene in which Kristina encounters Chase with his new wife?

Kristina's mother and stepfather want Kristina to heal. Why does Kristina journey down the wrong path again? What emotions exist between Kristina and her mother? Between her stepfather and Kristina?

Would you describe the way Kristina feels as "empty"? Explain. How much power do Kristina's parents have to help her? Could they have done anything to prevent her from spiraling downward again? If so, what?

Kristina became hooked on meth when visiting her biological father, a meth user. When her father pays a visit on her birthday, Kristina shares her own stash with him. Describe their relationship. In what ways is her relationship with her father similar to her relationship with her mother? How is it different?

Does Trey genuinely care for Kristina? Does Brad? Cite scenes to support your response.

Does Kristina feel parental attachment to Hunter in the beginning of the story? Explain. Do her feelings toward him change throughout the story? If so, in what way?

Does Kristina grow throughout the story? Why or why not? Cite passages to support your thoughts.

Kristina's mother "throws her out" and/or refuses to see her while she is addicted. Does her mother take appropriate steps by turning her away?

*Glass* contains numerous shape poems. Identify two shape poems and explain the meaning of these forms. What effect do they have on the overall story? Why do you think Hopkins chose these shapes?

*Glass* begs for another follow-up in the series. What might happen to Kristina now that she and Trey have been busted? Will she distance herself from Trey or will they continue their relationship? Will she rejoin her family and resist the monster?

## ACTIVITIES

Organize a drug awareness campaign in your school and/or community. You may develop brochures outlining the dangers of meth and invite a guest speaker (ex., adolescent therapist) to your school, church/synagogue, etc., to speak to your peers.

Re-examine the shape poetry found in *Glass*. Write your own poem in a shape that suits the poem's theme. You may create a Shape Poetry Collection that when read together convenes a theme or short story.

Research meth and its effects on the body. Develop a blog or wiki on the dangers of meth and include information about where teens can go for help. Share the site with others in your school.

Kristina is the "perfect" girl. She is pretty, smart, and lives a comfortable lifestyle with her family. Why might someone who seemingly has everything turn to drugs? Read nonfiction accounts of teens who turn to meth. Develop a presentation that outlines common reasons teens turn toward drugs.

Volunteer to work for an organization that supports high-risk children such as a Big Brother or Big Sister.

Read a follow-up fiction novel that addresses drug addiction (ex., *Candy* by Kevin Brooks or *St. Iggy* by K. L. Going). Compare and contrast the stories. What characteristics do the drug addicts share? How are they different?

Glass *guide written by Pam B. Cole, Professor of English Education & Literacy, Kennesaw State University, Kennesaw, Georgia.*

Turn the page to read Ellen's exclusive essay "You Can't Shutter the Truth."

# You Can't Shutter the Truth

My mother loved books. Poetry. Classic literature. Popular fiction. When I was little, she read to me every day, and taught me to read chapter books before kindergarten. My most cherished after-school activity was riding my bike to the library, where I stocked up on horse books and Nancy Drew. In sixth grade I blew through Tolkien, Dickens, Twain and Margaret Mitchell's *Gone with the Wind*. By the time I reached high school, the classics were mostly behind me and I was into sultrier fare—Jean M. Auel, Mario Puzo, Jacqueline Susann, Jackie Collins, Erica Jong. Plus my favorites, Stephen King, Ken Kesey, John Irving. Never, ever, did my mom censor a single word. She believed books were key to understanding the big, wide, beautiful, hideous, joy-filled, scary-as-hell world outside my door.

Our doors open first to our neighborhoods. These we understand and, to a degree, choose for ourselves, at least as adults. We know who our friends are and whom we should cross the street to avoid. When someone new appears on our block, we assess that person, usually with suspicion, until we can determine how he or she fits into our neat, little lives. Will that new person enrich us or, perhaps, destroy us? Should we shutter our windows, dead-bolt our doors?

To many, foreign ideas are as frightening as the stranger moving into the neighborhood. Their belief systems are at stake, as are those they've carefully constructed for their children. Books, of course, are full of ideas, some of which just might crack the walls they've built around their understanding of the world beyond their comfort zone—

a place brimming with difficult truths they refuse to accept because to acknowledge them would make them real.

This is where censorship begins. With ideas that make us uncomfortable, truths we'd rather avoid. Yes, my books are full of them, and so I understand that some people might, in fact, be afraid of what I write. But when I hear that libraries refuse to carry my books, that parents insist they be pulled from the shelves, it makes me sad because the disquieting truths inside them are realities for so many. Choosing to deny them won't make them go away. Choosing to understand them is the first step toward vanquishing fear.

The bigger issue is that when any one person manages to remove a book from easy access, he denies another person's understanding and therefore feeds the flames of fear. We cannot permit a single person or group to wield such power. Our society must be fearless and weigh all truths with equal importance. My truth cannot be allowed to supersede yours. And this is what would-be censors would do—hold their assumed personal truths as more important than another's.

Fear flourishes when you leave it locked up inside. It corrodes and finally eats right through, infecting all those around you. But eventually, after all the damage is done, the truth escapes anyway. You can't shutter it forever. Better to unlock the door, develop compassion for the stranger in the neighborhood, understanding of the foreign ideas books offer. Much better to embrace the big, wide, beautiful, hideous, joy-filled, scary-as-hell world beyond our comfort zones.

When the ride ends,
all that's left is the

Keep reading
for a taste.

# We Hear

That life was good
before she
met

                  the monster,

but those page-flips
went down before
our collective
cognition. Kristina

                  wrote

that chapter of her
history before we
were even whispers
in her womb.

The monster shaped

                  our

lives, without our ever
touching it. Read on
if you dare. This

                  memoir

isn't pretty.

*Hunter Seth Haskins*

# So You Want to Know

All about her. Who

        she

really is. (Was?) Why
she swerved off
the high road. Hard

        left

to nowhere,
recklessly
indifferent to

        me,

Hunter Seth Haskins,
her firstborn
son. I've been

        choking

that down for
seventeen years.
Why did she go

        on

her mindless way,
leaving me spinning
in a whirlwind of

        her dust?

# If You Don't Know

Her story, I'll try
my best to enlighten

you, though I'm not sure
of every word of it myself.

I suppose I should know
more. I mean, it has been

recorded for eternity—
a bestselling fictionalization,

so the world wouldn't see
precisely who we are—

my mixed-up, messed-
up family, a convoluted

collection of mostly regular
people, somehow strengthened

by indissoluble love, despite
an ever-present undercurrent

of pain. The saga started here:

# Foreword

Kristina Georgia Snow
gave me life in her seventeenth
year. She's my mother,

but never bothered to be
my mom. That job fell
to her mother, my grandmother,

Marie, whose unfailing love
made her Mom even before
she and Dad (Kristina's stepfather,

Scott) adopted me. *That was
really your decision,* Mom claims.
*You were three when you started*

*calling us Mama and Papa.*
*The other kids in your playgroup*
*had them. You wanted them too.*

We became an official
legal family when I was four.
My memory of that day is hazy

at best, but if I reach way,
way back, I can almost see
the lady judge, perched

like an eagle, way high above
little me. I think she was
sniffling. Crying, maybe?

Her voice was gentle. *I want
to thank you, Mr. and Mrs.
Haskins, for loving this child*

*as he deserves to be loved.
Please accept this small gift,
which represents that love.*

I don't really remember all
those words, but Mom repeats
them sometimes, usually

when she stares at the crystal
heart, catching morning sun
through the kitchen window.

That part of Kristina's story
always makes Mom sad.
Here's a little more of the tale.

# Chapter One

It started with a court-ordered
summer visit to Kristina's
druggie dad. Genetically,

that makes him my grandfather,
not that he takes much interest
in the role. Supposedly he stopped

by once or twice when I was still
bopping around in diapers.
Mom says he wandered in late

to my baptism, dragging
Kristina along, both of them
wearing the stench of monster

sweat. Monster, meaning crystal
meth. They'd been up all night,
catching a monstrous buzz.

It wasn't the first time
they'd partied together. That
was in Albuquerque, where dear

old Gramps lives, and where
Kristina met the guy who popped
her just-say-no-to-drugs cherry.

*Our lives were never the same
again,* Mom often says. *That
was the beginning of six years*

*of hell. I'm not sure how we all
survived it. Thank God you were
born safe and sound. . . .*

All my fingers, toes, and a fully
functional brain. Yadda, yadda . . .
Well, I am glad about the brain.

Except when Mom gives me
the old, *What is up with you?
You're a brilliant kid. Why do*

*you refuse to perform like one?
A C-plus in English? If you would
just apply yourself . . .*

Yeah, yeah. Heard it before.
Apply myself? To what?
And what the hell for?

# I Kind of Enjoy

My underachiever status.
          I've found the harder you
                    work, the more people expect

of you. I'd much rather fly
          way low under the radar.
                    That was one of Kristina's

biggest mistakes, I think—
          insisting on being right-up-
                    in-your-face irresponsible.

Anyway, your first couple years
          of college are supposed to be
                    about having fun, not about

deciding what you want to do
          with the rest of your life. Plenty
                    of time for all that whenever.

I decided on UNR—University
          of Nevada, Reno—not so much
                    because it was always a goal,

but because Mom and Dad
            did this prepaid tuition thing,
                        and I never had Ivy League

ambitions or the need to venture
            too far from home. School is school.
                        I'll get my BA in communications,

then figure out what to do with it.
            I've got a part-time radio gig at
                        the X, an allowance for incidentals,

and I live at home. What more
            could a guy need? Especially
                        when he's got a girl like Nikki.

# Picture the Ideal Girl

And you've got Nikki.
She's sweet. Smart. Cute. Oh,
yes, and then there's her body.
I'm not sure what perfect
measurements are, but
Nikki's got them,

all wrapped up in skin
like sun-warmed mocha silk.
Delicious, from lips to ankles,
and she's mine. Mine to touch,
mine to hold. Mine to kiss
all over her flawless

deliciousness. Plus,
she's got her own place,
a sweet little house near campus,
where I can do all that kissing—not
to mention what comes after
the kissing—in private.

I'm done with classes
for the day, and on my way
to Nikki's, with a little extra fun
tucked inside my pocket. Yeah, I
know getting high isn't so
smart. Ask me if I care.

Turn the page for a
first look at Ellen
Hopkins's riveting
novel SMOKE.

*Pattyn Scarlet Von Stratten*
## Some Things

You can't take back, no
matter how much you wish
you could. No matter how
hard you pray to

          some

all-powerful miracle maker.
Some supposed God of Love.
One you struggle to believe
exists, because if he did,

          things

wouldn't be so out of control,
and you wouldn't be sucked dry
of love and left to be crushed
like old brittle bones that

          are

easily ground into dust.
Hindsight is useless
when looking back over
your shoulder at deeds

          irreversible.

# Dear, Sweet God

Forgive me. I don't know what to do.
Where to go. How to feel. I'm perched
on the precipice, waiting for the cliff
to crumble. No way to change what

happened. What's done is done and I . . .
I can't think about it. If I do, I'll throw up
right here. Bile boils in my gut, erupts
in my esophagus. I gulp it down, close

my eyes. But I can still see him, lying there.
Can still hear the gurgle in his throat.
Still smell the rich, rusty perfume of blood
pooling around him. I so wanted him dead.

My father. Stephen Paul Von Stratten.
The bastard who beat my mother. Beat
my sister. Beat me. The son of a bitch
who was responsible for the accident

that claimed my Ethan—catapulted him
wherever you go when you die. Our unborn
baby rode into that wilderness with him.
Dear, cruel God. Why couldn't I go, too?

# Eye for an Eye

If ever a person deserved to die,
it was Dad. But when I saw the bullet

hit its target square, watched him drop,
surprise forever branded in his sightless

eyes; when his shallow breathing went
silent, I wanted to take it back. Couldn't.

The Greyhound shifts gears, cresting
the mountain. Donner Pass, maybe.

Can't tell, leaning my head on the cool
window glass. It's dark. After ten. Escaping

into the night. Into the unknown. It's warm
in the bus, but I can't quit shaking. I think

I'll be cold forever. Frozen. Soul-ripping
sadness ice-dammed inside of me.

I shouldn't have listened to Mom. Shouldn't
be here. Shouldn't be free. I should be in

handcuffs. Behind bars. Locked away
forever. That's what I deserve. Instead,

I'm on my way to San Francisco.
I want to see something I've never

seen—the ocean. They'll find me,
sooner or later. Put me away in a cement

box without windows, where I belong.
I want to carry a memory with me,

bury it inside my heart, treasure, to be
exhumed when I need something

beautiful. Peaceful. Pacific. Of course,
I'll probably never feel at peace again.

Dad had ghosts who visited him often,
demons he tried to drink away. Now

he'll be my ghost. A ghost, filled with
demons. Haunting me until I'm a ghost, too.

# The Bus Is Crowded

I chose a seat near the back, away
from the driver. Mistake. Too close
to the bathroom. It stinks of urine

and worse. Every now and again
someone goes in there and then it
smells like marijuana, though smoking

is prohibited on all Greyhounds.
At least that's what the signs say.
Not like the driver cares. Easier not

to interfere with derelicts, dopers,
failed gamblers, and crazies. Oddly,
I feel safe enough among them.

Like freeway drivers in separate cars,
all going the same direction at the same
time, each passenger here has a unique

destination. A personal story. I try
not to listen. Try to tune the voices
out. Don't need other people's drama.

## But Some I Can't Miss

Somewhere behind me, a couple
has argued for an hour. Seems
he was up two hundred dollars
at Circus Circus. But she dropped
that, plus three hundred more,
which explains why they're:
    *riding a piss-smelling bus home*
       *'stead of getting a little cooch*
          *in a cozy motel room before*
            *catching the morning Amtrak.*

Kitty-corner and a couple rows
up, two blue-silver-haired women
talk about their husbands, kids, and
grandkids. One of them got lucky
on dollar slots. Now she can pay
her electric bill and have enough
         *left over to put some back into*
       *our savings. Shouldn't have*
     *took it out for this trip, but I*
    *just had one of those feelings. . . .*

# Behind Me

The guy takes up two whole seats.
       No one wants to sit near him, mostly
because he smells like he hasn't had

a shower. Ever. Probably homeless and
       put on the bus by law enforcement. They
don't much like finding people frozen

to death in riverside cardboard boxes.
       Lots of homeless take up residence on
the banks of the Truckee. Wonder if one

of them will notice the metallic glint
       of a 10mm. The gun that killed Stephen
Von Stratten. Wonder if the cops will

check the river. After . . . it . . . Mom
       told me to take Dad's car and go far
away. Fast away. She gave me her money

       stash, packed a few clothes. *Once*
          *the cops come,* she said, *they'll*
       *look for the car. Dump it soon.*

Driving into Reno, it came to me—
        a scene from an old movie—to park
the old Subaru in the airport garage.

I took the overhead walkway, down
        the escalator, out the front doors,
carrying the tatters of my life in

an overnight bag. Walked the couple
        miles to the bus station, much of it
along the river. Seemed like a good

place to lose the gun Ethan gave me
        for protection. It did protect Jackie
from another fist to her face. But, oh,

the price was dear. For Dad. For me.
        For the entire family. What will happen
to Mom and the kids now? Tears

threaten, but I can't let them fall.
        Can't show weakness. Can't show
fear. Can't look like a girl on the run.